Willa wore her pride like an iron cloak.

But damned if she didn't look fantastic.

She had obviously just washed her hair, and the scent of jasmine drifting from it had nearly driven him wild. Usually she wore her hair in a braid or pulled back with a clip. Tonight that glorious ebony mane hung loose and arrow straight almost to her waist. Zach's fingers itched to dive into that thick mass, feel it warm against his skin, slithering through his fingers.

Mahoney, what the hell are you doing fantasizing about Willa Simmons? There was no way he was getting involved with that little spitfire.

Sure, they'd shared one mind-blowing kiss, but so what? She wasn't his type. He preferred women who were sweet and gentle and domestic. Not temperamental tomboys.

Zach watched Willa disappear into the upstairs hallway. "Damn prickly woman. One of these days you're going to collapse under the weight of that chip on your shoulder. If I don't break through it first, that is."

Get caught reading Silhouette.

Dear Reader,

May marks the celebration of "Get Caught Reading," a national campaign the Association of American Publishers created to promote the sheer joy of reading. "Get Caught Reading" may be a phrase that's familiar to you, but if not, we hope you'll familiarize yourself with it by picking up the wonderful selections that Silhouette Special Edition has to offer....

Former NASA engineer Laurie Paige says that when she was young, she checked out *The Little Engine That Could* from the library fifty times. "I read it every week," Laurie recalls. "I was so astounded that the library would lend books to me for free. I've been an avid reader ever since." Though Laurie Paige hasn't checked out her favorite childhood storybook for a while, she now participates in several local literacy fund-raisers and reads to young children in her community. Laurie is also a prolific writer, with nearly forty published Silhouette titles, including this month's *Something To Talk About*.

Don't miss the fun when a once-burned rancher discovers that the vivacious amnesiac he's helping turns out to be the missing Stockwell heiress in Jackie Merritt's *The Cattleman and the Virgin Heiress*. And be sure to catch all of THE CALAMITY JANES, five friends sharing the struggles and celebrations of life, starting with *Do You Take This Rebel?* by Sherryl Woods. And what happens when Willa and Zach learn they both inherited the same ranch? Find out in *The Ties That Bind* by Ginna Gray. Be sure to see who will finish first in Patricia Hagan's *Race to the Altar*. And Judith Lyons pens a highly emotional tale with *Lt. Kent: Lone Wolf*.

So this May, make time for books. Remember how fun it is to browse a bookstore, hold a book in your hands and discover new worlds on the printed page.

Best,

Karen Taylor Richman
Senior Editor

Please address questions and book requests to:
Silhouette Reader Service
U.S.: 3010 Walden Ave., P.O. Box 1325, Buffalo, NY 14269
Canadian: P.O. Box 609, Fort Erie, Ont. L2A 5X3

The Ties That Bind

GINNA GRAY

Silhouette®

SPECIAL EDITION™

Published by Silhouette Books

America's Publisher of Contemporary Romance

SILHOUETTE BOOKS

ISBN 0-373-24395-2

THE TIES THAT BIND

Books by Ginna Gray

GINNA GRAY

A native Houstonian, Ginna Gray admits that, since childhood, she has been a compulsive reader as well as a head-in-the-clouds dreamer. Long accustomed to expressing her creativity in tangible ways—Ginna also enjoys painting and needlework—she finally decided to try putting her fantasies and wild imaginations down on paper. The result? The mother of two now spends eight hours a day as a full-time writer.

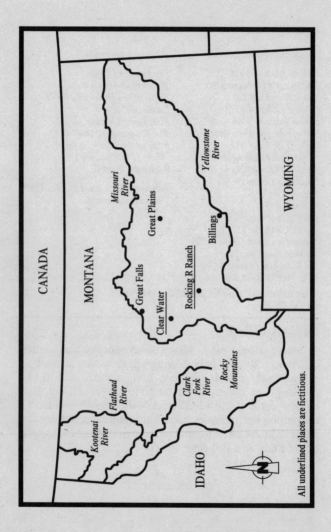

All underlined places are fictitious.

Prologue

*Welcome to Clear Water, Montana—
Population 1,474*

Scanning the sign at the edge of town, Zach Mahoney grimaced. "What the devil are you doing, Mahoney? You should be halfway to Sedona by now, not wasting time on a fool's errand," he muttered to himself.

At the time he'd agreed to this crazy plan he'd been reeling from shock. If he'd been thinking straight he would have told J.T. and Matt to count him out. Hell, he had a good mind to turn his rig around and head for Sedona, and the devil take it.

Zach ground his teeth, knowing he wouldn't. He didn't break his word.

Besides, Kate would give him a tongue-lashing that would blister his eardrums if he didn't see this thing through. His sister, like most women, got emotional when it came to family.

The two-lane highway ran through the center of town, and past the Mountain Shadows Motel on the northern edge. Zach parked his motor home in front of the motel and climbed out.

Inside, he learned from the desk clerk that J.T. and Matt were having lunch across the street at a place called Hodie's. They'd left a message for him to join them there.

Back out on the sidewalk Zach paused to replace his hat and look around. Clear Water nestled in a north/south valley with rolling foothills to the east and the towering peaks of the Rocky Mountains to the west. Other than the spectacular setting, the place was typical of hundreds of other western towns he'd seen while traveling the rodeo circuit—small, sleepy and rugged, a dot of what passed for civilization in a land of incomparable wild beauty.

Though it was April, snow still covered the mountains. They glittered a blinding white in the bright sunshine, and the breeze that swept down their rugged slopes held a bite. Tugging the rolled brim of his Stetson lower over his eyes, Zach huddled deeper into his coat and headed across the street toward Hodie's Bar and Grill.

Like many western "watering holes," Hodie's was a combination restaurant, pool hall and bar. It took a few seconds for Zach's eyes to adjust to the dimness inside, but when they did he homed in on the two men in a corner booth and headed in that direction.

J.T. was the first to spot him.

"Hey, Zach, you made it. Good to see you, bro. Have a seat," he offered, sliding over to make room.

The appellation jarred Zach, but his expression remained carefully impassive. He hung his hat and coat on the brass hook attached to the end of the booth and slid onto the bench seat.

Across the table he met Matt's penetrating gaze. More reserved than J.T., he merely nodded and said simply, "Zach."

"You're just in time to join us for lunch."

"No thanks. I've already eaten. I'll just have a cup of coffee." Righting the upside-down crockery mug in front of him, Zach signaled to the waitress.

"You sure you don't want something to eat? This place doesn't look like much, I know, but the food is great. I had dinner here last night after I got in."

"No, I'm good."

"How about—"

"He said he didn't want anything," Matt growled. "Let him be."

"Hey, I was just being friendly. Something you should try once in a while, bro."

Matt gave him a laser look. Unfazed, J.T. grinned back.

Zach took a sip of coffee. The brew scalded his tongue, but drinking it gave him an excuse to remain silent and observe.

No matter how hard he tried, he still had difficulty accepting that he and these two men were brothers. It just didn't seem possible.

Which, he supposed, was normal, given the circumstances. Hell, until six weeks ago, when J.T. and Matt had tracked him down and broken the news to him, he'd had no idea he even *had* brothers. Learning at age thirty-five that he was one of a set of triplets had been a shocker.

At first he'd been certain they were trying to pull some

sort of con, and he'd flatly refused to believe them. To be honest, he hadn't *wanted* to believe them. Kate was his family—all the family he needed.

However, there was proof. Most conclusive of which was the odd irregular-cut wedge of flat silver that each wore on a chain around his neck—a token from a birth mother none of them could remember. Unconsciously, Zach raised his hand and rubbed his through his shirt.

The three jagged, pie-shaped wedges fit together perfectly to form a silver medallion. When whole, etched on one side was an R with a curved line under it, on the other side, in block print were the words, Rocking R Ranch and a post office box in Clear Water, Montana. Beneath the address were the words, "Your Heritage."

Whoever she was, for whatever reason, the woman who had given each of them life had left this fragile link to one another and to their past.

Even so…it was still difficult to believe that they were related. They seemed to be as different in every way as any three men could be.

Other than all being six feet two inches tall and having the same general build, they looked nothing alike. Well…maybe, if you looked hard enough, you could see a slight resemblance between J.T. and Matt. They both had vivid blue eyes and dark hair, but Matt's was black, whereas J.T.'s was a mahogany-brown. Zach's own hair was the color of pale wheat, and if he spent too much time in the sunshine without a hat it bleached almost white, and his eyes were green.

The differences between the three of them went deeper than looks, though. Their personalities were nothing at all alike.

A former detective with the Houston police, Matt was tough and taciturn. To Zach's eye, he had the look of a man who had seen too much of life's seamy side to have any illusions left.

On the surface, J.T. appeared to be a lightweight. Movie-star handsome, charming to the ladies and amiable, he seemed to take little seriously. Before quitting his job to try his hand at novel writing, he'd been an investigative reporter for a Houston newspaper—an occupation that had often put him at odds with Matt. It did, however, require intelligence, talent and tenacity, and that made Zach wonder just how much of J.T.'s affability was a clever ploy he used to put people at ease to gain their trust.

He'd read J.T.'s first manuscript, and it was gut-wrenching, insightful and hard-hitting, hardly the work of a shallow playboy.

"By the way, Kate sends her love."

Zach turned his head and fixed J.T. with an unwavering look. "How is she?"

"Terrific. And happy. Did you think she wouldn't be?"

Zach let the question hang between them for several seconds, his eyes narrowing, searching J.T.'s face for the truth.

To his credit, J.T. met the stare without flinching.

At last Zach shrugged, which was as close to an apology as he intended to get. "I just can't get used to you being married to my sister, is all."

"Jeez, man, you make it sound like incest. Kate's your *adoptive* sister. You're not related by blood."

"Yeah, well, we grew up together. She seems a damn sight more like kin than you do."

Matt snorted. "I can sympathize with you there. My last eleven years as a cop, back when J.T. was a reporter, he was a constant thorn in my side. Imagine what a kick in the head it was for me when I found out that he was my brother. The two of us made the connection seven months ago and I still haven't gotten used to the idea.''

"Hey, it was no thrill for me, either," J.T. fired back, his perpetual good humor for once slipping. "But it's a fact, so we're all just going to have to deal with it."

"True. Maybe it'll be easier once we know more. Soon as we eat, we'll get directions to the Rocking R Ranch."

Zach frowned. "Are you two sure you want to do this?"

Matt gave him a sharp look, his coffee mug poised halfway to his mouth. "Why? Don't you?"

"I just don't see the point."

"The point is to get some answers. Maybe meet our mother. Find out why she gave us up."

"Why bother? Look, I've always known I was adopted, and it's never bothered me. Why should it? No kid could've asked for better parents than the Mahoneys. I've sure as hell never felt deprived or been haunted by nightmares, or even felt any curiosity about my biological parents. Maybe you two have some unresolved issues, but I don't. The way I figured it, our mother gave us away, so why should we go searching for her? As far as I'm concerned, the past is past. I say let it go."

Matt looked at J.T. "He has a point."

J.T. snapped, "Look, we're entitled to some answers. At the very least, we should find out our family's medical history in case any of us ever has kids of our own."

"I guess you're right," Matt conceded. "Anyway, Maude Ann and Kate would kill us all if we didn't see this through."

"Okay, fine. As soon as you two finish eating we'll go out to the ranch and get this over with. I wanta be outta here by morning. I got two days to get to my next rodeo.''

The waitress, a plump, fiftyish woman, bustled up to the table. ''Here you go, fellas. Anything else I can ge—''

Her breezy chatter ended abruptly when she glanced at Zach. Her jaw dropped almost to her chest. ''Oh, my stars! You're Colleen Rafferty's boy, aren't you?''

Zach exchanged a quick look with Matt and J.T. ''Maybe.''

''*Maybe?* You mean you don't *know?*''

''No, ma'am. I was adopted when I was two. All three of us were.''

''All three of you?'' Her gaze bounced from one man to the other. ''You mean…you're *triplets?*''

''Yes, ma'am.''

''Oh, my stars.''

''Actually, we came here looking for our birth mother. We have information that she might be from around here,'' J.T. said. ''Maybe you could help us.''

''Well, boys, there's not a doubt in my mind that your mother is Colleen Rafferty. She had a very distinctive face.'' She smiled at Zach. ''You, young man, are the spitting image of her. And I oughta know. Colleen and I were best friends. By the way, my name is Jan Prescott.''

''Nice to meet you, Ms. Prescott. I'm Zach Mahoney, and these are my brothers, Matt Dolan and J.T. Conway.''

''Three different names. Oh, that's just so sad.''

''So her name was Rafferty,'' Matt said. ''Can we assume that has something to do with the Rocking R Ranch? And that she's connected to the owners?''

''I should say so. That ranch has been in Colleen's family for four generations. Her great-great-grandfather,

Ransom Patrick Rafferty, was one of the first settlers around these parts. For the last fifty years or so the ranch has belonged to her daddy, Seamus Rafferty.'' Jan Prescott sniffed. ''A meaner old coot you'll never meet, I'm sorry to tell you.''

''Does Colleen still live at the ranch?''

''Oh, dear, I'm afraid not. Colleen lit out of here close to thirty-six years ago, as I recall. Just boarded a bus one day without a word to anyone, not even me. No one around these parts has seen hide nor hair of her since.

''The rumor going around at the time was that she was pregnant. Back in those days that was a disgrace. I didn't believe it. Gave a few folks a good dressing-down for even suggesting it. But, seeing as how you boys are here, looks like it was true.''

''Could you give us directions to the Rocking R?'' Matt asked.

''Sure. Just follow the highway north about ten miles and you'll see the sign.''

She hesitated, gnawing at her bottom lip, looking from one to the other. ''Look, fellas, I feel it's only fair to warn you, Seamus Rafferty is meaner than a snake. He's not gonna take kindly to you showing up on his doorstep. Fact is, you'll be lucky if he doesn't run you off at gunpoint.''

''We still have to give it a shot,'' J.T. said.

''We're not here to cause trouble,'' Matt added. ''All we want is some information.''

''Yeah, well, good luck getting it. Regardless of how it turns out, though, I want you to know that I'm just pleased as punch that I got to meet Colleen's boys. An' I sure hope you get the answers you want,'' she added, but her expression said she didn't think much of their chances.

* * *

After turning in at the ranch entrance they drove several more miles without seeing anything but rich, rolling grassland on either side of the SUV.

The land rose and dipped in undulating waves, stretching out as far as the eye could see to the east, north and south and to the base of the mountains to the west. Patches of snow still dotted the winter-brown pastures, but in protected spots green shoots poked up to brave the chill. Here and there stands of pine and spruce broke up the rolling landscape. Placid cattle grazed on either side of the narrow dirt road.

Now this was prime ranch land, Zach thought. Exactly the kind of spread he'd always dreamed of owning.

His mouth twisted. Yeah, right. In your dreams, Mahoney. If he saved his money until he was ninety, he'd never have enough to purchase a place even a fraction the size of this one.

The road went down a long incline into a wide, gently rolling valley. At its center sat the ranch house, a sturdy, sprawling, two story structure made of logs and stone. The logs were stained dark brown, the shutters and trim painted cream. A wide porch spanned the considerable width of the house, front and back. It had the look of permanence, as though it had been sitting there for a hundred years or more.

A couple hundred yards or so behind the house, cowboys worked in and around a maze of corrals and the gargantuan barn. Beyond that a bunkhouse, several open-sided hay barns and other outbuildings, which Zach knew probably housed tractors and cattle trailers and other ranch equipment, were scattered around. It was as fine a setup as he'd ever seen…and he'd darn near sell his soul to own it.

A Border collie lay sleeping in a patch of sunshine on the porch. When Matt drove up to the front of the house the animal sprang to her feet and streaked down the steps, barking furiously.

Zach, Matt and J.T. climbed out of the SUV, and the dog continued to growl. Following Zach's lead, they let her sniff their hands. When she was satisfied, the men went up the walk and climbed the steps, the Collie trotting along beside them, tail wagging.

Their knock was answered by an elderly Hispanic woman.

"*¿Sí, señors?*" Her face went slack with shock and she clasped her face between her palms. "*¡Aiee! ¡Madre de Dios!* It is you! Señorita Colleen's *muchachos!*"

Before any of them could respond the woman surged forward, hugging first one, then the other, weeping and babbling in an incoherent mix of English and Spanish.

"Dammit to hell, Maria! What in tarnation are you caterwauling about!" a male voice inside the house bellowed.

Boot heels hammered across the foyer an instant before a gray-haired man appeared in the doorway. Backing up a step, Maria wrung her hands, her worried gaze bouncing back and forth between the four males.

The old man's weathered skin resembled aged leather. He was shorter than Zach and his brothers by about two inches and lean to the point of boniness, but he looked as tough as a pine knot.

"Whoever you are and whatever you're selling, I'm not interested, so get the hell off my property."

As he spoke the old man's gaze skimmed over them, then did a double take, flashing back to Zach. His faded blue eyes narrowed and sharpened as recognition dawned. He stared for the space of three heartbeats before switching to the other two men.

Zach would not have thought it possible, but the old man's expression grew even harder, and his eyes narrowed with pure hatred when his gaze settled on J.T.

"So...she whelped three of you, did she?"

Maria made a distressed sound, which drew the old man's attention. "Get back to your duties, woman. This is no business of yours."

"Are you Seamus Rafferty?"

"That I am." His flinty stare returned to J.T.

"My name is Zach Mahoney. These are my brother's, Matt Dolan and J.T. Conway. We're here because—"

"I know who you are," the old man snapped. "No matter what you call yourselves, you're still Colleen's bastards." He jabbed a bony forefinger at the end of J.T.'s nose, "This one is a dead ringer for Mike Reardon, the sorry, no-good saddle tramp who seduced my daughter. And you." He turned his head and looked at Zach. "You're the image of her."

"So I've been told."

Seamus turned his attention on Matt. "Now, you—you don't favor either of them. You're just a mutt mixture of both." He looked down at Matt's cane, and his mouth curled with contempt. "Got a gimp leg, I see. Not much use to anyone, are you?"

Matt's jaw tightened and his piercing blue eyes flamed.

Zach made a subtle shift, placing himself between Matt and the old man. "We're looking for some information. We're hoping you can help us."

Seamus Rafferty's hard stare swung to Zach and held for an interminable time. Finally he snapped, "Come in. I don't conduct business on the porch." He stomped back inside, leaving them no choice but to follow.

As they walked through the entry hall a young woman dressed in snug-fitting jeans and a Western-style shirt and boots descended the stairs. She was small and wand slim. At first glance Zach took her for a teenager, but drawing nearer he realized she was in her mid-twenties. Her skin was ivory, her eyes blue, her hair black. The thick mane hung down her back almost to her waist, arrow straight and as shiny as polished ebony. Though she appeared to wear no makeup she had the kind of delicate beauty that took your breath away.

Zach wondered who she was. Another of Seamus's grandchildren, perhaps? Or a late-in-life child? Or perhaps his wife?

The last thought was so distasteful Zach dismissed it immediately.

The woman came to a halt on the bottom stair as they walked by, but even so she was still not eye-level with Zach. He realized that she could be no more than five feet two or three—and that her eyes were not blue at all, but a startling violet.

He thought surely Seamus would stop and introduce them, but the old man stomped past the stairs without so much as a glance in her direction.

"Seamus?" she called after him. "What's going on?"

The husky contralto coming from such a small, delicate woman surprised Zach, but he was given no opportunity to contemplate its sexy quality.

"This has nothing to do with you, Willie. Go on about your own business girl, and keep your nose out of mine."

He led them into a walnut-paneled office, took a seat behind a massive desk, then motioned impatiently to the leather sofa and chairs by the fire.

When they were seated he glared at them. "Well?"

"We came here hoping we'd find our mother, but we

learned in town that she left here years ago,'' J.T. said. ''We're hoping that you can tell us how we can get in touch with her.''

Seamus snorted. ''You expect me to believe that's all you want? Do you take me for a fool?''

''I don't think you want me to answer that.''

Matt's quiet comment gleaned a dagger stare from Seamus, but J.T. hurried on. ''I don't know what you think we're after, but I assure you, we did come here to look for our mother.''

''*You* can't assure me of anything. I don't trust you any more than I trusted that no-good daddy of yours.''

A muscle in J.T.'s cheek began to tic and his smiled slipped a bit. ''Nevertheless, it's true. We were adopted by different families, and until late last summer, none of us knew the other existed. Matt and I made the initial connection by accident.''

''With these,'' Matt said, pulling his medallion piece out from beneath his shirt and whipping it off over his head.

Zach and J.T. quickly followed suit. Gathering the three pie-shaped wedges, Zach rose and laid them on the desk in front of Seamus. With one finger, he slid the pieces of silver together into a perfect fit. The old man leaned over, scowling as he read the inscription.

''J.T. located Zach a few months ago,'' Matt continued. ''Now we're trying to find our mother. Or, failing that, to at least learn what we can about her. We were hoping you could help us.''

''You're barking up the wrong tree. I got nothing to say. That ungrateful girl has been dead to me since the day she confessed that she'd gotten herself knocked up. I threw her out and told her to never come back.''

''For getting pregnant?'' J.T. looked dumbfounded.

"Women have babies out of wedlock all the time. Some are even planned."

"Not thirty-six years ago they didn't," the old man snapped. "And I wouldn't stand for it today, either. I'll have no harlots or bastards in my family."

"How about her belongings?" Matt inquired. "She must have left something here. Could we take a look at those?"

"Burned it all years ago."

Seamus put his hands flat on the desktop and levered himself to his feet. "Let's cut the crap. I know damned well you didn't come here looking for your tramp of a mother. You came hoping to get your hands on this ranch. Well, I'm telling you that just ain't gonna happen. The Rocking R isn't going to fall into the hands of Mike Reardon's by-blows." He thumped the desktop with the side of his fist. "By heaven, I'll *give* the place away before I'll let that happen."

"That's it. I'm outta here. I told you two this was a bad idea." Zach headed toward the door.

"He's right. C'mon. We don't have to take this." Using his cane, Matt levered himself to his feet and followed.

Zach snatched open the door and strode out—and barreled into the young woman they had seen a few moments before. She hit his chest with an "Oof!" and bounced off.

"Damn." Zach grabbed her shoulders to keep her from falling, set her aside with a terse, "Excuse me, miss," and continued on toward the entrance.

He had a fleeting impression of startled violet eyes and skin like ivory silk, but beyond that he paid her no mind. He was too intent on getting the hell away from Seamus

Rafferty before he lost his temper and planted his fist right in the old coot's sneering face—grandfather or no.

"Seamus, is something wrong?" the woman asked as Matt and J.T. trooped past in Zach's wake. "Who are those men?"

Neither Zach nor his brothers waited around to hear the old man's answer.

"Of all the foul-tempered, suspicious, spiteful old bastards!" Matt snarled the instant they gained the front porch.

"Yeah, Gramps is a bit of a disappointment."

"If that's supposed to be funny—"

"Knock it off, both of you." Zach fixed his brothers with a hard look. "We gave it our best shot and got nowhere. Now can we just drop this whole thing and forget about the past?"

"Suits me."

"I don't think we ought to give up," J.T. argued.

Matt spat out an expletive and rolled his eyes.

"Look, you do what you want, but I'm out of here," Zach said. "As soon as we get back to town, I'm heading for Sedona."

"*¡Pssst! ¡Señors! ¡Señors!*"

As one, they turned to see the woman Seamus had called Maria peeking nervously from around a forsythia at the corner of the house.

"I must speak with you, *por favor. Es muy importante.*"

The brothers exchanged a brief look and moved down the porch to the woman's hiding place.

"Yes?"

Clutching a flat cardboard box to her breasts, Maria glanced around nervously. "You wish to know about Señorita Colleen, *sí? Sus madre?*"

"Yes," J.T. replied. "Do you know where she is?"

A stricken expression flashed over the woman's face. "I..." She shook her head, then cast a quick look over her shoulder and thrust the shirt-size box into Zach's hands. "You take this, *señor*. *La señorita* sent it to me over thirty years ago."

"What is it?"

"Her *diario*. How you say...journal. Also a photograph that I hid from Señor Rafferty so he would not burn it. Señorita Colleen, she beg me not to tell her *padre* I have the journal."

Matt snorted. "She probably knew he'd destroy it, like he did the rest of her stuff."

Maria nodded. "*Sí*, it is so. *La señorita*, she want me to keep the *diario* safe and give it to her *muchachos* if you ever come here. I am an old woman. I begin to think you will not come while I still live."

A door slammed at the back of the house and Seamus bellowed, "Dammit, Maria! Where the hell are you?"

She jumped guiltily. "I must go." Grasping Zach's arm, she urged, "*Por favor*. Read the *diario*. All your questions, they will be answered."

"To save time, I think we should read it out loud," Zach suggested when he and his brothers entered Matt's motel room a short while later.

"Good idea." J.T. stretched out on one of the double beds and laced his fingers together behind his head. "Why don't you start?"

Matt sat on the edge of the other bed, and Zach settled into one of the room's two chairs. Almost reverently, he lifted the cover off the box and found himself staring at a photograph of a young girl of about eighteen.

She was more striking than beautiful—a female ver-

sion of the face he saw in the mirror each day—the same
blond hair and green eyes, the same thin, straight nose,
sharp cheekbones and strong jaw. Her mouth was a bit
fuller and softer than his own, but the shape was identical.

It was eerie, looking at that face. The short hairs on
Zach's nape and forearms stood on end. No wonder the
waitress at Hodie's had been so shocked. And why Seamus
had known instantly who they were.

While his brothers studied the photograph, Zach lifted
the diary out of the box. The cheap vinyl cover was
cracked and split and the pages felt brittle, the edges
brown with age.

He looked at Matt and J.T. and cocked one eyebrow.
"You ready?" An edgy awareness that they were about
to uncover their past pulsed in the air.

"Yeah, we're ready," J.T. said, and Matt nodded
agreement.

Zach cleared his throat and turned to the first entry.

"'September 21st. I'm so scared. I'm on my way
to Houston, but I don't know what I'll do if my
mother's aunt Clara won't take me in. She's elderly,
and I barely know her, but other than Daddy she's
my only living relative. She never had children of
her own, and when she came to the ranch for a visit
a few years ago she was kind to me and urged me
to come stay with her for as long as I liked. I just
pray the invitation will still be open after I tell her
about my condition.

"'September 22nd. Heaven help me, I'm too late.
I arrived at Aunt Clara's this afternoon and found
her house full of people. They had just come from
her funeral.

"'I got hysterical, and I must have fainted. A while ago I woke up and found myself lying on a bed in my aunt's guest room. A lady was here with me. She introduced herself as Dr. Chloe Nesbitt and said she had been my aunt's doctor and friend. Then she asked if I was pregnant.

"'When I finally bawled out my story, Dr. Nesbitt was very kind. She said she would talk to Aunt Clara's pastor about my situation. In the meantime, she was sure that I could stay here, at least until the estate is settled. She told me to get some rest and not to worry.

"'How can I not worry? My darling Mike is dead, Daddy has tossed me out, I'm alone in a strange town where I know no one, I have no job, no money, no training other than ranch work and I'm expecting a child in five months! What am I going to do?

"'September 23rd. I can't believe it! Just when things look hopeless, a miracle has happened. Dr. Nesbitt returned this morning with Reverend Clayton and my aunt's attorney, Mr. Lloyd Thomas. Mr. Thomas said that as my aunt's only kin, I will inherit her entire estate! It isn't a great fortune—a modest savings and this small house, is all—but it's a roof over my head, and if I'm careful, the money will see me through until the baby is born and I can get a job. Bless you, Aunt Clara.'"

For the next hour Zach read from the diary. It told of Colleen's struggle to make the money last, her fear of living alone for the first time in her life, of being in a strange place, her shock and joy when she found out she was expecting triplets, and her worries over how she could support herself and three babies. Underlying it all was a desperate loneliness that colored every word and wrung Zach's heart.

Reverend Clayton and Dr. Nesbitt figured prominently in the entries over the next few months. The doctor saw Colleen through her pregnancy, and the reverend and others in his congregation took a special interest in her, offering spiritual guidance and practical assistance and advice.

    "'January 24th. Reverend Clayton is urging me to put my babies up for adoption as soon as they're born. He thinks that would be best—for them, and for me. Perhaps he's right. I don't know. But, God help me, I can't. I just can't. I love them so much already. Every time I feel them move, my heart overflows. I cannot bear to give them up, to have them whisked away from me the second they are born and never get to see their sweet faces, never get to hold them. No. No, I can't give them up. I love them. And they are all I have left of Mike.'"

Zach's throat grew so tight he had difficulty forming the words. He thrust the diary into Matt's hands. "Here. It's your turn," he said in a gruff voice.

Matt swung his legs up onto the bed and leaned back against a mound of pillows and continued.

    "'February 7th. I'm the mother of three beautiful, healthy boys! They arrived yesterday, two weeks early, but Dr. Nesbitt says they are all doing fine. I have named them Matthew Ryan, Zachariah Aiden and Jedediah Tiernan.'"

"Jedediah Tiernan!" Matt hooted. "No wonder you go by J.T."

"Stuff it, Dolan."

"Do you two mind? Could we just get on with this?"

"Okay, okay." Picking up where he left off, Matt continued.

"'February 9th. Reverend Clayton came by during visiting hours. He offered me a job working in the church's day care center. The pay isn't much, but Reverend Clayton says I can bring the babies to the center. That means I won't have to be separated from them or have the expense of child care. The reverend is such a good man. I don't know what I would do without his help and support.

"'February 10th. The first day home with the boys. I had no idea babies were so much work. I'll write more later when I'm not so exhausted.'"

The entry was typical of the ones during the following year. A picture began to emerge of a young girl struggling to support and nurture three babies alone. To make ends meet she took in ironing in the evenings and on weekends, often working late into the night.

A few weeks before their first birthday Colleen began to mention that she wasn't feeling well. By the end of February her boss at the day care center insisted that she see a doctor, in case she had something contagious. Then came the entry that stunned Zach and his brothers.

"'March 5th. I have advanced ovarian cancer.'"

"Ah, hell," Zach swore and raked a hand through his hair.

"Yeah," J.T. agreed in a subdued tone. "After all she'd already been through, she sure didn't deserve that."

Swinging his legs over the side, Matt sat on the edge of the bed. "Funny. That possibility never occurred to me. I always assumed she gave me away because she didn't want me."

"Deep down, I think we all did," Zach said quietly. "We were too young to understand anything else."

Matt thought that over, then nodded and resumed reading.

"'Dear Lord, what am I going to do? I can't afford to be sick. My babies need me. On top of that, I have no idea how I'll pay for the treatment, but without it I'll surely die. What will become of the boys if that happens? Daddy won't have them. Even if he would, I don't want my boys to grow up under his iron-fisted rule or to bear the brunt of his hatred for their father. God help me. And them.

"'March 6th. I started treatment today. Feel even worse. Nausea is awful.'"

For the next eight months the entries were about the treatment and the ghastly side effects. And her growing financial worries. Within weeks she could no longer work. It was all she could manage to take care of her three toddlers. Left with no alternative, she was forced to go on welfare.

Despite aggressive treatment, her condition continued to worsen, and in December, after nine months of struggle, Colleen accepted the inevitable and wrote of her decision to ask Reverend Clayton help her find homes for her sons.

"'November 23rd. Reverend Clayton and Mr. Thomas, Aunt Clara's attorney, are handling the adoptions. I would like to interview the prospective couples myself, but the family court judge will not allow it. Even though these are private adoptions he demands complete anonymity on both sides, and afterward the adoption records will be sealed.

"'The reverend and Mr. Thomas have tried but they couldn't find a family willing to take three two-year-olds so it appears the boys will have to go to different couples. Oh, how I hate to think of them being separated. They are not only losing me, but each other, as well. But what choice do I have?

"'January 10th. Reverend Clayton has selected three couples. I trust his judgment and I'm sure they will all be wonderful parents, but I can't quite bring myself to commit to them. It shreds my heart just to think about handing my babies over to strangers and never seeing them again. For the boys' sake, though, I have to stop being selfish. They are typical rambunctious toddlers, and I'm so weak now and in so much pain that I can barely get out of bed some days. I worry that I'm not giving them proper care.

"'January 15th. Well, I've done it. I've agreed to the adoptions and signed all the papers. Reverend Clayton had the medallion made and cut, like I asked him, and all the couples have agreed to give them to the boys when they are older. I just hope that someday it will help them find one another again.'"

Matt turned the page, scanned it, then flipped over several more before turning back. "Looks like there's just one more entry. After that there are just blank pages."

"Go ahead. Let's hear it," J.T. said.

"'February 24th. Today was the worst day of my life. I gave my babies away. Two social workers came and took them. I cuddled and kissed them for the last time, and I think they knew something was wrong. As they were being carried out they screamed and cried and held their arms out to me, calling 'Mommie! Mommie!' It broke my heart. Dear Lord, it hurts. It hurts so much I don't think I can bear it. I want to die. Without my babies I have nothing to live for. Please, God. Please. Let me die now. Please.'''

Matt exhaled a long sigh and slowly closed the journal. A heavy silence hung in the room.

Colleen Rafferty was dead. The rush of disappointment and grief took Zach by surprise. For Pete's sake. He had no memories of her. Until he'd seen that photograph he hadn't even known what she looked like. Why did it bother him so much to learn that she was dead?

"Well, that's it. Now we know," J.T. said finally.

Zach gave a little snort. "Yeah. Now we know. For all the good it did us."

Chapter One

The horse snorted and danced in the narrow chute. His ears lay back flat to his head and his eyes rolled, showing white all around.

"Better watch 'im, Zach. This here's one mean sidewinder," one of the handler's cautioned.

Zach nodded, studying the furious bronc with satisfaction. Hellbent was a good draw. Zach knew if he could hang on for the count he'd finish in the money. Maybe even in first place.

Ignoring the canned music and the announcer's deep baritone blaring from the speakers, the crowd cheering on the contestant in the ring, he kept a wary eye on the fractious animal and eased down from his perch on the side of the chute and into the saddle. Immediately he felt the horse's muscles bunch. Squeezing his knees tighter, he wound the reins around his left hand.

"Up next in the chute, from Gold Fever, Colorado, is Zach Mahoney."

A cheer went up, and Hellbent tried to rear, hammering the gate with his hooves.

"Zach is— Whoa! Watch out there, Zach. You got yourself a mean one today."

Between them, Zach and the handlers subdued the horse, but he felt the animal quiver with rage and knew he was in for a wild ride. He tugged his Stetson down more snugly on his head. Wrapping the reins tighter around his gloved hand, he adjusted his position and paused to gather his focus. When he was ready, he raised his right hand.

The gate flew open and Hellbent leaped out into the arena, eleven hundred pounds of bucking, snorting fury, his massive body arching and twisting and spinning.

Zach's hat went flying on the third buck. In rhythm with the violent movements, he raked his blunted spurs over the horse's shoulders and kept his right hand high in the air while his upper body flopped back and forth in the saddle like a rag doll. Every time Hellbent's front hooves hit the ground Zach felt the jarring impact shoot up his spine all the way to the top of his head.

The crowd in the stands became a blur as the horse spun and pitched and did everything in his power to dislodge him. Never had eight seconds seemed so long. Zach's thigh muscles began to quiver from the strain of gripping the horse's flanks, but he gritted his teeth and hung on.

After what seemed like forever, in his peripheral vision he saw a pickup rider move in, and an instant later the horn blared, signaling the end of the ride. Zach grabbed the pickup rider's arm and shoulder, lunged from the saddle and swung to the ground.

"What a great ride! Let's give Zach a big hand, folks," the announcer urged.

While the crowd clapped and cheered and the pickup riders caught Hellbent and led him away, Zach scooped up his hat, gave it three hard knocks against his pant leg to remove the dust, set it back on his head and ambled for the pens, doing his best to not limp. With each step pain shot through his left leg and hip—a nasty little memento from the enraged bull that had given him a toss four days ago. Damn. He was getting too old for this.

Most of the cowboys on the rodeo circuit were in their twenties. Some were even in their teens. Zach's mouth took on a wry twist. Yeah, and there's a reason for that, Mahoney, he thought. By age thirty-six they're either too busted up to compete or they've wised up.

Not until Zach reached the exit gate did he allow himself to look over his shoulder and check his score. Yes! The ride had put him in the lead. Not bad for an old man.

By the time he made his way through the clutch of riders and handlers and accepted their congratulations, the last contestant was picking himself up out of the dirt, and Zach knew he'd won the top purse in the bronc riding event. Maybe even Best All Around, as well, but he wouldn't know that for an hour or so when all the events were over. He'd come back then for the finale, but in the meantime he was going to his RV to apply heat to his aching hip and leg.

After retrieving his saddle and bridle, Zach slung them over his shoulder and headed back to his motor home in the camping area behind the rodeo arena. Halfway there a man in a FedEx uniform intercepted him with an overnight letter.

Zach frowned. Who the devil would be sending him a registered letter? He turned the envelope this way and that, but the return address was too faint to make out in the dim light of the parking lot.

When he stepped into the RV his cell phone was ringing. Zach dumped the saddle and bridle just inside the door, tossed his Stetson on the sofa and snatched it up. ''Yeah, Mahoney here.''

''Zach, it's J.T.''

Surprise darted through him. He hadn't heard directly from either of his brothers since they'd they parted company in Clear Water, Montana, nine months ago.

No matter how much Kate and Matt's wife, Maude Ann, might wish otherwise, the brotherly connection just wasn't there.

''Yeah, what's up?''

''Have you gotten an overnight letter from the Manning and Manning law firm yet?''

Zach checked out the return address on the envelope he still held. ''It just came. I haven't had a chance to open it yet. How did you know about it?''

''Because Matt and I each received the same letter a couple of hours ago.''

''Oh? What's going on?''

''You're not going to believe this. The letters are from Seamus Rafferty's attorney, Edward Manning, notifying us of the old man's death and that we're beneficiaries in his will.''

''You've got to be kidding.''

''Nope. The old coot passed away yesterday. I called the law firm and talked to Edward Manning. He's waiting to hear from us before scheduling the funeral so he can allow plenty of time for us to get there.''

''The hell you say. I'm not going to that old devil's funeral.''

''I understand how you feel. That was Matt's first reaction. Mine, too. But the Rocking R meant a lot to Colleen. She obviously felt it was our heritage. If Seamus leaves us so much as one square foot of the place, we owe it to her to accept it.''

Zach rubbed the back of his neck and looked up at the ceiling, torn between resentment and a nagging sense of obligation and loyalty to the mother he couldn't remember. Damn. He didn't need this.

Although…J.T. did have a point.

He sighed. ''All right. I'll go.''

The January wind swooping down the snowy mountain slopes cut to the bone, causing several people to huddle deeper in their coats and shiver. Gray clouds scudded overhead, heavy with the threat of more snow to come. The dank smell of freshly dug, frozen earth hung in the air. From the nearby stand of pines came the raucous cawing of a raven, and in the valley the cattle lowed mournfully, as though aware of the event taking place in the small family cemetery on the slope above the ranch house.

''Dear Lord, we commit unto your keeping the soul of Seamus Patrick Rafferty.'' The minister picked up a handful of dirt and dropped the frozen clods onto the coffin. ''Ashes to ashes. Dust to dust. May God have mercy on your soul.'' Clutching his Bible to his chest, he lowered his head. ''Let us pray.''

Reverend Turner's dolorous voice droned on, but Willa Simmons barely heard him. She was too angry and upset. Refusing to look at the three men standing shoulder to shoulder on the opposite side of the grave, she kept her gaze focused on the casket. They had no right to be there. No right at all.

The sun glinted off one of the coffin's silver handles,

and Willa's eyes narrowed. Her hands curled into fists. It's your fault that they're here. Damn you, Seamus. How *could* you?

"Amen," the reverend intoned, and everyone in the sparse band of mourners echoed the word—all except Seamus's three grandsons. They stood stony-faced and dry-eyed, as they had throughout the service.

Zach Mahoney, Matt and Maude Ann Dolan, J.T. and Kate Conway, Edward Manning, Maria and the ranch hands and herself were the only ones there. A pitiful turnout for a man's funeral, Willa thought.

It was sad, but Seamus had only himself to blame. Over the years, with the exception of Harold Manning and his son Edward, Seamus had alienated every friend he'd ever had and all of his neighbors and acquaintances around Clear Water.

For an awkward moment the cowboys stood with their hats in their hands and shifted from one foot to the other, looking from Willa to Seamus's grandsons, trying to decide to whom they should offer condolences first.

Edward solved the dilemma for them by turning to Willa with a murmured word of sympathy before skirting around the grave to speak to the three brothers and the wives of the two who were married. The reverend did the same, and the relieved hands quickly followed their example. After muttering a few words, each man wasted no time heading down the hill to the bunkhouse, eager to escape the unpleasant duty and shed his Sunday-go-to-meeting clothes.

When the last cowboy sidled away, Willa slipped her arm through the housekeeper's. "C'mon, Maria. Let's go."

"But, Willie, you have not spoken with the *señors.*"

"Nor do I intend to." Unable to resist, Willa glared

at the brothers before heading for the gate in the wrought-iron fence that surrounded the cemetery.

"Willie? Hold on." Edward called.

The housekeeper turned to wait for the attorney to catch up, leaving Willa no choice but to do the same.

Impeccably dressed as always in a custom-tailored suit, silk shirt and tie, and a cashmere overcoat, Edward looked painfully out of place on the ranch. He was huffing by the time he reached them. Exertion and the biting cold had chaffed his cheeks to a ruddy hue and his styled brown hair was windblown. However, if he was annoyed that he'd had to chase after her it didn't show. His face held only sympathy and tenderness when he took her hand and patted it.

"Willie, I know this is rushing things, but since everyone involved is here, I was wondering if we could go ahead with the reading of the will? I have an early appointment in Bozeman tomorrow."

Willa's gaze shot past him to Seamus's grandsons and the two women. Resentment flooded her. She had been shocked to learn only the day before that her stepfather had rewritten his will to include Colleen's sons. Willa had no doubt that Seamus had left each of them a sum of money merely to ease his conscience. Still, just thinking about it made her bristle.

"By all means. Let's get this over with. The sooner they get their windfall, the sooner they'll leave."

All the parties named in Seamus's will had gathered in the study when Willa arrived, including Maria, Pete Brewster and Bud Langston, the ranch foreman. Only Edward was missing.

Willa took a seat in one of the fireside chairs. Everyone was seated except Zach Mahoney. He stood to one side, by the built-in bookshelves, a little apart from the others, with his suit coat thrust back on either side and his hands in his trouser pockets. While his brothers and their wives talked quietly among themselves, Zach kept silent and waited and watched.

Willa eyed him askance, her mouth tightening. She resented all of the interlopers, but especially this one. There was something about Zach Mahoney—something she couldn't quite put her finger on—that made her edgy and set her temper to simmering. They had barely exchanged half a dozen words, but whenever she was near him her body seemed to hum as though a low-voltage current of electricity were running through her.

Surreptitiously, Willa studied him for a clue to what triggered the reaction, but his chiseled face revealed nothing. Zach wasn't as handsome as J.T., nor did he have Matt's street-tough appeal, rather he had the weathered ruggedness typical of a Westerner.

Even dressed in a suit and tie as he was now, it was apparent in the way he held himself, that loose-limbed walk, and most of all, that aura of quiet strength and self-reliance that radiated from him.

Squint lines etched fan patterns at the outer edges of his eyes and deeper ones ran from his nose to the corners of his mouth. Thick, wheat-colored hair created a startling contrast to his tanned skin. A strong, square jaw, straight nose, well-defined lips and cheekbones sharp enough to cut combined to create a face that had a certain masculine appeal, Willa supposed—if you liked those sorts of rough-hewn looks in a man.

As though he felt her inspection, Zach turned his head, and their gazes locked. The hum of electricity coursing through her body became a jolt. Determined to not let him fluster her, she ground her teeth to keep from shivering and stared back into those deep-set green eyes. They glittered like gems in his sun-scorched face, giving him the sharp, dangerous look of a hungry wolf.

Willa's heart began to pound and her mouth grew dry, but she could not look away. To her relief, the spell was broken when Edward came striding into the room.

"Sorry I'm late. I had to take an urgent call."

He sat at Seamus's desk, snapped open his briefcase, and withdrew a legal-looking document. "If everyone is ready, I'll begin." Edward slipped on a pair of reading glasses and picked up the document. "I, Seamus Patrick Rafferty, being of sound mind..."

The first few pages consisted of the usual convoluted legalese, the upshot of which was several small bequests to the University of Montana and a few charitable organizations. Maria, Pete and Bud were each to receive a modest lump sum and a guaranteed pension when they decided to retire, plus the right to remain on the ranch for life in one of the cottages scattered about the property, if they so chose.

Turning another page, Edward glanced over his glasses at Willa and the three brothers and cleared his throat. "To my grandsons, Matthew Ryan Dolan, Zachariah Aiden Mahoney and Jedediah Tiernan Conway, and to my step-daughter, Willa Grace Simmons, I bequeath the remainder of my estate, including the Rocking R Ranch and all its assets, to be shared equally among them."

"*What?*" Willa shot out of the chair like a bullet. Shaking with fury, she felt the color drain out of her face. "That can't *be!* Seamus wouldn't leave the ranch to *them.* He *swore* over and over that he wouldn't!"

"I'm sorry, Willa, but it's true," Edward said. "Seamus wasn't happy about it. However, despite his threats, in the end he couldn't bear to let the ranch slip out of the family.''

Willa opened her mouth to continue, but Edward stopped her. "Before any of you say anything else, you should know there are conditions attached."

"'Conditions'?" Willa repeated in a voice bordering on hysteria.

"Yes. And I feel I must warn you, you're not going to like them."

"Uh-oh, here it comes," J.T. drawled.

"Yeah," Matt agreed. "I knew there had to be a catch."

"Exactly what are these conditions?" Zach spoke quietly, never taking his eyes from the attorney.

"You must all live here in this house and work the ranch together for a period of one year."

"That's outrageous! I won't do it!" Willa declared.

"If you don't—if any of you refuses to accept the conditions, or leaves before the year is up, then none of you inherits. The ranch and all its assets will be sold in a sealed-bid auction. The money from the sale will be held in a trust fund, from which each of you will receive the sum of ten thousand dollars a year. The remainder of the profits from the fund will go to a number of western universities that offer agricultural and ranching studies."

"Who will be the executor of the trust?" Matt made no effort to hide the suspicion in his voice.

"I will."

"And the sealed-bid auction? Will you handle that, as well?"

"That's correct." Edward met Matt's hard stare. "I know what you're thinking—that's a lot of power for one man. You're right. Normally a board of trustees would oversee a fund of this size and handle the auction, as well. I tried to get your grandfather to set things up that way, but he wouldn't hear of it. Seamus was a difficult man, as I'm sure you discovered.''

"Say we comply with these conditions. What happens at the end of the year?'' Zach asked.

"At that time, if any of you wants out, you may sell your share of the ranch to one or more of the others, but no one else.''

"I should have expected something like this,'' Willa railed. "Seamus always was manipulative and controlling. I just never thought he'd go this far.'' Seething, she paced to the window with quick, jerky steps, then made a frustrated sound and swung around. "This is intolerable!''

Enraged almost beyond bearing, Willa turned the full force of her fury on the brothers, addressing them directly for the first time. "This is all your fault.''

"Now wait just a darned minute,'' Matt began, but Zach raised his hand and silenced him.

He stared at Willa. His face was impassive but those eyes glittered in his tanned face like green ice. "Let's get something straight right now, Ms. Simmons. Whatever devious reasons Seamus had for making us his heirs, my brothers and I did nothing to influence his decision. We came here last year for one purpose—to find our mother. Failing that, we were hoping to get some information about her. That's all.''

Willa's chin came up at a challenging angle. "Not according to Seamus. He said you were three greedy opportunists, just like your father had been, and that you came here hoping to get your hands on this ranch. When you found out your scheme wasn't going to work, you left in a huff.''

"That's not true.''

"Oh, right. I'm supposed to believe you? I don't think so."

"Believe whatever you want. It makes no difference to me. Nor does it change anything."

"It's just not fair," she raged. "Your entire lives you spent less than an hour with Seamus. I've lived here since I was seven years old." She thumbed her chest. "I'm the one who worked this ranch every day for the past twenty years, not you three. I'm the one who was here for Seamus. When he got too old to ride a horse, I relayed his orders to the foreman and the men and worked right alongside them. I'm the one who put up with his bad temper and maliciousness. If you hadn't shown up here, he would have left the ranch to me like he promised."

"Uh, Willie." Edward's expression was a mixture of pity and chagrin. "I'm afraid you're wrong about that."

"What?" Willa stared at him with a blank look. "What do you mean?"

"Before Seamus changed his will to include his grandsons, all he was going to leave you was a few thousand dollars. The only reason he gave you a share of the ranch in this will was to irritate them."

Willa swayed and gripped the back of a chair for support. She felt as though she'd been hit in the stomach with a battering ram. "But...but he always said I'd inherit the ranch someday. He said I deserved it because I was the only one who cared, the only one who'd stuck around. He *promised!* Why would he say that if he didn't mean it?"

"Probably to keep you here. You were a big help to him and he depended on you. As you said, he was good at manipulation. Once he was gone, though, you would no longer be needed."

Another wave of shock slammed into her, and her hold

tightened on the chair back, whitening her knuckles.
"You mean…are you saying that I would have had to
leave the ranch?"

"I'm afraid so," Edward said gently. "The Rocking
R would have been sold in a closed-bid auction, just as
it will be if any of you refuses to abide by the conditions."

And she would have been left out in the cold.

Willa closed her eyes. She knew that later, when the
hurt was not so fresh, anger would resurface and come
to her rescue, but at that moment all she wanted was to
curl up in a tight ball and wail out her misery until she
was nothing but a hollow shell.

The pain was so great she forgot for a moment where
she was, and with whom. Then she opened her eyes and
cringed when her gaze fell on the brothers. The knowledge that she had meant so little to Seamus was devas-
tating enough, but having that revealed in front of these
men compounded her humiliation. They had the grace to
avoid looking at her, but somehow that oblique act of
compassion made her feel worse than if they'd gloated,
as she had expected them to do.

Gathering her tattered pride around her like a cloak,
Willa lifted her chin, squared her shoulders and pulled
herself up to her full five feet three inches. Ignoring the
others, she turned to the attorney. "I'll challenge the will.
Other people heard Seamus promise me the ranch. Maria,
for one."

"That's your right, of course. But you should know it
will be expensive and it could take years. In my opinion,
in the end you'd lose. I'm telling you this as a friend,
Willie, not as your stepfather's attorney. Trust me, the
will is air-tight."

"I see." Her full mouth folded into a bitter line.

"Then I guess I have no choice but to accept the conditions."

"Maybe you don't have a choice, but we do," Zach said.

"Oh, please." She shot him a look of patent disbelief. "Surely you don't expect me to believe that you would actually turn *down* the bequest. Yeah, right."

"This may come as a shock to you, Ms. Simmons, but we had lives of our own prior to Seamus's death."

"That's right," Matt snapped. "I say to hell with it. And Seamus. I'll be damned if I'll let that old tyrant dictate to me how and where I live my life."

"I agree," J.T. chimed in.

Zach nodded. "I'll admit, that was my first knee-jerk reaction, as well."

"You fools!" Fear that she might actually lose all claim to the ranch wiped away every other consideration. "Do you city slickers have any idea what such a rash decision would cost all of us? What we'd be giving up? I don't like what Seamus has done any better than you, but only an idiot would toss away a fortune of this size. Tell them, Edward."

The attorney rattled off the appraised value of the ranch and last year's revenues.

Matt let out a low whistle, but J.T. was more vocal.

"Holy cow! This place is worth a freakin' fortune!"

"The Rocking R is one of the largest ranches in this part of the country, and our firm's most important client." Edward paused.

"You have exactly two weeks from today, both to make up your minds and to do whatever you need to do and move in. Once you do that, the year begins."

"Mmm. Two weeks isn't much time. We need to talk it over before we make a decision," Zach said.

"Of course. I understand."

"Well, I don't," Willa snapped. "What is the matter with you people? You can't seriously be thinking of refusing? No one throws away a chance like this."

"Miss Simmons, if we do this, it's going to change all of our lives. Yours included. The least we can do is talk it over calmly and take a vote. So why don't you sit down."

"I don't need to talk it over. I can give you my vote right now. I detest the very idea of sharing the Rocking R with you people, but this is my home, and I'll do whatever I have to to keep it. Even if that means putting up with a bunch of greenhorn freeloaders." She stormed out and slammed the door behind her.

Edward winced. "I'm sorry about that. I do hope you'll excuse Willie." Standing, he slipped his reading glasses into a leather case and put them and the will into his briefcase and snapped it shut. "I know it doesn't seem so now, but she's really a nice person and normally quite good-natured and easy to get along with."

"We understand. She's upset, and apparently with good reason."

Matt rolled his eyes at his wife's comment. "Spoken like a psychiatrist. You ask me, she's a spoiled brat."

"That's not fair," Maude Ann protested. "From the sound of it, Seamus has been stringing that poor girl along for years."

"You don't know the half of it," Edward said. "Now, if you'll excuse me, I really must be going. It's a long way to Bozeman. When you've reached a decision, give me a call. If I'm not at my office you can reach me on my cell phone," he said, handing each of them his business card.

He turned to leave, then hesitated. "Uh...it's true that

the Rocking R Ranch is a sizable inheritance, but I feel I must warn you, if you decide to stay you'll earn every penny you get from it. Running a ranch this size is far from easy, and nothing is guaranteed. A poor calf crop, a string of bad luck, a few slaps from Mother Nature can hurt even a place this size. It won't be a piece of cake.''

Zach didn't need anyone to tell him about the hardships and perils of ranching. He knew them firsthand. In college he'd earned degrees in ranch management and business and before going out on the rodeo circuit he'd been general manager of the Carter Cattle Company, better known as the Triple C, a huge spread near Ridgeway, Colorado. Zach, however, saw no need to mention that to the attorney.

''Well, this is certainly an unexpected turn of events,'' Kate said when Edward had gone. ''From what you told Maude Ann and me about Seamus, I thought we'd attend a funeral, then go home with five dollars or some such slap-in-the-face bequest.''

''Yeah, we all did,'' Matt agreed. ''I wonder what made the old man change his mind?''

''My guess is, during our first visit here he somehow picked up on the strain between us,'' Zach said. ''The old coot probably took sadistic delight in that. Like Manning said, he cooked up this whole thing to stir up trouble and make claiming the inheritance as difficult as possible.''

''Right,'' J.T. agreed. ''Wherever he is, he's probably laughing himself silly right now.''

''He's got us in a bind, that's certain. If just one of us refuses to go along with the conditions, we all lose.'' Matt swept the others with a regretful look. ''Much as I hate to, I'm afraid I'm going to have to be the bad guy.

Maudie and I can't just abandon Henley Haven and pick up and move here. The kids we foster need her care."

"Yeah, well, if it makes you feel any better, I can't ask Kate to give up the Alpine Rose, either. Her parents spent years restoring that house and she's turned it into a profitable business. Added to that, she grew up in Gold Fever. It makes no difference to me where I live. I can write anywhere, but I won't rob her of her home."

"Before you two start making any noble sacrifices, don't you think you should ask Kate and me what we think?"

"Maude Ann's right. What kind of wife would I be if I stood in the way of your inheritance? Besides, I wouldn't have to sell the bed-and-breakfast. I'm sure I could hire someone to run it for me. And while it's true that I love the Colorado mountains, have you looked around? It's not too shabby here, either."

"The same applies to Henley Haven," Maude Ann stated emphatically. "I can get another psychiatrist to take over for me, and Jane will stay on. And there's no reason why I can't continue to work with abused children. I'm sure there are some here in Montana who need my help."

"But what about our own kids? They—"

"Will love it here," Maude Ann insisted before Matt could finish. "Can you think of a better place to raise five rambunctious children than on a ranch? Or to shelter others? The wide-open spaces will be good for them. And the drier climate will be good for your leg."

Matt frowned at the mention of his disability. It had been seventeen months since he taken that bullet that had ended his career as a detective with the Houston Police Department and left him with a permanent limp.

"Still...I don't know."

According to J.T., Matt had become more flexible since marrying Maude Ann, but it was still his first instinct to resist change of any kind. Watching him, Zach could see the struggle going on inside his taciturn brother.

"We're talking about a complete change in lifestyle and careers," Matt argued. "I don't know anything about ranching. Neither does J.T."

"No, but Zach does," J.T. said in a thoughtful voice, beginning to warm to the idea. "And you and I can learn."

"Maybe. Still, we all have to live together in this house," Matt said.

And that, Zach thought, was the real crux of the problem. He, J.T. and Matt might be brothers, but they didn't really know one another. A year ago they had made contact again, but a lifetime apart had created a chasm between them that they couldn't seem to breech.

Kate said they didn't try, and maybe that was true. At best, their relationship was distant, with currents of disquiet and wariness, even an undefined resentment running just below the surface, making them guarded with one another. For whatever reason, the fact remained that they *were* strangers.

"It will be awkward, I guess," J.T. agreed. "But it's not as though it'll be forever. Let's not forget that we're talking about a fortune here. And regardless of what Willa Simmons thinks, we are the rightful heirs. We'd be fools to turn it down. Surely we can manage to rub along together for a year. At the end of that time if anyone is miserable, they can sell out."

Matt looked at Zach. "You've sure been quiet. What do you think?"

"I think I should stay out of this discussion and let the four of you decide. All of you know that owning a ranch is my dream. I'd put up with anything, even Ms. Simmons, to own a part of this place, but I don't think it would be fair for me to try to influence you.''

"Yeah, but do you think we could live and work together for a whole year?''

"Maybe. Maybe not. I'm sure Seamus figured if he threw us together we'd be at one another's throats inside of a week. But one way or another, we won't know unless we try. One thing is certain, though. It's what Colleen would have wanted us to do.''

Chapter Two

Sadie's furious barking and the sound of vehicles approaching caught Willa's attention. Tossing aside the curry brush, she gave her horse an absent pat and walked over to the barn door, arriving just in time to see a caravan of vehicles—a pickup loaded with boxes, three SUVs towing rented moving trailers and a minivan—pull into the ranch yard at the back of the house. Instantly her whole body tightened.

Pete Brewster left the tack he'd been repairing and came to stand beside her. "Looks like they's here."

Gritting her teeth, Willa folded her arms and narrowed her eyes. She watched Zach hop out of the pickup cab and go over to one of the SUVs and say something to Kate as she climbed from behind the wheel.

"Made it just in time," the old man continued, undaunted by Willa's hostile silence. He paused to squirt a stream of tobacco juice into the ground to one side of the door, then added, "Be two weeks t'morra since the funeral."

"Oh, there was never any doubt they'd make the deadline," Willa muttered. "I'm sure they couldn't wait to get here and claim the lion's share of the ranch."

"'Pears to me you oughta be glad 'bout that, 'stead of standin' there looking like you just swallered a lemon. The way I heard it, if they hadn't'a accepted the inheritance, you'd be out on your ear."

Willa glared at the old man, but he paid no attention. With a huff she returned her gaze to the line of vehicles.

Pete had worked on the Rocking R for almost sixty years, even before Seamus had inherited the ranch. He'd taught her to ride and rope and brand, how to string barbed wire, build a campfire, inoculate and castrate cattle and the other myriad skills that ranch life entailed, skills Seamus either had not had the time, patience or inclination to teach her. When Willa had been a child Pete had been the one who bandaged her cuts and scrapes and dried her tears if her mother or Maria wasn't around. He'd also given her backside a wallop a few times when he'd thought she deserved it. Willa's temper didn't faze Pete.

"Yes, well…that's what makes it so galling. That and the fact that they have no to right to this place."

"Well, now, I don't rightly know as how I'd agree with you there, Willie, seeing as how they's old Seamus's grandsons, wrong side of the blanket or no. You'd best accept it, girl. Blood counts fer a lot, 'specially to a feller like Seamus."

"So I've discovered." She tapped one booted foot against the hard-packed ground, simmering inside. "Maybe they have the legal right, but they don't deserve it. They've never put in so much as a day's work on this ranch. While I was pouring my blood, sweat and tears into the place all those years, where were they? When Seamus needed them, where were they? They never bothered to call him or write to him or come for a visit their whole lives. Then, when he was so old it was obvious he couldn't last much longer, they showed up with their greedy hands out.''

"You know that fer sure an' certain, do ya?'' Pete rolled his cud of tobacco to his other cheek and slanted her a glinty look out of the corner of his eye.

"Seamus said— Good grief! I don't believe it! Look at all those children! One, two, three—why there's *five* of them."

"Looks like it," Pete agreed.

"Just what we need," Willa mumbled. "A bunch of chattering kids underfoot. They'll be nothing but a nuisance."

"Oh, I dunno 'bout that. When you was no bigger than a button you tagged after me or Seamus all the time, soakin' up ever'thing like a sponge. Tell you the truth, I plum enjoyed it. Ya ask me, havin' younguns around sorta brings a place to life."

Willa made a noncommittal sound. It wasn't so much the children who worried her, it was the adults, the five strangers with whom she would have to share her home. Her gaze zeroed in on Zach again. That one in particular bothered her. Just watching him, even from that distance, made her edgy and irritable. What was it about the man?

Willa watched as Maria bustled out the kitchen door onto the back porch, wiping her hands on her apron. The elderly housekeeper hurried down the gravel walkway and greeted the adults effusively then made a big fuss over the children.

She could see that Matt was having a difficult time

persuading the oldest boy to leave the horses in the corral, but after a brief exchange the sulky child climbed down off the corral fence and stomped after the others.

Everyone disappeared inside, and Willa turned to go back into the barn but she stopped when she spotted a red pickup cresting the rise at the top of the road.

Visitors to the Rocking R were rare enough that Willa experienced a dart of surprise. Thanks to Seamus's rotten disposition, with the exception of his grandsons, about the only outsiders who ever set foot on the property were George Pierce, the local veterinarian, and Edward Manning.

Shading her eyes with her hand, she squinted against the glare of the sun and watched the truck descend the road into the valley. It wasn't one of theirs. All the Rocking R pickups were silver-gray. Willa couldn't see who was behind the wheel, but the truck looked vaguely familiar. Who in the world…?

Recognition came with a jolt. Before the shock wore off, her legs were moving. By the time the truck came to a stop in the ranch yard behind the line of parked vehicles she was there to meet it.

"What are you doing here, Lennie?" she demanded, making no effort to hide the irritation in her voice. Not that it mattered. Lennard Dawson was much too self-involved to notice. The man had the sensitivity of a stump.

He flashed what he fancied to be a killer grin. "Why, I came to see you, gorgeous. I figured since Seamus wasn't around to object anymore, I'd drop by and see if you'd like to go out tomorrow night."

Willa barely stifled a groan. She might have known. Eight months ago she'd made the mistake of going out with Lennie. It had been only one date, and she never would have accepted that if Seamus hadn't butted in and forbidden her to go.

Lennie was handsome and as the only child and heir of another local rancher he was probably the most eligible bachelor in that part of Montana. The trouble was, he knew it. Willa hadn't liked him when they were kids, and in her opinion he had not improved with age.

In addition, there had been bad blood between Seamus and Lennie's father, Henry Dawson, for years. Over what, Willa had no idea, as Seamus had refused to discuss the matter, but for that reason alone, had he given her the chance, she would have refused the invitation without a qualm.

Her entire life she'd gone out on only a few dates, and never twice with the same man. Somehow Seamus had managed to run off every male who had ever shown an interest in her. That night his high-handedness had been the last straw, and for once she'd defied him and agreed to meet Lennie in town for dinner.

She'd been ruing that rare act of rebellion ever since.

It had taken no more than five minutes in Lennie's company for her to realize that she still could not abide the man, but he was too conceited to notice. Ever since that night, he'd been acting proprietorial toward her whenever they bumped into each other in town. She'd even heard that he'd been telling people they were a couple. Willa had taken him to task at the first opportunity, but Lennie had just laughed and brushed aside her ire, saying if it weren't for Seamus, they would be. So far, nothing she said made the slightest difference.

Lennie reached for the door handle, but Willa stopped him. "Don't bother getting out. My answer is no."

"Look, we could drive over to Bozeman and take in

a movie. Or just go out to dinner and see what happens after," he said with a suggestive wiggle of his eyebrows.

"Nothing is going to happen, because I'm not going out with you. Will you get it through that thick head of yours that I'm not interested?"

Lennie hooked his left elbow over the window frame and gave her a coaxing look. "Aw, c'mon, Willie. Seamus kept you on a short lead from the time you turned fourteen and developed knockers. It's past time you kicked up your heels, babe."

"Don't call me babe," Willa snapped. "And trust me, if I ever decide to kick up my heels, it won't be with you."

Willa heard the back door open and close, and when Lennie glanced in that direction his cocky smile collapsed.

"Who's that?" he demanded, scowling.

She looked over her shoulder in time to see Zach lope down the porch steps and head for his pickup. He glanced in her direction and nodded, but otherwise ignored them and began untying the ropes securing the boxes in the truck bed.

"That's Zach Mahoney, one of the new owners of the Rocking R," she said, unable to hide her resentment. "He and his brothers and their families arrived just a few minutes ago."

"One of Colleen's bastards, huh. Everybody in town in talking about them. Is he married?"

"No, just Matt and J.T."

Lennie's scowl deepened. "I don't like it."

"Don't like what?"

"Him living in the house with you."

"*What?* You don't have the right to like or dislike anything that goes on here, Lennie Dawson."

She could have saved her breath.

"Damn that Seamus. Don't you see what that scheming old devil was up to? He figured he'd throw you and his bastard grandson together and let nature take its course."

"Seamus may have been autocratic about a lot of things, but he wouldn't go so far as to pick out a husband for me."

"Why not? He tried to force Colleen to marry my old man. He and Seamus even shook hands on a deal. Dad would marry Colleen and take over the ranch when Seamus kicked the bucket."

"That's a lie! I don't believe you."

"Believe it or not, it's true. Hell, Willie, the old coot was a control freak. It bugged the hell outta him that Colleen escaped, so he dangled the ranch in front of her bastards to rein them in. And you're the honey that sweetens the trap. That's the only reason he bothered to include you in his last will."

The statement hit her like a slap in the face. Willa trembled with anger and hurt…and uncertainty. "Get out of here!" she stormed. "Get off this ranch this minute."

"Willa?"

Her head snapped around, and she realized that her raised voice had drawn Zach's attention. He tossed the rope he had just wound into a neat coil onto the tailgate of his truck and took a couple of steps in their direction. "Is there a problem?"

She didn't know which stung the most—Lennie's disgusting insinuations, or having Zach come to her aid.

"No. There's no problem. Mr. Dawson was just leaving."

Lennie's mouth tightened and his face flamed an angry red. Clearly he did not take kindly to being dismissed.

He stared at Willa for a long time, his gaze flickering now and then to the other man. Though Zach's stance was deceptively casual and loose there was no doubt that he was braced for trouble.

"Dammit, Willa—"

"*Goodbye,* Lennie."

A muscle twitched in his cheek. He swore and reached for the door handle again but hesitated when Zach moved closer.

"All right, all right. I'm going." He twisted the key in the ignition and the truck roared to life. "You're obviously too emotional to discuss this rationally. When you've calmed down, think about what I said. You'll see that I'm right."

"Don't hold your breath."

Lennie stomped on the accelerator and the pickup fishtailed as he spun it into a U-turn. Gunning the engine, he tore out of the ranch yard, his tires rudely kicking up dirt and gravel.

Watching the truck shoot up the road at breakneck speed, Willa experienced an odd mixture of fury and disquiet. Lennie was a hothead. She and everyone else around Clear Water had witnessed his temper many times, but she had paid no more attention to his tantrums than she would a small child's. This time, though, she had seen something wild and dangerous simmering in his eyes, and that glimpse had sent an icy trickle down her spine. It galled her to admit it, but she was certain if Zach hadn't been there Lennie would not have let her order him off the ranch.

"Was that guy giving you a hard time, or was that just a lovers' quarrel?"

The question made her jump, and she was even more startled to realize that Zach now stood just behind her left shoulder. Willa was shorter than most men, but he seemed to tower over her, topping her five foot three inches by almost a foot. She was suddenly, uncomfortably aware of his broad shoulders and lean, muscular build, that raw masculinity that surrounded him like an aura, and her nerves began to jitter.

She stepped away and gave him a cool look. "Neither. Lennie Dawson is a neighbor. His father owns the Bar-D, the ranch that borders us to the east. I've known him since I was six."

"Mmm," Zach replied, watching the red pickup disappear over the crest of the hill. "Has he always had a bad temper?"

Willa stiffened, and immediately her anger with Lennie transferred to Zach. "Look, I can handle Lennie. In the future just mind your own business."

Zach shrugged. "Fine by me. I was just trying to help."

"I don't *need* your help. I don't need anything from you." She spun away and stomped back to the barn.

Watching her, Zach shook his head. That's where you're wrong, lady, he thought. You need me, all right. Like it or not, you need me and J.T. and Matt to hold on to this place.

Everything about the woman radiated anger, from those snapping violet eyes to her rigid spine to the defiant set of her jaw. Though on the small side, she was beautifully proportioned, and her leggy stride ate up the ground. Today all that ebony hair was confined in one long braid as thick as his wrist, which bounced and swayed against her backside with each furious step.

He could understand her anger—up to a point. She felt cheated and ill-used, and who could blame her? In her place, he'd feel the same. Seamus had strung her along with false promises, and after putting up with his foul temper and rigid control for most of her life, losing three-quarters of the Rocking R to strangers, never mind that they were the rightful heirs, had to have been a low blow. Discovering that without them she would have lost it all must have been even more galling.

Hell, he couldn't blame her for resenting them. Seamus was the real villain in all this, but the old bastard was gone, and her fury needed a live target.

Okay, he could live with that for a while. It wouldn't be easy, but he'd cut her some slack. At least until the raw hurt eased enough for her to gain a little perspective and look at the situation fairly.

Willa entered the barn muttering a litany of colorful epithets aimed at Zach, Lennie, Seamus and men in general. Sitting on a nail keg in the sunshine spilling in through the open double doors, Pete cast her a cautious glance, then wisely went back to stitching the saddlebag he was repairing.

"How dare Lennie accuse Seamus of using me to further his own agenda," she snarled as she paced to the far end of the barn. "How *dare* he! Idiot. Jerk. Hopeless Neanderthal!"

True, Seamus may not have loved her as his own flesh and blood, as she'd so desperately wanted, but he had accepted her as his stepdaughter and assumed responsibility for her, honoring that obligation even after her mother's death.

Willa had been only fifteen at the time. Seamus could have shipped her off to live with distant relatives, but he had not been a man to shirk his duty.

Still, the sad truth was, Seamus had been perfectly capable of scheming to make a match between her and

Zach. Was that why he had made her a beneficiary in his last will? So propinquity could do its work? He'd clearly had no intention of leaving her any portion of the ranch until after his grandsons showed up.

Seamus may have resented Zach and his brothers, but they had the Rafferty blood that had been so important to him and she had the experience and dedication and love for the Rocking R. If her stepfather had gotten it into his head that a marriage between her and Zach would benefit the ranch, he would have schemed and manipulated to make it happen.

In all things, Seamus had always been so absolutely certain that his way was the right way that he would not have considered such a maneuver wrong. Or insulting to her. Willa snorted. He probably would've thought he was doing her a favor.

"Well, if that was Seamus's plan, it's doomed to failure," she swore. "By heaven, I won't be anyone's brood mare.

"Men!" she spat, earning another wary look from Pete.

Though she'd paced the barn's cavernous length three times, fury still bubbled inside her. Finally she picked up a pitchfork and attacked the stalls, even though they had been mucked out only that morning.

She worked steadily for a couple of hours, until her shoulders ached and the muscles in her arms quivered from the strain. After the stalls were clean and spread with fresh hay she filled the feed and water troughs in the corrals as well as those inside the barn. Occasionally, through the open doors, she glimpsed Zach and his brothers and the children retrieving things from their vehicles and toting them into the house.

When Willa could find nothing else to do she fetched

a can of neatsfoot oil and a soft chamois from the tack room and started applying the lubricant to her saddle.

"I just oiled that saddle two days ago," Pete growled, never taking his gaze from his work. "It don't need it again." Pete had gotten too old to ride and he refused to retire, so Seamus had put him in charge of the tack room, and he guarded his domain with the fierceness of a stock dog with his herd.

"It looked a little dry," Willa said defiantly, and continued to rub the leather.

Pete stood and hung the bridle on a nail. He crossed the barn to Willa's side, took oil and cloth from her and set them aside, then cupped her elbow with his gnarled hand. "C'mon, Willie," he said gently, steering her toward the door. "You can't avoid them folks forever, so you might as well go on inside. Maria's bound to have dinner ready by now. An' from the smells coming from the cookhouse, Cookie's got the men's grub ready, too."

Willa sighed, knowing that Pete was right. "All right, I'm going. I'm going," she mumbled.

Outside twilight had fallen. She murmured good-night to Pete and headed toward the house on leaden feet. She'd rather take a whipping than sit down to a meal with those people.

The heavenly smell of fried chicken greeted her as she climbed the steps to the back porch, and despite the dread she felt, her stomach growled in anticipation. Opening the door, she stepped inside the kitchen and came to an abrupt halt.

For the last eleven years she, Maria and Seamus had rattled around in the huge ranch house. Seamus had not been a talkative man, nor had he been tolerant of what he'd called "women's chatter" at the table. As a result, meals had been eaten mostly in silence, the three of them often exchanging not so much as a word. Now the chatter and bustle of six adults and five children filled the huge old kitchen.

The children were setting the table and indulging in a bit of bickering and shoving as they darted and dodged around each other. J.T. and Matt sat on opposite sides of the long trestle table, drinking coffee and arguing quietly about something. The women carried on a conversation of their own while they helped Maria— Kate at the stove assisting with the cooking and Maude Ann washing the pots and pans and mixing bowls as quickly as the other women finished with them.

Standing a little apart in the doorway that lead into the hall, one shoulder braced against the frame, Zach sipped a mug of coffee and took in the scene in silence, those sharp green eyes missing nothing, including her.

The cacophony of laughter, voices and activity assaulted Willa's senses, making her nerves jump.

"Hello, Willa. We wondered where you were," Maude Ann greeted when she spotted her.

Kate's gaze flickered in her direction. She offered a cautious hello, and J.T. and Matt interrupted their discussion long enough to do the same. Sensing the adults's wariness and the sudden strain in the air, the children stopped what they were doing and stared at Willa with distrust. As though *she* was the one who didn't belong, Willa thought.

Wiping her hands on a towel, Maude Ann turned from the sink with a tentative smile. "I was beginning to worry that you'd miss dinner, but you're just in time."

"Watch out, Willa," Matt drawled. "Maudie's a mother hen. She'll tuck you under her wing with the rest of her chicks if you let her."

"Don't be silly. I just didn't want her to go hungry,

that's all,'' his wife said with a huff, but her eyes danced with affection and humor as she yanked a lock of his hair.

"Ah, the biscuits, they are ready," Maria announced.

"So is everything else," Kate said, carrying a steaming gravy boat and a bowl of salad to the table. "Everybody sit down while I dish up the rest."

The children whooped and made a dash for the table, elbowing one another and jostling for position, but a firm order from Matt put an instant end to the unmannerly behavior.

Kate noticed that Willa still stood rooted to the spot just inside the back door and motioned to the table. "Have a seat. You must be starved after working all day."

Willa wanted to refuse, but she was so hungry she was shaky, and the aromas filling the kitchen were driving her crazy. She shifted from one foot to the other. "I, uh…I have to wash up first. Excuse me."

She expected Zach to move out of the doorway, but he merely shifted a bit to one side to allow her to squeeze by, those cool eyes tracking her all the while.

As Willa scooted past him, her shoulder brushed his chest and a tingle trickled down her spine. He had recently showered, and the smells of soap and shampoo and clean male enveloped her. The heady combination made her light-headed and self-consciously aware that after working in the barn all afternoon she smelled of horses, straw, neatsfoot oil and old leather. Gritting her teeth, she marched down the hall to the powder room.

When she returned everyone was seated, and she took the only chair left, next to the angelic-looking little blond girl.

Matt offered the blessing, and as the bowls and platters

were being passed around the table, Willa felt a tug on her left sleeve. Startled, she looked down into a pair of wide, innocent blue eyes, fixed on her with unwavering directness.

"You ith pretty," the child lisped.

Disarmed, Willa blinked. "Uh…thank you."

"My name ith Debbie, and I'm five. Whath yourth?"

"Willa."

"Wiwa. Thath a pretty name."

"Uh…thanks."

"Not Wiwa, you dumb girl," the African-American boy jeered, rolling his eyes. "She said Willa."

"Tyrone, no name-calling," Maude Ann warned. "You know the rules."

"But she talks like that dumb ole duck in the cartoons."

Tears welled in Debbie eyes and her protruding lower lip trembled. "I ith not dumb. Am I, Daddy?" she appealed, turning her pathetic little face to Matt.

"No, of course not, sweetheart." He gave the boy a stern look. "Apologize to your sister, Tyrone."

"Aw, do I gotta?"

"Yes. Now."

The boy stared down at his plate, his jaw set in a mulish pout. "Sorry."

Maude Ann sent Willa an apologetic look. "Sorry about that. But you know how children are."

"No, actually I don't. I've never been around children."

"Oh. I see." Willa's cool tone was not lost on Maude Ann, and for the first time her own voice had a guarded quality. "Well, we all have adjustments to make. And so you'll know who you're dealing with, let me introduce you to the rest of the children. This is Yolanda."

Starting with the Hispanic girl, Maude Ann worked her way around the table. With the exception of twelve-year-old Yolanda, the Dolans's adopted brood were stair-step in age. In addition to Debbie and eight-year-old Tyrone, there was seven-year-old Jennifer, a quiet, plain child who seemed to be trying to make herself invisible, and a frail-looking six-year-old named Tim.

Willa responded to each child with a cool hello that didn't encourage conversation and returned her attention to her meal as soon as the introductions were finished. They were well behaved, and she supposed they were appealing, but they didn't belong there, and she wasn't interested in getting to know them.

"I know there are a lot of us, and this probably seems like a huge imposition to you, after living here so quietly with your stepfather all those years, but I assure you, the children won't be a problem," Maude Ann added when the introductions were over.

Willa gave a little snort of disbelief and slanted her a look. "Actually, I'm surprised that you brought them here."

Around the table everyone stopped talking and the clank and ping of silverware ceased. Willa could feel ten pairs of eyes fix on her, and in her peripheral vision she saw Maria shaking her head sadly.

As though an iron rod had been rammed down her spine, Maude Ann sat up straighter. Her chin rose and the almost perpetual impish twinkle in her eyes turned to frost. "Really? And just what did you expect me to do with my children during the year we all must be here?"

"Technically, you and the children and Kate don't have to be here at all. The conditions only apply to your husbands and Zach and me."

"Now wait just a minute—" Matt began, but his wife held up her hand to stop him.

"No. I'll handle this." She turned to Willa with an implacable expression. "Where my husband goes, I go, and so do our children. We're a family. If you don't like that, too bad."

"The same goes for J.T. and me," Kate agreed. "You have a lot of nerve even suggesting that we shouldn't be here."

"Look, all I'm saying is, this is a busy ranch. A lot of the work we do is dangerous and cattle and horses are unpredictable. It isn't the safest place to bring a bunch of children."

"Oh, please," Maude Ann scoffed. "Children have grown up on ranches for hundreds of years."

"That's right. You were raised here, weren't you?" Matt demanded.

"Yes, but I was born on a nearby ranch. I wasn't a city kid when my mother and I came to the Rocking R." Willa shrugged. "Actually, you're all going to have a difficult time. There aren't any fancy stores or coffee-houses or restaurants or even a movie theater in Clear Water."

"Don't worry about us. We'll manage," Maude Ann said. "What we don't know, we'll learn."

Zach sat quietly, taking in the clash, but the other adults murmured agreement while the children stared at Willa as though she were a monster with two heads. All except Tyrone, who glared at her and bragged, "Yeah. I'm gonna learn to ride a horse and rope cows an' ever'thing."

Willa shrugged. "Suit yourselves. Just don't say I didn't warn you."

She picked up her fork, took a bite of mashed potatoes.

For the remainder of the meal the others talked among themselves. The only one who spoke to Willa was Maria, and then only to give her a scolding in rapid-fire Spanish, which Willa knew she richly deserved.

It had been a stupid thing to say. The instant the words had left her mouth she'd known that she had gone too far. But, darn it! She was feeling so prickly and on edge. Out-of-sorts and outnumbered.

Zach said little, but the others, including the children, carried on a lively conversation.

Willa's appetite had fled, and she spent most of the meal moving the food around on her plate. When the children were sent upstairs to brush their teeth and shower and get ready for bed, she scraped back her chair. "I'm going to turn in, too."

She made it only as far as the front hall when Zach caught up with her.

"Willa. I want to talk to you."

"Not now. I'm tired. I'm going to bed." She put her hand on the newel post to start up the stairs, but Zach clamped his hand around her upper arm and spun her around to face him.

"What do you think you're doing? Let go of me! I have nothing to say to you."

"Good. Just keep your mouth shut and listen." He bent forward until his face was mere inches from hers. Willa's heart skipped a beat. Fury blazed in his normally cool green eyes. His face was a taut mask, his jaws so tight he spoke through his clenched teeth. "Listen to me, Willa Simmons. You can unleash your anger on me and Matt and J.T. all you want, but if you ever, *ever* again strike out at those kids or my sister or Maude Ann, or upset them in any way, you'll answer to me. Is that clear?"

"I didn't mean to upset anyone. I was only trying to point out the downside of living here."

"Bull. You're between a rock and a hard place, and that frustrates the hell out of you. You can't run me or my brothers off without losing the ranch, so you thought you'd see if you could get rid of the wives and kids. That way you wouldn't feel quite so outnumbered. Nice try, but it won't work. We're here to stay. All of us. Is that clear?"

Humiliation, shame and temper tangled together inside Willa, but it was pride that saw her through. She tilted her chin at a regal angle. "Yes. Perfectly."

"Good."

Chapter Three

Willa rose earlier than usual the next morning. In the kitchen, over Maria's objections, she grabbed a couple of hot biscuits and made her escape, and moments later she drove her pickup out of the yard.

At the ranch entrance she turned north onto the highway and headed for Helena.

It wasn't Willa's nature to run away, and her conscience pricked her as she punched the accelerator, but she kept going. She simply wasn't up to facing Zach and his family just yet, not after the night she'd just had. She had behaved badly and she'd paid the consequences. Long after she'd heard the others come upstairs she'd lain awake, staring at the ceiling, wrestling with her guilt and anger. Even when she'd finally fallen asleep she had tossed and turned fitfully.

Willa justified the trip by telling herself she had to pick up the new boots she'd had made. Never mind that there was no hurry, and that anyone from the ranch who was going to Helena within the next few weeks could have picked them up for her. She wanted to do it herself. Anyway, she deserved a day off now and then, didn't she?

Willa was so unaccustomed to having leisure time she hardly knew what to do with herself, but she forced herself to delay her return as long as possible.

At ten after eleven that evening she pulled into the ranch yard. The house was dark except for the light in the kitchen, but Willa wasn't surprised that Maria had left it on for her. Intent on getting upstairs without waking anyone, she eased open the back door as quietly as possible.

"Oh. What are you doing still up?"

Seamus's grandsons sat at the kitchen table, watching her.

"Waiting for you." Zach gestured toward the chair opposite his. "Have a seat. We need to talk."

Willa didn't budge. "What now? It's late and I'm tired."

"And whose fault is that? If you hadn't run off, we would have had this discussion at breakfast."

"I did not 'run off.' I had some errands to run."

He simply looked at her. She tried to weather that steady gaze, though she felt a guilty blush spread over her face. "Oh, all right. We'll talk." She jerked out a chair and plopped down with a huff. "What is so important that it couldn't wait until morning?"

"Before we go any further, we need to decide who's going to be in charge of the ranch operation."

Shock slammed through Willa, jerking her head back. "What do you mean, who's going to be in charge? *I'm* in charge."

An uncomfortable silence filled the room as the three

men exchanged a look. Finally, J.T. cleared his throat. "Well, the thing is, since we all own equal shares of the Rocking R, my brothers and I feel that we should take a vote on that."

"That's right," Matt agreed. "Let's face it, you can't run a place like this by committee. There can only be one person giving orders."

"I agree with that. I just don't understand why we're having this conversation. None of you city slickers knows beans about ranching. I'm the only one with experience."

"Uh...that's not exactly true," J.T. corrected. "Zach has ranching experience."

"A rodeo cowboy?" She gave a scornful laugh. "You want to put a rodeo cowboy in charge of this ranch? Are you crazy? This may surprise you, but on the Rocking R we don't spend a lot of time riding our bulls."

"Actually, Willa, Zach has worked on a ranch before."

"Oh, please. Hiring on as a wrangler at some hardscrabble little spread between rodeos hardly qualifies him to ramrod a spread the size of this one."

"You don't understand. Zach is highly qualified for the job. He has—"

"Never mind, J.T." Zach watched Willa, his expression inscrutable. "I don't think she wants to hear any of that."

"But—"

"No, it's okay. She's entitled to her opinion. Just as we are to ours. Which is why we're going to vote."

"Then I vote that Zach should be in charge," Matt said.

"So do I," J.T. concurred.

"Since I agree with them, that settles it." Zach's cool

gaze drilled into Willa. "From now on, I'll be giving the orders. Are we clear on that?"

Willa's hands curled into fists. The fierce emotions roiling through her set off a trembling deep inside her body. She gritted her teeth and glared at him, too furious to speak.

Zach cocked one blond eyebrow. "Well?"

"Fine!" she snapped. "Go ahead and play cowboy. Just don't come whining to me six months from now when we go belly up." She exploded out of the chair so fast it toppled and crashed to the brick floor, but she paid it no mind and stomped toward the back door. She had to get out of there—*now*—before she blew apart.

"Willa, wait. We have some other decisions to make."

"Make them yourself. No matter what I want, the three of you will outvote me, anyway."

The back door slammed with a force hard enough to rattle the windows and make the brothers wince.

J.T. gave a long, low whistle. "Man, that is some temper."

"Yeah." Zach stared at the door, a furrow creasing between his eyebrows. "But she has reason to be angry. I hated to deal her another blow, but I don't think we had a choice."

"Maybe we could have been a little more subtle about it."

Matt snorted at J.T.'s suggestion. "And just how were we supposed to do that, Einstein? There is no gentle way to strip someone of their authority."

"Oh, I don't know. Zach could have taken over bit by bit over a period of time."

"And you don't think she would've notice? Yeah, right. That lady is as possessive of this ranch and her position as a dog with a meaty bone."

"I agree," Zach said. "You don't maneuver around a strong-willed woman like Willa. Anyway, clean and quick is usually less painful in the long run.

"As for the other things we need to hash out, I think we'd better give her time to cool down. We'll continue this discussion in the morning."

"Fine by me. I'm ready to turn in. I'm beat." Matt stood and stretched, then unhooked his cane from the back of his chair. He limped away a couple of steps, then stopped and looked back at his brothers with a wry half smile. "The funny thing is, Willa assumes because we're triplets we're going to agree on everything. Man, is she in for a shock."

Willa always rose early, and the following morning was no exception, even though once again she had gotten little sleep.

After storming out of the house the night before, she'd made a beeline for the barn, as had been her habit in the past whenever she'd been upset or smarting from Seamus's criticism. There she had paced and ranted and cursed at the rafters. At one point she'd hauled off and kicked a galvanized pail almost the length of the structure. Of course, that had made a terrible racket and frightened the stock, and she'd had to take time out to quiet them, but, oh, it had felt good to vent her fury.

Finally, with the worst of her rage spent, Willa had wrapped her arms around her horse Bertha's neck and poured out her woes into the animal's sympathetic ear. Of all the unpleasant changes and low blows she'd endured in the past few weeks, this one was by far the worst. The usurpers were taking over, and there wasn't a blessed thing she could do to stop them.

It wasn't until hours later that Willa had returned to

the house and tiptoed upstairs to her room. Still upset, she had slept poorly until just before dawn when she had to get up.

Confident the others were still asleep, Willa dressed and braided her hair and went downstairs. She intended to once again grab a biscuit then saddle up and ride out before anyone stirred, but to her surprise, when she approached the kitchen she heard raised voices.

"No, dammit! I won't do it."

"Why not? You're the logical one."

Stunned and fascinated by the unexpected friction between the brothers, Willa paused outside the swinging door.

"Why? Because I've got a busted leg? Just because I walk with a limp doesn't mean I can't ride a horse or drive a truck."

"Have you ever ridden a horse?"

"No, but I can learn. I'd helluva lot rather be out in the fresh air than cooped up inside all day."

"Actually, Zach, it would be better for Matt to be involved in some sort of physical work," Maude Ann offered cautiously. "He needs to exercise his leg as much as possible."

Willa slipped inside the kitchen in time to see Zach rake his hand through his wheat-colored hair. The others were so intent on their discussion they didn't notice her standing just inside the doorway.

The three brothers and Maude Ann and Kate sat at the table, drinking coffee, while Maria prepared breakfast.

"All right, then J.T. will keep the books."

"The hell I will!"

"Dammit, J.T., what's *your* problem? You're a writer. You're going to be inside working at a desk a lot of the time, anyway."

Well, well, isn't this interesting, Willa thought. She looked from one man to the other, enjoying herself immensely.

"All the more reason to get away from a desk for part of each day. You're nuts if you think I'm going to be stuck inside while you and Matt are out enjoying the wide-open spaces and the fresh air. Besides, I'm lousy at figures."

Zach heaved a long-suffering sigh and massaged the back of his neck. "Look. First of all, ranching isn't fun and games or some kind of lark. It's long hours of hard, back-breaking, muscle-straining, dirty, sweaty physical labor. Sometimes it can be damned dangerous, as well."

"Don't worry about me. I can handle it," Matt vowed.

"Me, too," J.T. echoed.

"How? Neither one of you has ever even been on a horse before, for Pete's sake."

"Then teach us to ride."

"I won't have time."

"Fine, then I'll find someone who will. Because there's no way you're going to turn me into a pencil pusher. I quit the police force rather than take a desk job, and I'm sure as hell not going to be stuck with one here. You got that, Mahoney?"

"For once, I have to agree with Matt," J.T. said.

"Oh, great. Just what this place needs—*three* greenhorns on horseback."

The drawled statement brought six heads swiveling in Willa's direction in time to see her hook her thumbs into the front pockets of her jeans and saunter toward the table. Matt and J.T. shot her an annoyed look, but the women regarded her with a mixture of wariness and concern.

Willa tilted her chin. No doubt they knew about that

discussion last night and that Zach had usurped her place as boss. Well, if they were looking for signs of tears, they were going to be disappointed. She was mad as hell, not hurt.

"Good morning." Kate gestured toward the chair beside her own. "Come join us. We're trying to decide who does what."

"So I gathered."

Zach focused on his most pressing problem. "Can you keep books?"

"No." It was a bald-faced lie. In Seamus's later years, when his eyesight had begun to fade, she'd helped him with the accounts, but of all the jobs on the ranch, bookkeeping was her least favorite, and she wasn't about to take it on to help Zach.

"Great. That's just great."

"I'll do the books, Zach," Kate offered quietly. "Giving Maria a hand with meals and doing the books should keep me busy."

"The children and I will help out around the house, too," Maude Ann volunteered. "And we can put in a garden. I noticed there isn't one now, and I do love fresh veggies. Maybe we can build a coop and raise some chickens, too. It would be nice to have fresh poultry and eggs."

The changes were coming too fast. For Willa it was like being chased by a swarm of bees, and she instinctively resisted.

"And what about me? What am I supposed to do?" Everything about Willa—her expression, the thrust of her chin, her tone—was a belligerent challenge. If Zach thought he could stick her in the house with the women, he had another think coming.

"What were your duties before Seamus became ill and you started relaying his orders?"

"I did whatever needed doing. Usually I worked alongside the men."

"Then that's what you'll continue to do," he said matter-of-factly, taking the wind out of her sails.

At the very least she had expected he would assign her menial chores that were reserved for the newest, most inexperienced hands. At worst, that he would relegate her to the house and domestic chores. She'd been prepared to fight him tooth-and-nail over either.

Zach turned to his brothers. "I want to make one thing clear. If you two insist on working outdoors alongside me, then you're going to darn well pull your own weight and put in an honest day's work. Is that clear?"

Both men bristled.

"Hey! I may have a bum leg, Mahoney, but I'm no slacker. I can work you into the ground any day of the week."

"That goes for me, too," J.T. declared.

"Fine. Just so we understand one another." Zach looked at Willa. "Can you give them riding lessons?"

"No." She sipped her coffee and eyed him defiantly.

"Okay, who do we have on the payroll who can teach these two yahoos to ride and rope and the rest of the basics?"

Willa gritted her teeth. She was spoiling for a fight and wouldn't you know he'd refuse to cooperate. "Your best bet would be Pete. He's almost eighty and arthritic but he was practically born in the saddle. He's been working here since he was sixteen, and he taught me to ride."

"Okay, I'll talk to him after breakfast. Now, the next—"

A high-pitched scream from the front of the house cut

him off in midsentence. The shrill sound made the hairs on Willa's forearms and the back of her neck stand on end.

"What the hell!"

"Holy—!"

"That's Jennifer!" Maude Ann bolted out of her chair. She shoved open the swinging door at a dead run and raced for the front hall. Everyone else followed right on her heels.

The screams continued, running together in one long, ear-piercing sound. By the time they burst into the foyer Willa was at the back of the group.

Jennifer stood by the open front door, rigid, trembling with fright and shrieking. Her face was chalk white, her stricken gaze fixed on the outside of the door.

Both Zach and Matt cursed and Kate and Maude Ann gave a shocked cry.

"*¡Dios mio!*" Maria closed her eyes and crossed herself and began to recite a fervent prayer under her breath.

"Aw, hell," J.T. muttered. "What a thing for a kid to see."

"What? What is it?" Skidding to a halt behind them, Willa wriggled her way to the front of the group, and gasped. "Oh, my, Lord."

Nailed to the outside of the front door was a dead gopher. Between the animal and the door hung a bloodied piece of paper.

Maude Ann dropped to her knees and snatched the child into her arms. Turning away from the gruesome sight, she pressed the girl's face against her shoulder.

"It's all right, baby. It's okay. Momma's here, love," she crooned over and over, stroking the child's back.

The girl locked her arms around Maude Ann's neck in a death grip. "I—I'm s-sorry, Momma. I w-wasn't·going anywh-where. I—I just w-wanted to...pet the d-d-doggie," she sobbed against her mother's shoulder.

"That's okay, baby. You didn't do anything wrong. It's okay, baby. It's okay."

Striding forward, Zach snatched the paper free and slammed the door shut, removing the animal from view.

"There's writing on it," J.T. pointed out. "What does it say?"

Zach scanned the sheet of paper. It was lined and ragged along the left side, obviously torn from a spiral notebook. "It says, 'Get out, Bastards. You're not wanted here.'"

His head snapped around toward Willa. "Is this your doing?"

"*Me?* Of course not!" she denied, but all around the others were staring at her, their expressions accusing. Even Maria looked sad. "How can you even ask that?"

"Easy. You've made it plain that you don't want us here."

"That's true, but I'm not a fool. Why would I try to run you off? If any of you leave, I lose everything I've ever wanted. Do you honestly think I'd do something that stupid?"

"What I think is that temper of yours sometimes overrules your common sense."

"That's not true!"

A stony silence stretched out as everyone eyed her with suspicion and hostility. Zach stared at her so long she had to fight the urge to squirm.

The tense silence was broken when the other four children came clamoring down the stairs, barefoot and in their pajamas and still rumpled and rosy from sleep. "What's goin' on? What's Jennifer screaming about?" Tyrone demanded, knuckling both eyes.

"Yeah, she woked me up," Debbie grumbled.

"Nothing to worry about. She just had a little scare, is all," Matt said. "But since you're up, you kids go get dressed. Maria will have breakfast ready in two shakes, so move it."

Taking charge, Kate hurried up to where the children stood. "C'mon, gang, you heard your dad. Time to rise and shine." That produced a chorus of grumbling, but she herded them back up the stairs.

"C'mon, let's get Jennifer out of here." Matt glared at Willa one last time and put his arm around his wife and daughter and led them into the parlor. "It'll be okay, sweetheart. I won't let anything hurt you," he murmured, stroking the shivering child's arm.

"I'll get a crowbar and take care of that mess on the door," J.T. offered quietly. "Maria, would you get me a scrub brush and a pail of soapy water and some rags."

"Ah, *sí*. Come, with me, *señor*."

As the pair headed for the back of the house, Willa risked another glance at Zach. Those cool green eyes still bore into her.

"I didn't *do* it," she insisted through clenched teeth.

He continued to stare at her, so long she began to think he wasn't going to speak to her at all. Finally he nodded. "Okay. If you say so. But if you didn't, who did?"

Chapter Four

Over the next few days the question seemed to hang in the air. Unanswered. Silently accusing.

Zach and the others said they believed her, but Willa knew that they were merely withholding judgment. She could see it in their eyes, hear it in their carefully neutral tones.

Matt was barely civil, and even gregarious J.T. had become reserved toward her. The women were polite, but they'd dropped all previous attempts at friendliness.

"Well, fine. Let them believe whatever they want. What do I care, anyway?" Willa muttered to the blazing sunset. Her horse snorted and bobbed her head, as though in complete agreement.

Willa sat slumped in the saddle, her lower body moving to the rhythm of Bertha's plodding walk. They had been riding fence line all day, and both she and the horse were bone-tired.

Those people were nothing to her, she told herself adamantly. Just a bunch of greedy city slickers and a pack of rowdy kids. Fact was, she didn't like them any more than they liked her. Not any of them.

No matter how many times she said it, however, the truth was, like them or not, it hurt that anyone could think she was capable of such a vile act. Willa felt maligned, and even after five days her pride still smarted from the insult, which kept her temper simmering.

Most of the blame she put squarely on Zach. He was supposed to be the boss, wasn't he? The leader? If he truly believed her, he could have convinced the others.

She avoided them all whenever possible, especially Zach. If he gave her a choice, each morning she opted to tackle jobs that took her as far from where he was going to be as she could get. Those times when she was forced to endure his company she tried to ignore him, but so far she had not succeeded even once.

Despite her best intentions she always ended up taking verbal potshots at Zach. She criticized every decision he made, everything he did, the way he did it and when he did it, even when she knew he was right. She constantly compared his methods to Seamus's and sneered at any changes Zach implemented.

It was foolish of her and nonproductive, and she knew it, but she could not seem to restrain herself. Merely being around the man made her hackles rise and her skin tingle as though it were covered in a prickly rash.

For his part, Zach never flared back at her, no matter how much she picked at him or how cutting her comments, and that was the most irritating thing of all. He would simply give her one of those long, unreadable looks and go about his business, as though she were no more than a pesky mosquito buzzing around.

"Insufferable jerk," she swore. "The man either has a thick hide or the patience of Job. Or he's dumber than dirt."

Willa sighed. Much as she'd like to believe the latter, she knew it wasn't true. After being around him only a few days, it was obvious that Zach was an intelligent, logical man.

Everything was changing, Willa thought morosely. And she was powerless to do anything about it.

She looked around at the glorious sunset backlighting the mountains and streaking the sky with reds and purples and golds, and she sighed again. The only thing that remained the same was the land.

Her previously quiet home was now a beehive of activity and noise, and she resented it. Never mind that she'd always hated the tomblike quiet and emptiness of the huge house in the past, or that she'd often longed for some female companionship, women her own age with whom she could talk. She hadn't chosen to share her home or the ranch or her life with these people. They had been thrust upon her.

Worst of all, she was turning into a shrew, and she hated that.

What in heaven's name was the matter with her? It was true, she'd never been a pushover. From an early age she'd learned to stand her ground, even if it meant locking horns with Seamus. If she hadn't he would have run roughshod over her. Even so, contrariness and bad temper had never been part of her basic makeup.

Inevitably after every attack on Zach, Willa felt small and ashamed—but she simply couldn't stop herself from lashing out at him. Or bring herself to apologize.

Deep down, though she didn't like to think about it, Willa knew that, at least in part, her reaction to Zach sprang from fear that Lennie was right about Seamus scheming to get her and Zach together. No way was she going to let that happen.

There was more behind her prickliness than just self-protection, though. It was also a reaction to Zach usurping her position at the ranch.

She had expected at least some initial resistance from the hands, but none had materialized. It was painful and demoralizing to stand back and watch how easily Zach stepped into Seamus's boots. All the men, including the old-timers she had known all of her life, not only accepted him as their boss, they looked up to him and obeyed his orders over hers. Even Pete.

Maria had accepted the newcomers totally, as well. She adored the children and was devoted to Kate and Maude Ann and thought the three men were *"Muy macho."*

Willa felt betrayed on all sides, unfairly accused and more alone than ever. Her response was to lash out—and to attack whatever job that needed doing with a vengeance. Driven by hurt feelings, simmering temper and offended honor, she worked herself into a state of near exhaustion every day.

The sun went down in a blaze of glory as Willa dismounted and led Bertha into the barn. Zach's horse was in his stall, contentedly munching grain, and the rest of the horses were in the corrals. As usual, she was the last one to come straggling in. She was probably late for dinner again and in for a lecture from Maria.

Willa unsaddled the mare, gave her fresh food and water and a cursory rubdown. "I'll be back later, girl, and give you a good currying. I promise," she said, and hurried toward the house.

To her surprise and delight, Edward Manning sat at the kitchen table drinking coffee with Zach. Maude Ann and Kate were helping Maria prepare dinner, and from the den came the sounds of the television and children squabbling.

Like the gentleman he was, Edward rose as soon as he spotted her. "Ah, Willie. There you are."

"Edward, it's so good to see you." She flashed him a beaming smile and rushed forward with her arms outstretched.

He was taken aback by her enthusiastic greeting, which didn't surprise her. They were casual friends and had never been particularly close. However, since the funeral she'd been feeling woefully outnumbered, and she was so happy to see a friendly face she couldn't restrain herself.

With his usual aplomb, Edward recovered quickly and accepted her hug, though he couldn't quite suppress a little grimace of distaste when he got a whiff of the "horsey" smell that clung to her.

As Willa stepped back from Edward's embrace they heard groaning and the sound of footsteps. Walking with a painfully slow, slightly bow-legged gait, J.T. and Matt entered the kitchen from the main hall. Every step produced a groan and a grimace of pain from both men.

When he spotted their guest, J.T. gritted his teeth and stretched his lips in a strained smile. "Hey, Edward, good to see you."

Matt just nodded.

Grinning, Willa watched them hobble to the table. Matt carefully lowered himself into a chair, groaning louder as his sore backside came into contact with the seat.

"Aren't you going to have a seat, J.T.?" she asked, making no effort to hide her amusement.

"I'll stand, thanks." He cautiously leaned a shoulder

against the wall, making certain his rear end did not come into contact. "In fact, I may never sit again."

"Matt and J.T. have been learning to ride," she explained to Edward with a grin.

"Ah, I see. That explains a lot."

Willa turned her attention back to Edward. "I haven't seen or heard from you since Seamus's funeral, and that was almost a month ago. I was beginning to think you'd forgotten me."

"Hardly. I could never forget you, Willie, you know that. The Rocking R is still my number-one client. But I do apologize for neglecting you. For the past two weeks I've been tied up in political business in Helena. Although I did asked my secretary to convey that message. Don't tell me she didn't call."

"No, I haven't heard from her."

"She called," Zach said.

Willa shot him an accusing glare. "Why wasn't I told?"

"The message didn't seem to be directed to you personally, and I wasn't aware that you were expecting Mr. Manning."

Ever the diplomat, Edward jumped in before Willa could utter a blistering retort. "Oh, well. No harm done. You all seem to be settling in nicely, and I assume, since you haven't contacted my office, that no legal problems or questions have arisen so far."

"Now that you mention it, we have had one disturbing incident," Zach said.

Willa stiffened, but he ignored her and explained about the dead gopher and the note. By the time he was done, the attorney was frowning.

"Do you have any idea who would do such a thing?"

"No. We've drawn a blank." Zach and his brothers

carefully avoided so much as a glance Willa's way. On the other side of the kitchen the women were suddenly busy.

"It doesn't make any sense." J.T. grimaced and adjusted his position against the wall. "What motive would anyone around here have to run us out? We haven't had time to make enemies."

"Ah, but Seamus didn't exactly endear himself to the folks around Clear Water," Edward replied.

"What's that got to do with us?"

Edward shrugged and spread his hands wide. "Who knows? Sins of the father, maybe?"

"Or in this case, the grandfather," J.T. muttered.

"The motive could be simple jealousy," Matt said. "Or greed."

"Greed?" Edward shook his head. "How can that be? The only ones who would stand to gain if you were to give up the ranch are a few universities. I can't believe anyone from those institutions would stoop to scare tactics to drive you out."

"Neither can I. However, there is one individual who would profit." Matt stared at Edward. "You."

"Me?"

"I don't believe it," Willa exclaimed. "First you accuse me. Now Edward?"

"You accused Willie?" Edward looked stunned. "But…that doesn't make any sense."

"I agree," J.T. said. "And neither does accusing you. What's the matter with you, Matt? That's just plain crazy."

"He's right, you know. All I would get is the normal executor's fee."

"I've done some checking. That fee is a percentage of

the trust, which in this case would amount to a hefty sum.''

''So is my annual retainer as your attorney.''

''True, but it's not nearly as much as you'd get as executor of the trust.''

Exasperated, Willa threw up her hands. ''For Pete's sake, Matt! The Mannings have been our attorneys for years. Seamus had absolute trust in Edward's father and Edward. They were his friends!''

''Do you seriously believe I would risk my professional reputation and my political future, not to mention possible criminal prosecution, to sneak out here and kill some hapless creature and nail it to your door?'' Edward shuddered fastidiously. ''Please. Anyway, I've been in Helena for weeks. You can check that if you'd like.''

''I intend to.''

Edward tipped his head to one side and studied Matt's tough-as-nails face. ''You don't like me much, do you, Matt?''

''I don't know you.''

J.T. groaned. ''Don't pay any attention to him. Matt was a cop. He has a suspicious mind and an innate distrust of lawyers.''

''I can't say that I care much for reporters, either,'' Matt added, fixing J.T. with a pointed look.

''Hey, bro, lighten up, will you? I repented my ways, remember. I'm a novelist/cowboy now.''

Matt snorted. ''Some cowboy. You can barely stay in the saddle.''

''Hey! You're one to talk.''

''All right, that's enough, boys,'' Maude Ann drawled, dumping a stack of place mats on the table. ''It's time for dinner. Darling, would you go tell the kids to wash up and come set the table?''

Matt groaned as he started to rise, but J.T. waved at him to stay put. "I'll go. I'm already on my feet."

"Edward, you will join us, won't you?" Kate asked as she and Maria began to placed platters and bowls of food on the table.

"Thanks, but—"

"Please, Edward, do stay," Willa urged, laying her hand over his. "We can do some catching up over dinner. You can tell me how your political plans are going. Are your friends in Helena still urging you to run for mayor?"

"Ah, no fair," he teased. "You know how much I love talking politics."

"Then you'll stay?"

The other women added their pleas, and he gave in.

Willa made certain that Edward was seated next to her, and throughout the meal she devoted all her attention and conversation to him and ignored everyone else. She listened attentively to his every word and laughed at his attempts at humor.

When dinner was over she tried to persuade him to spend the night, but he insisted he had to return to Bozeman.

Willa walked with him to his car, which was out front where he always parked. It would never occur to Edward to enter the house through the back door.

"How is it going?" he asked kindly when they reached his car and were alone for the first time. "Everything working out all right?"

Crossing her arms over her midriff, Willa shrugged and looked away at the night sky. "Okay, I guess. I still hate this arrangement, but there's nothing I can do about it. At least none of us has committed murder yet."

Edward chuckled, then patted her shoulder. "Buck up.

You can take it, kiddo. I promise to stop by more often in the future, and you know you can always call me at my office or at home if you have a problem, don't you?''

''I know. Thanks, Edward.''

He dropped a brotherly kiss on her forehead and climbed into his car. Willa stood where she was, watching him drive away. When his car's taillights disappeared over the crest of the hill, she headed for the barn.

She was halfway down the wide middle aisle before she realized she was not alone. ''Oh.'' She stopped abruptly. ''I didn't know you were in here.''

Zach squatted on his haunches, examining the gate of the stall two down from Bertha's. An open toolbox sat on the ground at his side.

He glanced over his shoulder at her. Those cool green eyes did a quick sweep of her face and body. ''What? Has your lover gone already? I thought you'd still be making out in his car.''

Willa narrowed her eyes. ''First of all, I do *not* 'make out in cars' as you so elegantly put it, and second, Edward is *not* my lover.''

''Yeah, well, you'd never know it by the way you hung all over him during dinner.''

Willa sucked in a sharp breath, so incensed all she could do for a moment was gape at him. ''I *did not* hang on Edward,'' she denied hotly when she found her tongue. ''I was merely enjoying a conversation with an old friend. Trust you to read something dirty into a perfectly innocent act.''

''All I know is you sure seem to have a lot of 'good friends.' First Lennie Dawson, now Edward.'' He fished a screwdriver out of the toolbox and went to work tightening the screws on the stall gate. ''Do they know about each other, by the way?''

"There is nothing to know," she snapped. "Not that it's any of your business."

Willa turned to leave, then changed her mind and spun around again. Jaws clenched, she stomped to Bertha's stall, jerked the gate open and stepped inside. She had as much right to be there as he did. She'd be darned if she'd let him run her off.

Bertha whinnied a greeting and nudged Willa's shoulder. Despite her anger, she smiled and reached into her shirt pocket for the sugar cube she'd stashed there during dinner. Bertha lipped the treat from her palm, and Willa leaned her forehead against the horse's neck and stroked her. "You big baby," she murmured.

She loved Bertha more than anything or anyone on earth. Seamus had surprised her with the ten month old filly for her twenty-first birthday. The animal was the only thing of any great value that he'd ever given her. For that matter, it had been the first time since her mother's death that he had bothered to acknowledge her birthday at all.

Ever since then Bertha had been her most prized possession. Not just because she had been a gift from Seamus, but because the animal loved her in return—totally and unconditionally. That was something Willa had never been sure of from any of the people in her life—not her mother, not Seamus, not even Maria or Pete.

For those few moments as she petted Bertha, Willa forgot about everything else, including Zach, but when a quick glance revealed that he was watching her she stiffened and snatched up the curry brush.

Sweeping the brush over Bertha's hide in long, vigorous strokes, she studiously ignored him. She was braced for more of his sarcastic remarks but after several moments when none came she risked another sidelong glance and saw that he'd returned to working on the gate.

They worked in silence for several more uncomfortable moments, but then some imp of mischief prodded Willa. Casting another look his way, she smiled slyly and began to softly sing "Rhinestone Cowboy."

From the corner of her eye she had the pleasure of seeing Zach stiffen. The screwdriver stilled and his jaw clenched. Willa fought back a grin. Until now, her gibes and insults had had no effect whatsoever on Zach, which had exacerbated her anger all the more. No matter what she'd said or done, it had all slid off him like water off a duck's back. It was insulting. He might as well have come right out and said her opinion of him was of no importance.

Enjoying herself, Willa sang a little louder and put an extra twang into the lyrics.

She expected him object at any second, but instead he flexed his shoulders and went back to tightening screws. She sang the entire song twice, but for all the reaction she got you would think that Zach was deaf. By the time she'd finished she was seething. Was the man made of stone?

Unable to bear his silence an instant longer, she finally snapped, "What are you doing over there, anyway?"

"Isn't it obvious? I'm repairing this gate."

"What for? We keep only the most valuable horses in here. The rest of the riding stock is kept in the corrals or the pasture next to the yard. Bertha, here, is out of a long line of prize cutting horses, and I assumed you stabled that stallion you ride for the same reason, but the rest of our stock are just work horses."

"Not that black stallion in corral four. He's a beauty."

"True, but he's also meaner than a snake and unridable. That's why he's being sold."

"Not anymore, he's not."

"What do you mean? I've already found a buyer in Dallas willing to take him." Bertha nickered and shifted uneasily at her harsh tone. "Mr. Henderson is driving up next week to pick him up."

"I called Henderson and canceled the deal."

"You *what!*" Willa slammed down the brush. "You can't do that!"

"It's done." He tossed the screwdriver back into the toolbox and closed the lid, then stood up and swung the gate back and forth to test it.

Willa let herself out of the stall and marched over to him. "You had no right—"

"I had every right. I'm in charge now. Remember?"

She ground her teeth and glared. Paying no attention to her impotent rage, Zach calmly picked up the toolbox and headed for the back of the barn to place it on a shelf. Willa followed right behind.

"It makes no sense to keep that animal. If you'd bothered to ask, anyone could have told you that Satan can't be ridden. All he's good for is breeding. This is a cattle ranch, not a horse farm. If a horse can't be ridden he's no good to us."

"I'll ride him."

"Ha! Better men than you have tried. At one time or another every hand on the place has. Satan has been the cause of more broken bones than I care to count. Sooner or later he's going to seriously injure someone, maybe even kill them. And you think you're going to break him. Fat chance."

"I said, I'll ride him."

Zach placed the toolbox on the shelf and strode back

down the aisle toward the front of the barn. Willa dogged his steps.

"Oh, of course. How silly of me. I forgot, you're the big rodeo star." Dropping the simpering voice, she made a disgusted sound. "Believe me, it'll take more than a broken down bronc buster to ride that horse. Who do you think you are, John Wayne? You're going to have to stick on his back a heck of a lot longer than a measly nine seconds to break him, and that can't be done."

"I don't intend to break him. I'm going to gentle him first, then ride him."

She let out a derisive hoot. "That'll be the day. Do let me know when you plan to perform this miracle, won't you? I'd like to sell tickets."

"That's it!" He stopped and whirled around so quickly that she slammed into his chest and would have bounced off if he hadn't grasped her upper arms.

Surprise formed Willa's mouth into an O, but the fury in those silvery eyes silenced her. "Dammit, woman! You've been snapping at my heels like a vicious little terrier for weeks now," he snarled. "I know you got a raw deal from Seamus, and for that reason I've tried my damnedest to be patient with you, but enough is enough."

His explosive reaction had taken her by surprise, but Willa wasn't one to remain intimidated for long. She tipped her chin up at a pugnacious angle. "Oh? And what are you going to do about it? Beat me?"

"Don't think I'm not tempted to turn you over my knee and blister your butt. But I won't. I've never struck a woman in my life and I don't intend to start now."

"Then there's not much you can do about it, is there?" she said smugly.

Zach's eyes narrowed. "Don't count on it, little girl. There's more than one way to shut you up."

His mouth slammed down on hers, cutting off the sassy retort that was forming on her tongue before she could make a sound. Willa was so stunned she froze.

Then the heat seared through the icy shock. It slid through her veins like molten lava, flushing her skin, melting her bones. The smell of him was all around her—a potent male scent, musky and erotic. It made her light-headed and weak and sent a tingle down her spine.

Zach was in complete control. His mouth rocked over hers, hard, insistent, devouring. Unbearably exciting.

Silently, he commanded her to open to him, and she obeyed mindlessly. When his tongue plunged into her mouth and stroked against hers, passion flared like a gas-oline-fed bonfire. The greedy flames shot skyward, consuming her.

Willa moaned as her knees buckled, but when she began to slump, Zach simply tightened his hold on her arms. She hung there between his big, calloused hands like a rag doll as the kiss went on and on. Her heart thrummed and her head spun and her body throbbed and yearned as it never had before.

As suddenly as it had begun, the kiss ended. Zach set her away from him at arm's length, holding her steady while she settled. She blinked at him, bewildered and disoriented, still lost in the daze of passion. "Wha...? Why....?"

Slowly, his stern face came into focus, and as the reality of what had just passed between them came crashing down on her she felt the cold slap of rejection, followed instantly by the most pride-rending mortification she had ever known.

Then, from outside the barn she heard the noisy approach of a group of riders, and she knew why he had ended the kiss so abruptly. That knowledge, however, did not alleviate the terrible humiliation.

"We don't have much time before someone barges in here, so listen up," Zach growled, giving her a little shake. "Let that be a warning. Those who play with fire can expect to get burned, so unless you want more of the same, in the future you had better keep that sharp tongue of yours sheathed. Got it?"

Too embarrassed to fight back, Willa bobbed her head once and prayed the ground would open up and swallow her. When Zach released her she staggered back a couple of steps. The instant she regained her balance she bolted for the door.

"Hey, Willa, how's it goin'?" one of the cowboys called when she emerged from the barn. The others offered similar greetings.

Normally she would have stopped and shot the breeze for a while, but this time, muttering a barely audible, "Evening," Willa ducked her head and stomped past them, her knees threatening to buckle with every wobbly step.

The men stared after her, slack-jawed. "Well, if that don't beat all. Whaddaya s'pose put a burr under her saddle?"

"More likely who. She's prob'ly been buttin' heads with the boss again."

The comments brought a blush to Willa's cheeks, making her profoundly grateful for the darkness.

To her great relief, no one was in the kitchen when she entered the house. Maria always retired to her quarters and put her feet up after dinner, and from the sounds coming from the den, everyone else was in there.

When she reached the safety of her room she leaned

back against the closed door and squeezed her eyes shut, nearly sick with shame and self-loathing.

What on earth was the matter with her? Why hadn't she fought him? She could have kicked or bitten. Or used her fists, for that matter. Instead she had just stood there like a stump and let him kiss her senseless.

Groaning, Willa folded her arms over her middle and rocked back and forth as though she had a bellyache. Dear Lord, she had just meekly let him do as he pleased, docile as a sacrificial lamb. Worse, she'd actually enjoyed the searing rush of sensations and emotion, wallowed in them, mindless to everything but Zach and the way he made her feel. The way he made her burn for him. Like some love-sick teenager.

Most humiliating of all, the kiss had not affected Zach in the least. He hadn't been trembling or flushed or weak in the knees. He had just stood there, pinning her with those icy eyes, steady as a rock. She wanted to kick him. Hard. Then she wanted to shrivel up and die.

The instant Willa disappeared through the barn door Zach relinquished his steely self-control, and as his knees buckled he plopped down onto a bale of hay, shaken to the core. The kiss was supposed to have been a warning to Willa, but it had backfired on him. He felt like he'd been run over by a loaded cattle truck. He propped his elbows on his knees and held his head in his hands. "Aw hell!"

Chapter Five

Willa had never dreaded anything in her life as much as she did facing Zach the next morning, but when she entered the kitchen he barely glanced her way. Throughout breakfast he behaved the same as he always did, saying little beyond discussing the work schedule for the day or any possible change predicted for the weather. After a while she realized that he had put that sizzling kiss in the barn out of his mind, just as though it had never happened. At first Willa didn't know whether to be relieved or insulted, but his disinterest grated on her and set her temper to simmering.

So did the memory of his warning. Playing with fire, indeed. If he thought the encounter would scare her into meekly accepting his dictates, he was sorely mistaken.

He had caught her off guard, that was all. That's why she had behaved like a docile idiot. It wouldn't happen again.

Neither her anger nor Zach's maddening indifference lessened her need to escape, however, and when he mentioned that he wanted someone to drive to Bozeman and pick up the tractor engine they'd had rebuilt, she volunteered.

The trip took most of the day. When Willa drove into the ranch yard that afternoon she spotted the Dolan kids sitting on the top rail of the corral, cheering and clapping. She parked the truck by the tractor barn and walked over to see what all the fuss was about.

She arrived just in time to see the chestnut gelding J.T. was riding rear up when he jerked the reins too hard. He let out a shout and slid backward over the cantle and right off the horse's rump, and hit the ground flat on his own behind, raising a cloud of dust and a chorus of groans from the kids.

Then all hell broke loose.

Matt doubled over the front of his saddle and guffawed. The sudden loud sound so close to his mount's ear startled the horse. The Appaloosa whinnied and rolled his eyes and went into a side-stepping dance.

Matt's laughter cut off instantly. Dropping the reins, he flung his arms around the animal's neck and held on for dear life, scaring the horse all the more and sending the animal into a series of bucks. Inspired, J.T.'s loose mount ran around the perimeter of corral, tossing his head and kicking out with his hind legs every few steps.

"Dang blast it!" Pete roared.

J.T. scrambled to his feet, hobbled over to the side and hopped up on the first board of the corral fence to avoid being kicked or trampled. Grinning, he called, "Hey, Matt! Having a little trouble with your horse?" He let out a whoop. "Ride 'um, cowboy!"

Pete chased after horse and rider with his funny, bow-

legged gait, shaking his fist. "Dang blast you dang-
blasted ornery good-fer-nothin' critters!" After several
tries the old man finally snagged the Appaloosa's trailing
reins, but the horse merely pulled him along. Digging in
his heels, Pete grabbed the bridle with both hands and
hauled back on it. "Whoa, horse. Whoa. Settle down you
good-fer-nothin' hay-burner." The horse kept going, and
heels of Pete's worn boots dug twin tracks in the dirt.
"Leggo o' his neck, dang it! You're gonna choke the
beast!" he barked at Matt.

When the Appaloosa finally steadied and came to a
stop, Pete swung on J.T. "Dag nab it, man, don't just
stand there laughin' like a fool! Catch your horse!"

Willa crossed her arms on the top rail of the corral
fence and grinned. This was the most fun she'd had in
months.

Both men were ready to call it a day, but Pete wouldn't
allow that. He believed in getting right back on a horse
after a fall. "Now get back up on them horses and let's
see if you can get it right this time."

Reluctant and grumbling, Matt and J.T. remounted and
cantered around the perimeter of the corral, their back-
sides slapping leather with each stride.

"Move with your horse, dammit! Catch his rhythm! I
don't wanta see no daylight 'tween your arses an' them
saddles. An' keep them heels down!"

Willa shook her head. Pitiful. Just pitiful.

Disgusted, she turned away. After stopping by the barn
for a bridle, she headed toward the fenced pasture that
butted up to the ranch yard. That morning when she'd
realized that she wouldn't be riding out with the men,
before leaving for Bozeman she had turned Bertha out to
graze.

Tyrone raced up from behind and fell into step beside her.

"Whacha doin'?"

Willa gave the boy a sideways glance and kept moving. So far she'd managed to avoid the children except at mealtime. She had no idea how to deal with kids and was uncomfortable around them. "I'm going to saddle my horse and go join the men."

Tyrone scrambled onto the board fence and looked around at the thirty or so head of horses scattered over the pasture. "Which one's yours?"

"The black mare with the white star on her forehead." Willa unlatched the gate and stepped inside.

"What's a mare?"

"A female horse."

"Man, you ain't ever gonna catch 'er," he said with cocky certainty. "Uncle J.T.'s still chasing his horse around, an' that's a little bitty ole pen."

"Yeah, well, I'm not your uncle J.T." She stuck two fingers into her mouth and produced a piercing whistle. The black's head came up and she trotted over to Willa.

"Hey, cool! How'd you get 'er to do that?"

"She's my horse. I trained her." Willa patted Bertha's neck and let the mare nuzzle her hand, then slipped the bridle over her head.

The boy fell into step beside her again as she headed back to the barn. She kept her eyes straight ahead and pretended he wasn't there, but Tyrone was not a child who would be ignored.

"Will you show me how to train a horse?"

"You don't have a horse."

"My momma says I can have one soon as I learn to ride. We're all gonna learn. 'Cept for Debbie. She's just a baby."

Willa led Bertha into the barn. Tyrone dogged her heels, peppering her with questions about everything he saw. She kept her answers short, almost curt, but that didn't discourage him.

"Whacha putting that on 'er for?" he ask when Willa positioned the saddle pad on Bertha's back.

"It protects her hide from chaffing." She slung the saddle over the animal's back, hooked the near stirrup over the horn and began to fasten the cinch. Tyrone crowded in so close to watch the operation he got right under the mare's belly, and she had to yank him back and give him a sharp reprimand. That didn't deter the boy one iota.

"Will you teach me to ride?"

"I don't have time. Ask Pete."

"He's busy teaching Dad and Uncle J.T. They're at it every day. An' he says after that it'll be time for roundup and he'll be busier than a one-armed paperhanger."

Willa bit back a grin. How many times had she heard Pete use that expression?

It was true, though. They would all be putting in long hours in the saddle, which meant a constant stream of tack repairs. "Well, I guess you'll just have to wait until summer when spring roundup is over."

"I can't wait that long. I gotta learn now."

"What's the rush?"

"I just gotta, that's all."

"In that case, you'll have to find someone else."

Tyrone cocked his head to one side and studied her with disconcerting directness. "Miss Maudie said you'd say no."

Willa slanted him a look of mild surprise. "You call your mom by her first name?"

"Sometimes." He skipped ahead of her as she led Bertha back out into the sunshine. "She's not my real mom, you know. My real mom didn't want me. Miss Maudie says that's just 'cause she's a drug addict."

Willa stopped in her tracks. "What?"

"Yolanda's folks didn't want her none, either. They dumped her on the side of the highway. An' Jennifer's old man blew away her real mom, an' Debbie was abused. Tim, too." The boy narrowed his eyes. "His old man was one *meeean* dude. He's the one who shot Matt in the leg."

"Good Lord."

"That's why we was all sent to live with Miss Maudie. She's a sigh-ki-trist," he added proudly. "She coulda made big bucks if she'd'a wanted to, but she loved kids so she took in fosters like us."

"Maude Ann's a psychiatrist?" Willa's gaze darted to the woman who was hammering together a chicken coop on the other side of the ranch yard. That gorgeous earth mother was a shrink? She couldn't believe it.

"Yeah. An' when she married Matt they 'dopted all five of us. Now we're a family and cain't nobody take us away from 'um. An' we got two new uncles and Aunt Kate, too."

Willa had no idea what to say. How *did* one respond to such stunning revelations? All she managed was a wan smile.

Feeling a need to escape those big brown eyes and that disturbing innocent candor, she climbed into the saddle. She'd hoped the boy would take a hint, but Tyrone wasn't finished.

He shaded his eyes with one hand and squinted up at her. "An' you know what else? Momma says now that we're livin' here, you're part of our family, too."

"What?" Stunned anew, Willa glanced at Maude Ann

again, then back at the boy. "You must have misunderstood her."

"Nuh-uh. That's what she said." The boy looked down at the ground and scuffed the toe of his athletic shoe in the dirt, then slanted her a sly look out of the corner of his eye. "So, you gonna teach me to ride or not? Momma says family is s'posed to help each other out."

Willa's mouth twitched. *Why you crafty little devil,* she thought with reluctant admiration. *You almost had me there for a second.* "Sorry, kid. Like I said, I'm too busy."

"Aw, shoot." He kicked a clod of dirt across the yard, then hooked his thumbs into the side pockets of his jeans and trudged away, the picture of dejection.

Willa watched him for a moment. Pete was right—that one was a pistol.

Zach slung a hundred pound sack of seed into the back of his pickup, then paused to arch his back and glance around. It was only the first of March and snow still covered the ground, but from the number of people in Clear Water it looked as if he wasn't the only one gearing up for spring.

As he turned to retrieve another sack from the stack piled up next to the door of the ranchers's co-op a red pickup screeched to a stop beside his truck and Lennie Dawson and two other men climbed out. Sparing them no more than a glance, Zach walked by the trio, hefted another sack onto his shoulder and carried it back to the pickup.

"Hey, you! You're Zach Mahoney, aren't you?" Lennie barked. "One of Seamus's bastard grandsons."

Zach's jaw clenched, but he kept working. "That's right."

"I want to talk to you."

"Oh? About what?" Zach slung a sack into the pickup bed and turned back for another one without breaking stride.

Lennie followed on his heels. "I'm Lennie Dawson."

"I know who you are."

"Yeah, well, here's something maybe you didn't know." He stuck out his jaw. "Willie Simmons belongs to me."

Zach experienced a rush of distaste. Willa was a high-tempered, annoying thorn in his side, but the thought of her being romantically involved with this guy was unsettling.

Outwardly he didn't react in any way. He simply continued transferring sacks, working in a steady, slow rhythm.

"Hey, Mahoney! Did you hear what I just said?"

"I heard you."

"Yeah, well I'm warning you—stay away from her."

"That's going to be difficult, since we live in the same house." Zach dumped a sack and turned to go back for another but this time Lennie blocked his path.

The first time he'd encountered this man Zach had pegged him for a swaggering bully, and nothing he'd seen so far had changed his mind. Though several inches shorter than Zach, and probably twenty pounds lighter, he stood braced for a fight, his hands fisted and his chin outthrust. Flanking him on either side, his buddies had assumed the same challenging position. Zach doubted that he would have been quite so eager for a confrontation if he'd been alone.

"You know what I mean, smart guy." Lennie reached

out and poked Zach's chest with his forefinger. Zach narrowed his eyes. "You keep your hands off of her, you hear? Willie is mine. An' I don't share what's mine." He poked him again. "You got that?"

Zach stared at him. He itched to ram his fist into the arrogant little weasel's face just on general principles, but he resisted the urge. The locals were already wary of him and his brothers simply because they were Seamus's grandsons. They hoped to eventually overcome the old man's reputation, but getting into a brawl after being in the area only a month wasn't exactly the best way to start off.

For all he knew, Dawson could be telling the truth. Willa had denied any involvement with the guy, but who knew. Maybe that scene he'd witnessed had been a lovers' spat, after all.

Finally he nodded. "Yeah. I understand. Now, if you excuse me, I have more seed to load."

Lennie appeared taken aback by Zach's attitude. He clearly had expected an argument, had probably hoped for one. After a moment his surprised expression turned into a smirk. "Sure. Just don't forget what I told you, Mahoney. C'mon, fellas." Motioning for his friends to follow, Lennie swaggered back to his pickup.

Zach watched them drive away, his eyes narrowed beneath the broad brim of his Stetson. Had Willa told him about that kiss they'd shared in the barn? Was that what had prompted that attempt at intimidation?

If so, Lennie had wasted his breath. He'd already decided that nothing like that would happen again. He didn't even want to think about it.

He had meant the kiss to be punishment. Yeah, right. That plan had backfired on him the instant their lips had touched. He had never experienced passion that strong before. It had sizzled and arced between them like lightening, and rocked him right down to the ground. He knew that Willa had been just as stunned.

And just as displeased.

Zach was grateful that the men had returned when they had and interrupted them. Otherwise, he was very much afraid that within minutes he and Willa would have been rolling in the hay in one of the empty stalls, tearing off each other's clothes.

That would have been disaster, of course. An affair between them was out of the question. Not to mention just plain stupid. The woman couldn't stand him, for Pete's sake. To her, he was the enemy. They were reluctant business partners, and that's all they would ever be. Period.

Still, merely thinking about how she had felt in his arms sent heat straight to his loins. Annoyed, Zach cursed and went back to loading seed. When done, he slammed the tailgate shut, climbed into the cab, gunned the engine and made a screeching U-turn out onto the highway, headed for the ranch.

Beyond being a royal pain in the rear, Willa meant nothing to him, he told himself. But he sure as hell couldn't say much for her taste in men.

Willa spent two days helping a crew of men repair a stock tank in a part of the ranch that was inaccessible by truck. Unable to get a front-end loader to the site, they had to do the job by hand. It was backbreaking work, but since Zach was busy elsewhere, it seemed to her the best place to be.

Willa put her back into the work, shoveling dirt, hauling rocks and stacking them against the earthen bank for reinforcement, right along with the men. They finally finished close to sundown the second day, and the men headed for the ranch headquarters and the hearty supper Cookie was sure to have simmering on the stove. Willa, however, declined to go with them, saying she wanted to check the fence line in the next pasture before calling it a day.

The truth was she was not in any hurry to return home. Most evenings she delayed doing so until the last possible minute, even though that usually earned her a scolding from Maria. In addition, tonight she simply wanted some time to herself. In the past, she'd done some of her best thinking riding fence.

By the time Willa finally returned to the ranch house and saw to Bertha's needs it was full dark. Expecting to find the others seated around the table, she braced herself, but when she entered through the back door Maria was alone in the kitchen and pots still simmered on the stove. The housekeeper looked up and smiled.

"Ah, there you are. The others, they were getting worried about you, *niña*."

"Where is everyone?" Willa asked.

"Upstairs, getting dressed. Today is Tyrone's birthday, remember? Dinner tonight, it will be special. A birthday party."

Willa groaned. "And I suppose everyone else has gotten him a gift."

"*Sí.*"

"Oh, great. That's just terrific. Somebody might have told me."

"But, *niña*…everyone, they have been talking about it for days." Maria's confusion turned into a scowl. "You were not listening, again, eh, *muchacha?*"

"No, I was listening, I, uh…I guess I just forgot." Maria had been right, though. Most often she simply tuned out the conversation around the table. Partly out of exhaustion, but also to maintain a distance from the others. It was easier that way.

"Humph!" The look in Maria's eyes said she didn't believe her, but she shooed Willa toward the door. "At least go shower and make yourself pretty for the boy. You smell of horse. Now go, go. It is getting late."

Willa started for the door, then paused and gave Maria a considering look.

No matter how hard she worked or how far she rode, she had not been able to dismiss from her mind the shocking things Tyrone had told her. Over and over she'd told herself that it couldn't be true. What kind of people—parents, no less—would do such things to children? He must have made it up. Or at the very least he'd exaggerated.

"Uh, Maria…has Maude Ann or Matt said anything to you about the children? Why they were in foster care?"

"Ah, *sí.*" She crossed her hands over her heart and shook her head sadly. In an emotional voice, and pausing now and then to dab at her eyes with the hem of her apron, she related each child's story, confirming in ghastly detail what Tyrone had said earlier. By the time the housekeeper had finished, Willa was appalled and outraged. And sick at heart.

She had always considered her own childhood a miserable one. Most of her life she had striven in vain to win Seamus's love and approval. Almost from the day that she and her mother had arrived at the ranch she had figured out that the only thing that mattered to her stepfather was the Rocking R. So she had thrown herself into ranch work and learned everything she could about the business and tried to make herself indispensable to him.

It had been a foolish quest that had been doomed from the start, she realized now. Seamus had wanted a son, and nothing any girl child could have done would have ever been enough.

Still, those years of verbal abuse and emotional coldness she'd endured from him were nothing compared to what these children had survived.

"Life has been cruel to these little ones. But that is all over. They belong to Señor and Señora Dolan now. *Gracias a Dios.*"

"Yes. Yes, thank, God." Willa left the kitchen and climbed the stairs in an appalled daze. She felt as though an aching, fist-size knot had lodged beneath her breast bone. Suddenly she was fiercely glad that Maude Ann and Matt had adopted Tyrone and the other children, and that they'd brought them there, to the Rocking R, where they would be safe and loved.

In honor of the occasion, dinner was in the dining room that night. Willa couldn't remember the last time they had used the impressive formal room. Probably when her mother was still alive.

She dressed in her new burgundy-and-gray-print, ankle-length skirt, burgundy sweater and gray suede dress boots, her freshly washed hair loose. She felt a bit self-conscious, but when she entered the dining room and saw that everyone else had dressed up, her misgivings faded. It helped that Kate and Maude Ann's eyes lit up when they spotted her.

"Willa! How pretty you look," Maude Ann exclaimed.

"You certainly do." Kate circled around her. "Oh, my, I love your outfit. You should wear a dress more often."

"There's, uh...there's not too many occasions that call

for dressing up around here. Jeans are more practical." She didn't bother to mention that Seamus discouraged the practice. The few times she had bothered to put on a skirt or dress he'd snarled that she looked like a gussied-up tart.

"If this is the kind of merchandise they have in Helena I can see that one of these days the three of us are going to have to drive over there together and hit the shops," Kate said, fingering the soft drapy skirt.

Together? The three of them on a shopping spree? Like…like girlfriends? Willa blinked at the two women. Was this Kate's way of saying she wanted them to be friends?

The idea was alien to Willa, and it filled her with both dread and longing. She had never, not once in her life, had a close female friend. Or gone shopping with another woman, other than her mother or Maria.

Willa had no experience with girlfriends. Even though she'd yearned for female companionship for most of her life, the very idea made her feel awkward and uncomfortable. She wasn't sure she knew how to relate to women as friends.

The door between the kitchen and dining room swung open, and Maria entered carrying an enormous dish of enchiladas, which Tyrone had requested for his birthday dinner.

While Kate and Maude Ann helped Maria bring in the steaming platters, Willa pulled an envelope from her pocket and slipped it in among the gaily wrapped gifts stacked on the sideboard.

She turned from doing so, and her heart skipped a beat when she discovered that Zach was staring at her. He stood by himself by the bay window on the opposite side of the room drinking a beer, those green eyes glittering at her over the rim of his glass.

Resisting the urge to turn away, she set her chin at a mulish angle and stared right back. Instead of having the good manners to look away, as she expected, he held her gaze for an interminable time, while her heart thudded against her ribs and a hot blush rushed to her cheeks. Then his gaze slid slowly down her body, from her loose swinging hair all the way to her fancy new boots, lingering along the way at her breasts, her waist, and the flare of her hips beneath the swirly skirt.

The intense scrutiny unnerved her, but as panic began to beat its wings against the walls of her stomach, Maude Ann announced that dinner was served. Relieved, Willa hurried over to the table.

Tyrone was seated in the place of honor at the opposite end of the table from Zach. Beaming from ear to ear, the boy made the most of his privileged status and soaked up all the attention coming his way. After dinner he blew out his candles with one gusty exhale and ripped into his gifts like a tornado while all the other kids crowded around his chair.

He received a video game player and several games from his parents, a robot action figure from J.T. and Kate, a baseball glove from Maria and various toys from his siblings. When all the boxes were opened he picked up Willa's envelope and tore it open without much interest. Willa could see by his bored expression he was expecting it to be a card.

"It's just a dumb ole note," he said, making no effort to hide his disgust when he pulled out the single sheet of paper.

"Tyrone, mind your manners," Maude Ann warned.

"Yeah, before you get too bummed you'd better read it, sport. It might be a treasure map, for all you know."

Tyrone shot his father a "yeah, right" look and unfolded the paper. "This en...tit..."

Kate leaned over and scanned the first line. "Entitles."

"This entitles the bear...er to one pair of cowboy bo...oots and—" He looked up, his eyes growing huge. "One pair of cowboy boots! Wow!" His gaze darted back to the paper, his face growing more animated as he read. "And free...ri...riding les...sons. Hot dog! Riding lessons! I'm gonna have riding lessons!"

"Hey, great, tiger. Whose gift is that?" J.T. asked.

Tyrone's gaze shot down to the bottom of the page. He looked up again, his eyes wide. "It's from Willa!"

A stunned silence followed, and Willa found herself the focus of ten pairs of eyes.

"What? Why are you all looking at me like that?"

"Oh. Nothing," Maude Ann replied. "It's, uh...it's just that...well...this is very kind of you, Willa."

"I thought you said you didn't have time to teach me how to ride."

"I don't. But I decided to take the time. I'll knock off early on Tuesdays and Thursdays and you meet me in corral one at five sharp. Okay?"

"O-*kay!*"

"Good. Tomorrow I'll take you to town for those boots."

"You mean...just you and me?"

"Sure."

To Willa's astonishment, Tyrone's eyes grew suspiciously moist. Suddenly he scrambled down from his chair, raced around the table and flung his arms around her neck. "Thanks, Willa."

She patted the child's back awkwardly, at a loss.

Like most children, Tyrone rebounded quickly and the emotional moment passed. He and the other kids inhaled bowls of chocolate cake and ice cream before the adults had eaten half of theirs and took off for the den to play with his loot.

Still shaken by the boy's reaction, Willa excused herself as soon as they'd gone.

"Don't rush off. Stay and have some coffee, why don't you," Kate urged.

"No. Thank you. I, uh, I'm tired. It's been a long day. Good night."

She barely made it to the bottom of the stairs when Zach caught up with her.

"Willa, wait up."

She stopped with one foot on the first step and shot him a wary look. "What do you want?"

His lips twitched. "Nothing bad. Relax, will you? Not everything between us has to be a battle, you know." She jumped when he put his hand over hers on the newel post, and her heart took off at a gallop. The touch of that calloused palm against her skin sent heat zinging up her arm. "I just wanted to say thanks. That was a nice thing you did. Tyrone is in heaven."

She could see that he hadn't expected that kind of gesture from her. Actually, she was having second thoughts herself. It had seemed like a good idea when she'd written the note, but now she wasn't sure. What did she know about kids? Especially a rambunctious one like Tyrone? What if she couldn't handle him? What if he got hurt?

"I'm glad he's happy," she replied stiffly.

"Yeah, well…Tyrone can be a handful. I thought maybe I'd give you a hand with those lessons. If that's all right with you?"

Willa narrowed her eyes as a painful suspicion began

to take hold. "Why don't you be honest? You didn't follow me out here to thank me. You and the others still think I'm responsible for scaring Jennifer. Now you're worried that I mean to harm that boy." She snatched her hand from beneath his. "Regardless of what any of you think, I'm not a monster."

"I wasn't implying that you were. I simply thought you could use some help. Dammit, Willa, will you wait a second."

Ignoring him, she climbed the stairs with her back ram-rod-straight.

Zach watched her go, exasperated and at the same time filled with reluctant admiration. Willa wore her pride like an iron cloak.

But damn if she didn't look fantastic in that swirly skirt and sweater. He couldn't recall ever seeing her in anything but jeans and a shirt before.

She had obviously just washed her hair, and the scent of jasmine drifting from it had nearly driven him wild. Usually she wore her hair in a braid or pulled back with a clip. Tonight that glorious ebony mane hung loose and arrow-straight almost to her waist. Beneath the entryway chandelier the shiny strands shone with the blue-black sheen of a raven's wing, swaying and sliding like a silk curtain with every furious step she took.

Zach's fingers itched to dive into that thick mass, feel it warm against his skin, slithering through his fingers.

Damn, Mahoney. What the hell are you doing fantasizing about Willa Simmons? The woman despises you. Even if she didn't, there was no way he was getting involved with that little spitfire.

All right, so there was some sort of weird chemistry going on between them. After that mind-blowing kiss in the barn a couple of weeks ago, he could hardly deny that. But so what? Hell, she wasn't even his type. He preferred women who were sweet and gentle and domestic. Not temperamental tomboys.

Willa disappeared into the upstairs hallway, and Zach heaved a sigh. "Damn prickly woman. One of these days you're going to collapse under the weight of that chip on your shoulder. If I don't knock it off first, that is."

Chapter Six

Willa was convinced that cattle were the most ornery critters God ever made. After a winter of drifting the range, they had grown wild and balked at being driven anywhere, especially cows that had recently dropped spring calves. The stubborn beasts hid out in the most inaccessible places, invariably bolted in the wrong direction when flushed out, and did their best to make a cowboy's life miserable.

Willa spent hours in the saddle riding hell-for-leather through brush and rocky gullies and up and down steep slopes, flushing out strays and recalcitrant new mothers and their young. It was dirty, strenuous work that she could have left to the men, but she used her simmering anger to push on, even when she was close to dropping.

After working without letup for more than an hour, Willa paused on a bench of land above the meadow where they were gathering cattle that day and dismounted to give the mare a rest. She ground-hitched the horse and left her cropping grass, and walked over to the edge of the drop-off to watch the busy scene below.

Even from that height she could hear the incessant racket made by the two hundred or so head they had rounded up so far. Kept bunched in a circle by four men and Sadie, the cattle milled about restlessly, bawling and clacking horns and kicking up a cloud of dust, even though patches of snow still covered much of the ground. Periodically other hands rode up, driving in one or more animals to add to the herd.

Willa's gaze locked on the big man wearing a sheep-skin-lined denim jacket and a gray Stetson. Her mouth tightened. Arrogant, overbearing oaf.

By the morning following Tyrone's birthday and that insulting encounter with Zach, her hurt had turned to full-blown anger. Even now, three weeks later, the memory of the doubt and worry in his eyes—and the others', as well—still rankled. That they could think she would de-liberately hurt a child was the most scurrilous, contemp-tuous insult she had ever endured.

So far she had given Tyrone four lessons without any serious mishaps. The boy had missed a lesson when he'd been kept after school one day, and another time she had gotten so busy she'd forgotten to knock off early, causing him to miss another. Wisely, Zach had kept his distance.

Tyrone was awkward and—despite his bravado—a bit afraid of the horse, which had made progress slow, but he was hanging in there. The little cuss was determined, she'd give him that. With that kind of gutsy focus Willa was certain that he would eventually overcome his fear and get the hang of it.

Below, Zach rode over to the herd and said something to J.T. and Matt. Watching him, it annoyed Willa that even from that distance he stood out from the rest of the cowboys. Like it or not, she had to admit there was something about him, something that drew your eye, that set him apart from the other men.

Zach was a commanding figure, a big, broad-shouldered, imposing man in his prime who sat a horse with a loose, easy grace. Still...it was more than just his height and impressive build. He seemed to have an aura of quiet authority about him.

Zach worked right along side his men, charging in and out of ravines and thick brush at breakneck speed and doing any other dangerous or dirty job that needed doing, but no one would ever doubt that he was the man in charge.

On foot, Zach's brothers had the same commanding air about them, even Matt, despite his limp.

As Zach rode out of camp again, Willa's gaze wandered over to Seamus's other grandsons. A reluctant half smile played around her mouth as she watched Matt cut off a cow that tried to bolt. She had to hand it to them. He and J.T. had stuck to the riding lessons with a gritty determination that she hadn't expected of two city boys.

Over the past weeks their riding ability had improved enough that Zach now allowed them to work with the men. However, they did not yet display the same confidence and prowess in the saddle as Zach, nor had they quite mastered the skills of roping or bulldogging, which was why he had assigned them the relatively simple task of riding herd on the stock that had been brought in.

Willa's gaze drifted irresistibly back to Zach as he came riding up out of a draw, driving a bawling cow and her two calves into camp. A tingle danced over her skin, as it always did whenever she saw him, even from afar.

She gritted her teeth and told herself the sensation was the result of intense dislike.

In the distance south of camp a cowboy crested a rise, riding flat-out. When he spotted Zach he waved his hat above his head and began to shout. Willa tensed.

Zach had been about to ride out after more strays, but he whirled his horse around and waited. When the rider pulled his lathered horse up alongside Zach he started gesturing wildly, and even from that distance Willa could sense his agitation.

Something was terribly wrong.

Willa raced back to her horse, vaulted into the saddle and headed down to camp as fast as Bertha could safely pick her way down the slope.

When she arrived in camp Zach was shouting orders. Already she could see some of the men riding south, slapping leather all the way.

"What is it?" Willa demanded, riding up beside him. "What's happened?"

"Stretch! Dooley! Come with me! We got trouble!" Zach shouted to the two men who came riding into camp driving three cows and two calves. He whirled his horse and raced over to where his brothers were circling the herd. Willa followed.

"What's up?" J.T. asked.

"We've got a half mile of fence down on the southern border. All the cows we've rounded up so far are out on the highway. Several have already been hit by motorists and killed."

"A half a mile of downed fence? That's impossible. Unless…"

"Unless it was cut," Zach finished for Willa, his mouth grim.

He turned back to his brothers. "You two and Jake

stay here with the herd. I'll send someone out later to relieve you and spend the night with this bunch. Send the next man who rides into camp to the barn to load a pickup with reels of barbed wire and staples and get it out there, pronto. As soon as they come into camp, tell the rest of the men to hightail it to the south border along the highway. C'mon, Sadie,'' he commanded, and when he kicked his horse into a gallop, the dog raced alongside him.

Willa dug her heels into Bertha's flanks and took off after them.

''Go back. Stay with Matt and J.T.'' he shouted when she rode up beside him. ''The men and I will handle this.''

''Forget it. I'm going. Those are my cattle, too, remember?'' Besides, she wanted to get a look at that fence.

Zach didn't waste time arguing.

They found pandemonium when they reached the southernmost boundary of the ranch. At least three hundred head of cattle had wandered out onto the highway. An eighteen-wheeler had slammed into a small bunch and jackknifed. Willa could see at least five dead cows scattered over the asphalt and along the verge. The big rig sat askew across the highway and partly in the bar ditch, blocking traffic.

This part of Montana was sparsely populated, making traffic light, but even so lines of pickups and semi-rigs were backed up in both directions.

It took the better part of four hours to clear the carcasses and wrecked truck off the highway and to round up the meandering cattle. Some had wandered more than two miles. Willa, Zach and several of the men drove them back onto Rocking R land while another crew frantically worked to repair the fence. The last thirty yards or so of wire was strung by lantern light.

It was close to nine when Willa, Zach and the men came dragging in. She was so exhausted she could barely put one foot in front of the other. Worse, she was very much afraid that she had sprained her right wrist, possibly even cracked a bone. She held her arm close to her body, hoping to hide the injury. Later, she'd catch Maria alone and get her to bind it for her.

Zach didn't look as though he felt much better than she did. His face was smudged with dirt and sweat and gray with fatigue.

They were met at the back door by three worried women.

"Ah, *muchacha. ¡Pobrecito!*" Maria exclaimed, wringing her hands. "Sit. Sit, before you fall on your face, and I will get your dinner."

"Don't bother. I'm too tired to eat. All I want is a hot shower and a chance to sleep for about twelve hours straight," Willa mumbled.

"What foolishness is this? You must eat to get your strength back. Now sit."

She gave Willa's shoulder a downward push, and her knees buckled. With a groan, she collapsed into the nearest chair like a dishrag. She crossed her arms on the table, carefully cradling the injured one, and lay her head down.

"First let's see about that wrist."

Willa was so tired she barely heard Zach, and the next thing she knew his calloused hand clasped her forearm. Despite exhaustion and pain, his touch set her nerve endings to tingling.

Her head popped up and she tried to pull away, but it was hopeless. Though gentle, his grip remained firm.

"Let me go. What do you think you're doing?"

"Be still. This arm needs tending. It's already swelling."

"No, it's fine. Just a little strain is al— Ow!"

Zach probed the puffy flesh, then clasped her hand and gently rotated it. Willa groaned and put her head down again, fighting nausea.

"It doesn't appear to be broken, but to be safe you should have it X-rayed tomorrow. In the meantime it should be tightly wrapped."

"Out of my way. I will take care of my *niña*. Ah, *pobrecito*. Such a foolish girl."

Willa heard a thunk, and the next instant she felt her hand being immersed in warm soapy water. Maria fussed and tutted while she washed her hand and arm up to her elbow, then dried it tenderly and wound an Ace bandage around the injured wrist.

"There. All done. Now you will eat."

Willa didn't have the strength to argue, or to even go wash up the rest of the way. Besides, she knew she wouldn't win. Vaguely she was aware of Kate and Maude Ann fussing over Zach. She heard plates clunk down on the table, one just inches from her face. The tantalizing aroma of roast beef drifted to her nose. Her stomach growled, but she was too tired to stir herself.

"Have J.T. and Matt gotten back?" Zach asked.

"Yes. About an hour ago," Kate replied. "They ate and went upstairs to shower. They should be down any minute."

As though on cue, the two men came through the door from the hall. "Hey, Zach. How'd it go?" J.T. said.

"We had a helluva time doing it, but I think we rounded up all of the cattle that weren't killed. It took a while to get that semi-tractor out of the bar ditch and clear the highway. And to get the fence mended, but we finally managed it."

"How many did we lose?" Matt ask.

"Seven cows, nine calves."

Maria poked Willa's shoulder. "Wake up, *muchacha,* and eat."

Groaning, Willa forced herself upright and picked up her fork. Her stomach growled when she took a bite of roast beef, but she could barely summon the energy to chew…or to hold her eyes open.

"Was it deliberate sabotage, like you suspected?"

"Oh, yeah. Dobie and Chuck were repairing fence in the far south pastures today. They said when they rode by that section this morning the fence was fine. When they came back by this afternoon on their way to the barn it was down. Every strand of wire had been cut off at the posts.

"My guess is, it was done as soon as our men were out of sight. Some of the stock had wandered so far by the time we got there they had to have gotten out hours before." Zach reached into the pocket of his shirt, withdrew a folded piece of paper and tossed it to Matt. "I found this nailed to one of the posts."

Willa sat up straighter, her attention caught. "You didn't say anything to me about finding a note."

Zach shrugged. "You were busy."

"What does it say?" J.T. demanded.

Matt unfolded the paper and frowned. The lined sheet had been torn from a spiral notebook and was ragged along one edge—just like the one that had been nailed to the front door a few weeks ago. "It says, 'You were warned. Get out now while you still can, or you'll regret it. This is just the beginning.'"

J.T. gave a low whistle. "Damn. Somebody wants us out of here bad."

"Yeah, but who?" Zach looked at Willa. "Do you have any ideas?"

She stiffened. "What's that supposed to mean?"

"I was hoping you might think of someone who'd do something like this. Like maybe your boyfriend."

"Which one," she asked with nasty sweetness. "You seem to think I have so many."

"Oh, c'mon, Willa. You can hardly blame Zach if he does," Maude Ann gently scolded. "A pretty girl like you? Why, you ought to have men lined up from here to the highway."

That caught Willa by surprise. She blinked at Maude Ann, delighted by the compliment and not wanting to be.

"I'm talking about Lennie Dawson. I ran into him in town a few weeks back. He went out of his way to let me know that you belonged to him."

Willa's gaze snapped back to Zach. "He did *what?*"

"He also warned me to keep my hands off of you." Those steady green eyes bore into her, and she knew he was remembering that night in the barn. He'd certainly put his hands on her then. And kissed her senseless, to boot.

She felt her cheeks heat, but she refused to let him make her squirm. "Damn that Lennie," she snarled. "I'll kill him."

"So...does that mean he isn't your boyfriend?"

"Of course he isn't! I told you that."

"You've never gone out with him?"

Willa winced. "Once. *Once!* And then only because Seamus forbade me to."

"Now there's a good reason," Matt muttered. His wife elbowed him in the ribs and shushed him.

J.T.'s forehead wrinkled. "I don't get it. If you're not involved with this Lennie character, then why is he telling everybody that you are?"

"For one thing, he's full of himself. Lennie always wants what he can't have. Telling him no is like waving a red flag in front of a bull. Plus, he wants—"

Willa could have kicked herself. She hadn't meant to mention Lennie's ridiculous claim to anyone. It had been a blatant lie. She stared down at her plate and hoped Zach would let the matter drop. She should have known better.

"He wants what?"

She shot him an annoyed look. "If you must know, I think he and his father want to get their hands on the Rocking R. Before you three showed up they, and everyone else around here, thought I would inherit the entire ranch, which is why Lennie started pursuing me. I figured out that much long ago."

"What about now?" Zach probed. "You think he's willing to marry you for a quarter of what he'd originally hoped to gain?"

Willa's cheeks heated. Put so bluntly, the question was insulting, but since she had brought the matter up, she couldn't very well object, although she suspected Zach was enjoying her discomfort.

Tipping up her chin, she looked him in the eye. "Yes, I do. Even a quarter share of the Rocking R, added to the Bar-D, would more than double the Dawsons' holdings.

"Besides, I think Lennie and his father are determined to at least get my part of the Rocking R. They've got this crazy notion that the whole shebang should have gone to Henry when Seamus died."

"What? Why would they think that?"

"It doesn't matter. I'm sure Lennie made the whole thing up to annoy me."

"Tell us, anyway."

"It's ridiculous. Lennie claims his father and Seamus had a deal. Henry would marry Colleen and take over the Rocking R after Seamus died. But I don't believe him. Seamus wouldn't do that. Lennie will say anything to get what he wants."

"No, *muchacha*. It is true."

Six pairs of eyes turned to Maria. The housekeeper stood by the kitchen sink, wringing her hands, her expression pained.

"Maria, what are you saying?" Willa demanded.

"When *la señorita* is seventeen, the *señor* he betroth her to Señor Dawson, a man twenty years older than *la señorita*." Maria huffed and made a face. "The Bar-D, it is not so *grande* as the Rocking R. Señor Dawson, he is a greedy man and he has much envy for this place. To get his hands on it, he is willing to sacrifice his pride and change his name to Rafferty so the babies from the marriage will carry on the name. Señor Rafferty, he say Señorita Colleen, she owe him this much."

"And our mother agreed to that?" Zach demanded.

"Oh, no, no. Señorita Colleen, she had much spirit, and she refuse to marry Señor Dawson. She love Señor Mike. He is one of the *vaqueros* who works for Señor Rafferty. When she tell him, the *señor* is *furioso*. He dismiss Señor Mike and order him to leave Montana.

"But Señor Mike, he love Señorita Colleen. He get a job at another ranch near Clear Water, and he and *la señorita*, they meet secretly and make plans to...to..."

"Elope?" J.T. suggested.

"*Sí*, elope." Maria sighed. "Before they can marry, Señor Mike, he is killed. Something frighten his horse.

The animal, he rear and fall on top of him. Not long after that, the *señorita* knows she is with child.''

''And when Seamus found out, he tossed her out on her ear,'' Zach finished for her with disgust.

''*Sí.* She ruin his plans, and he go a little *loco.* By the time he cool off, his pride will not let him go after her.''

''That's assuming he wanted to,'' Matt mumbled.

''*Sí.* With the *señor,* it is not easy to know what is in his heart. In the beginning he believe the *la señorita* will not survive alone, that she will give up her baby and come crawling back, begging his forgiveness, and marry Señor Dawson, as he wishes. But the years they go by, and the *señorita,* she does not come.

''Then a minister in Houston, he telephone Señor Rafferty and tell him Señorita Colleen *es muerto.*''

''So he knew when we first came here that she was dead?'' Matt snapped. ''Why the hell didn't he just tell us straight-out?''

''I do not know, *señor.* Señor Rafferty was an unhappy man. Sometimes he strike out in strange ways.''

''I didn't notice our mother's grave when we buried Seamus,'' Zach said quietly. ''I'd like for you to go up there with us tomorrow, Maria, and point it out.''

Her eyes filled with tears and her chin began to quiver. ''I cannot do that, *señor.* The minister who called, he say it is *la señorita*'s last wish to be buried beside her *madre* in the family cemetery here on the ranch.'' She made the sign of the cross and dabbed at her eyes with her apron. ''But the *señor,* he say no. He told the man of God to bury her in…in…*la sepultura de los pobres.*''

J.T. and Matt exchanged a puzzled look. ''Where?''

''A pauper's grave,'' Zach supplied in a voice tight with fury.

''Why that sorry—'' Matt bit off the tirade and

clamped his jaw tight. Anger radiated from him like a red aura.

Shocked, Willa stared at the housekeeper. Seamus had always been foul-tempered and unforgiving, but even so, she couldn't believe he would do such a thing to his own child. Apparently, however, he had.

Zach looked at his brothers. "I think we should find Colleen's grave and have her body brought here for reburial. Agreed?"

Without hesitation, J.T. and Matt nodded and murmured their approval.

Zach turned his attention back to Willa. "Do you think Lennie's father has been nursing a grudge all this time?"

"Probably." She yawned and fought to stay awake. "There's been bad blood between him and Seamus ever since my mother and I came here. I never knew why, but this explains it."

"Do you think Henry Dawson is bitter enough to be behind these incidents?"

"It's possible, I suppose."

"I see where you're going with this, Zach," Matt said. "But it doesn't hold up. Why would Dawson try to run us out? Unless he can afford to purchase the ranch in the event we default, he'll be better off if his son marries Willa."

Zach looked to Willa again. "Can he afford to purchase the Rocking R if it went up for sale?"

"I doubt it. Even if he used the Bar-D for collateral, he couldn't borrow enough for the purchase price."

"So Matt's right. The only way Dawson and his son would gain is if Lennie married you."

"Please. There is no *way* I'd ever marry Lennie Dawson."

"Yes, but does he believe that?"

"He should. I've told him often enough." Willa sighed and her shoulders slumped. "But knowing Lennie, probably not. His ego is so big he can't imagine there's a woman alive who wouldn't jump at the chance to be Mrs. Leonard Dawson.

"Look, I'm too tired for this. Could we continue this discussion in the morning?"

Without waiting for an answer, Willa scraped back her chair and stood up.

"It seems to me that pretty much eliminates the Dawsons as the ones behind the attacks," J.T. said as she trudged across the kitchen. "Which means we still don't have a clue who's behind this."

"You're right." Matt tossed the note down onto the table. "We don't have any more to go on than we did before."

As exhausted as she was, the remark still set fire to Willa's temper. At the door she paused and looked back at them over her shoulder, her expression tight with resentment.

"Wrong. This note may not tell us who is behind the vandalism, but it certainly proves that it wasn't me. In case you've forgotten, I was working up at Henchman's Meadow with the three of you all day."

"My alarm clock didn't go off."

Willa burst through the kitchen door, hopping on one foot while pulling a boot on the other one, no easy task using one hand. "Usually I wake up before it makes a sound. Wouldn't you know, the first time I oversleep the blasted thing doesn't go off."

"It is no big thing, *nina*. You needed to rest." Maria plunked an iron skillet down on the stove. "Sit down and relax and I will cook you breakfast. Last night you took only a bite of food.''

"Don't bother. Just wrap up a couple of biscuits. I'll eat them on the way to Henchman's Meadow. There are still plenty of cattle up there that need to be rounded up.'' She held on to the back of a chair and stomped her foot down into the boot.

Kate stood at the sink washing dishes while Maude Ann dried them. The two younger women and Maria exchanged a wary look. Maude Ann cleared her throat. "Uh…actually, Willa, you aren't working today.''

She looked up and blinked. "Excuse me?''

"Zach asked Kate to take you to the hospital in Bozeman to have your wrist X-rayed.''

"He what?''

Doing her best to ignore Willa's dangerously quiet tone, Maude Ann rushed on. "I would take you, myself, of course, but I always try to be here when the kids get home from school.''

"I've already called and made an appointment,'' Kate added. "We should leave in about an hour.''

"Forget it. No one is taking me anywhere.''

"Now, *nina,* Señor Zach, he is only trying to do what is best for you. He say you need to rest. And you know you must have a doctor look at your arm.''

Willa's gaze flashed to Maria, who was wringing her hands and looking incredibly guilty. "You turned off my alarm clock, didn't you? He told you to turn it off. Why that —''

"Ah, no, *nina.* The *señor,* he is worried—''

"Yeah, right.''

"Willa, wait! Where are you going?'' Kate cried.

"Where I go every day. To work. Zach Mahoney may

have taken over the Rocking R but he is *not* taking over my life."

"But what about your appointment?"

In reply, she slammed the door behind her.

Willa fumed every step of the way to the barn. By the time she reached it she had worked up a good head of steam.

"Here now. What're you doin' here?" Pete demanded when she stormed inside. "I 'spected you'd be halfway to Bozeman by now to see the doc."

"My wrist is fine. It's just a slight sprain."

"Izzat so? Then why're you holdin' it against your belly that'a way?"

"I'm fine. Don't fuss." She lifted her bridle off the nail with her good hand and stepped into Bertha's stall. "Would you please come help me saddle her? It's a bit awkward with one hand."

"Uh-uh. Not me. Zach left strict orders that you was to see the doc and rest today, an' that's all. I ain't about to cross the man just 'cause you got a burr under your saddle."

"He left *orders?* Why that arrogant, overbearing... Fine, then. I'll do it myself."

"Suit yerself. Just don't 'spect any help from me."

Putting a bridle and saddle on a horse one-handed proved to be incredibly difficult. Willa grunted and strained and cursed and struggled. Pete watched the whole thing with a disgruntled expression, shaking his head occasionally. The operation took her the better part of an hour, and by the time she had finished she was panting and exhausted and her injured wrist was throbbing like a son of a gun. Nevertheless, she grabbed the pommel with her left hand and swung herself up into the saddle. As she walked Bertha out of the barn, Pete followed behind her.

"Now that you're saddled up, just where is it you plan on goin'?" he asked dryly.

"Up to Henchman's Meadow to help with the roundup."

Pete snorted. "Well, then, little gal, you jist wasted all that time and effort fer nothin'. Zach's just gonna send you right back here."

"He wouldn't dare."

"Oh, he'd dare, all right. Why, he's jist liable to toss you over his shoulder and haul you back hisself. Face it, Willie, when it come to strong wills, you've met your match in that man. He's a patient one, but if I was you, I wouldn't push him too far."

Grinding her teeth, Willa held her throbbing arm against her side and glared down at the old man, but she knew he was right. Her act of defiance could well turn into humiliation if she showed up at the roundup camp. But dammit! There had to be something she could do to show him he couldn't run her life.

She glanced around. Two men were repairing a corral gate nearby and another was filling the water troughs. A second later her gaze lit on the group of cattle in the pen next to the barn. She stared at the small herd as an idea began to take shape in her mind.

Standing up in the stirrups, Willa called out to the men. "Skinny! Leroy! Taggert! Stop what you're doing and come over here."

"What're you up to now, little gal?" Pete demanded, glaring at her suspiciously.

"I'm going to take those men and drive this bunch up to the high country."

"What! Are you crazy?"

"There's no reason they can't be driven to summer pastures. None of the heifers is going to drop a calf and the bulls we didn't want to use for breeding have already been castrated."

"There's plenty a reasons 'sides them. The main one bein' Zach ain't ready to move them animals yet. He plans to take them up with the rest of the herd when roundup is over."

"In the meantime, they're just standing around consuming feed."

"Zach thinks it's too early to move 'em. We could have us a blizzard up in the high country yet. It's happened a'fore."

"It won't this year. Spring has settled in nicely."

The three men walked over. "You wanted us for something, Willie?"

"Yes. Saddle up and get those cattle out of the pen. We're taking them up the mountain."

The men exchanged an uncomfortable look. "Uh, the boss said we was to get these repairs done."

"Now I'm telling you to stop and help me drive these cattle."

The tall, lanky man called Skinny scratched the back of his neck. "I don't know. The boss didn't say nothing about moving cattle."

"I don't care what Mr. Mahoney said. I'm ordering you to saddle up and move these cattle. Now."

"Yes, ma'am."

"I'm tellin' you, Willie, you're making a mistake," Pete argued when the men disappeared into the tack room to get their gear. "Zach's gonna have a conniption."

"Let him. I'm moving those cattle."

Chapter Seven

The first thing Zach noticed when he rode into the ranch yard a few hours later was the empty pen.

He dismounted in front of the main barn and stalked inside. He found Pete in the tack room.

"Where the devil are the cattle that were in the holding pen?" he demanded.

The old man glanced up at Zach's thunderous expression and winced. "Willie's drivin' 'em up to the summer pasture on Devil's Cup Mountain."

"She's *what?* Why didn't you stop her? I made it clear that I didn't want to start the drive to the summer ranges for another two or three weeks. The weather this time of year is too unreliable."

"I tried to tell 'er, but she weren't in no mood to listen. Come tearin' in here madder'n a wet hen 'bout three hours ago, bound and determined to defy you." Pete shot a stream of tobacco juice into his copper spittoon and darted Zach a sly look. "Willie always was an independent little cuss. She don't take kindly to being ordered 'round, even when it's fer her own good."

Zach bit out an expletive. "That little idiot. I knew sooner or later that temper of hers would land her in trouble. Dammit! This morning the weather channel predicted a severe snowstorm would hit the high country by late afternoon."

The old man's head jerked up, alarm clouding his faded blue eyes. "By now they're over halfway there. We gotta do somethin'."

Zach spun on his heel and stalked toward the door. "Saddle a fresh horse for me. And add a bedroll and saddlebags. And a bag of grain. I'll go round up emergency supplies."

Zach rode hard, following the swath of churned earth the herd had left across the rangeland and up into the foothills. Once through the cut in the mountains the trail began a steep climb, leaving him no choice but to slow the gelding's pace.

Frustrated, Zach urged the horse upward at a speed just shy of reckless, giving silent thanks for Pete's years of experience. The old man had chosen well. The barrel-chested gray wasn't the fastest or the biggest, or even the handsomest horse on the ranch, but he had stamina and he was sure-footed as a cat.

There were several places on Devil's Cup Mountain that the Rocking R used for summer pasture, but from the direction Willa was taking she was heading for a high meadow called Cowboy Basin. She and the men had better than three hours' head start on him, but Zach knew the herd would slow them down. Cattle balked at climbing and had to be prodded every step of the way up a mountain. He figured he'd catch up with them a mile or two before they reached the summer range.

He clucked his tongue and nudged the gray's flanks almost constantly, urging him upward, all the while keeping a wary eye on the sky. Ominous, low-hanging clouds were moving in fast from the northwest. The higher he climbed, the darker the sky became and the colder it got.

Just past the halfway point he felt the first sting of sleet hit the back of his neck. He pulled a long fleece scarf out of his coat pocket, looped it over his Stetson to hold it on and wound the ends around his neck and the lower half of his face. Turning up the collar of his coat, he kicked up the gray's pace. A quarter mile farther up the trail the sleet turned to snow.

Zach's heart began to pound. Surely by now Willa would have realized what a precarious position she had gotten herself and the men into and turned the herd around, he told himself. Any minute now he should meet up with them coming down the mountain. When he did and he got his hands on Willa…

Clenching his teeth, he pushed the thought aside and forged on doggedly.

Five minutes passed. Ten. Twenty. The wind kicked up and the temperature began to plummet. The farther up the mountain Zach went, the harder it snowed and the worse visibility became. Snow quickly covered the ground, obliterating all sign of tracks and it swirled so thick that Zach had to lean forward in the saddle and strain to make out landmarks.

Luckily, he'd spent most of the previous two weeks riding the high country with a couple of the old hands. Taking advantage of the spell of mild weather, they had led pack trains to each of the line camps and stocked the cabins with supplies for the cowboys who would be riding herd on the cattle throughout the summer. In the process he had learned the territory.

It was bitter cold and getting colder. The snow was blowing almost sideways now. Worry gnawed at Zach's gut like a sharp-toothed animal. He had grown up in a small mining town high in the Colorado Rockies. He knew how easy it was to get disoriented in a snowstorm.

His heart gave a leap. Up ahead through the curtain of white he thought he saw something move. Nudging his horse forward, he cupped one gloved hand to his mouth and called out. "Hell-looo!"

The wind whipped the greeting back in his face, but as he drew nearer he could make out a large, dark, shifting mass and beside it the hunched shape of a rider on horseback. He rode within five yards of the herd before the man spotted him.

"Zach? Is that you? Man, am I glad to see you."

"Dammit, Skinny! What the hell are you doing up here?"

"Well, uh…you see, boss, Willie, she ordered us to help her move these cattle, an'—"

"You take your orders from me, not from Willa. You're supposed to be repairing corrals. When I assign a man a job, unless I tell him otherwise, I expect him to complete it. You got that?"

"Yessir, boss."

Zach cast a furious look around. Bunched together in a tight circle, their backs dusted with white, the cattle appeared as a shifting grayish-brown blob through the blowing snow. On the far side of the herd, he could barely make out the shadowy shapes of two other riders, but both were too large to be Willa.

"Where is she?"

"Looking for strays. Willie'd decided to turn around

and head back when five or six head took off into the brush. She told us to hold the herd here and wait for her. But me'n Leroy and Taggert, we're gettin' worried. She's been gone 'bout twenty minutes. Maybe a little longer.''

Zach's head snapped around. The look he gave the cowboy was hard enough to cut steel. "That's too long. Why the devil haven't you already been out looking for her?''

Skinny's Adam's apple bobbed. He looked like a man going to his own execution. "Willie ordered us to stay with the herd.''

"If you yahoos had followed my orders as well as you seem to follow Willa's, none of us would be in this mess.'' Fighting to control the fury and fear swelling inside him, he clenched his jaw and looked around. "Which direction did she take?''

"North, right through them bushes.''

"All right. While I go look for her I want you three to take this herd down the mountain as fast as you can.''

Even through the swirling white, Zach thought he saw the man pale. "In this? We'll be lost in ten minutes. If we don't fall off a cliff first.''

"Here, take this.'' Zach dug into one of the saddlebags and pulled out a compass and handed it to him. "Tell the point man to keep a close watch on the ground and keep a steady southeast course. In an hour or so you should be out of the worst of the storm, and if you don't dawdle you'll make the foothills by dark. From there the going is fairly easy. Now get these cattle moving. You're burning daylight.''

Zach didn't wait around to listen to any excuses. He nudged the gray and rode into the brush.

Conditions were growing worse. The snow fell faster and thicker and the wind began to howl, whipping the icy flakes into a frenzy. Within minutes Zach found himself in a whiteout.

He didn't bother searching the ground for her horse's tracks. The snow had wiped out all traces of those. In any case he knew how easy it would be to miss seeing her in the swirling maelstrom. While he stared at the ground he could pass within a few feet of her and never know it. So he rode slowly, his eyes constantly moving, straining to peer through the shifting white veil. Every few seconds he pulled down the scarf, cupped his mouth with both hands and yelled Willa's name.

He had no idea how long he searched. It seemed like hours. He was cold to the bone. Icy crystals clung to his eyebrows and lashes above the scarf. He was beginning to lose feeling in his toes and the tips of his fingers. Zach knew he had to seek shelter soon or perish, but he couldn't bring himself to stop searching. Willa was out there somewhere.

It was pure accident that he found her. He stopped to get his bearings, and in a brief instant of partial clearing he spotted the ghostly form of a horse and rider slowly crossing his path a few feet ahead.

"Willa!"

Giving no sign that she'd heard him, she rode on at the same plodding pace, hunched over, her coat collar turned up all around. Then the wind shifted, and the curtain of white swallowed her up again, and terror grabbed Zach by the throat.

"Willa, stop!" He kicked his horse's flanks, and the startled gelding leaped forward. In three long lopes he had her in sight again, but her lack of response and slumped posture only increased his fear. Lord, had she frozen to death in the saddle?

"Wil-laaa! Wil-laaa!"

Her head came up like a deer testing the wind for a sound.

"Here! I'm here." Shouting over the howl of the wind, he rode up beside her, grabbed Bertha's reins and brought her to a stop.

"Z-Zach?" She stared at him, her frost-rimmed lashes blinking owlishly.

"Yeah, it's me. Are you all right?"

First shock then abject relief flashed across her face. "You found me. You found me." She grabbed his arm as though making sure he was real, then squeezed her eyes shut and pressed her quivering lips together. "I thought...I thought I was going to die."

"Yeah, well, we both may yet if we don't get out of this storm. C'mon." He expected her to argue when he pulled the reins from her stiff fingers, but she was either too scared, too exhausted or too frozen to complain. He wrapped Bertha's reins around his gloved palm, turned in the opposite direction and led her through the blinding whiteness.

It would be dark soon. Zach knew that to attempt to descend the mountain at night in a blizzard would be suicide. In any case, the trip would take too long. Willa was half frozen and needed shelter—now. Their only hope was to find the line camp.

Seconds before spotting Willa he'd caught a glimpse of a giant tree that had been struck by lightning and split into a huge vee. He knew that the cabin was approximately ten feet due east of the dead pine. Willa had ridden right past it.

Luckily, Zach possessed an unerring sense of direction. He'd also taken the precaution of bringing another compass.

In good weather, from where they were he could have

tossed a stone and hit the log structure, yet it seemed to take forever to reach it. The exhausted horses plodded through the drifts with their heads down.

The puffs of vapor from the animal's nostrils froze instantly into tiny ice crystals. The wind shrieked around them like a banshee, tearing at their clothes and stinging their exposed skin.

Zach had expected Willa to question and argue, but she remained silent, which kicked his anxiety up another notch. He glanced over his shoulder and saw that she sat hunched deep in her coat. She had her head down and the wide collar turned up to meet the brim of her Stetson, shielding her face. She didn't utter a sound until he brought the horses to a stop.

Looking up, she saw the cabin, and surprise then utter relief passed over her face. Zach couldn't hear her over the wind, but he saw her lips form the words, "Thank God."

Focused on keeping them alive, he wasted no time on conversation. He dismounted and tied the horses to the hitching rail. Willa was so cold and stiff he had to lift her out of the saddle and carry her inside. For once she didn't fight him.

He shouldered the door shut behind them, muting the howling fury of the storm. The weak, grayish glow seeping in through the lone window provided barely enough light to see, but Zach strode directly to the small table in the center of the room. Hooking the toe of his boot around a spindly leg, he pulled out a wooden chair and sat her down.

The temperature in the room was only slightly warmer than that outside. Willa hugged her arms tight and shivered.

"I'll get a fire going," Zach said tersely.

He pulled a box of kitchen matches from a shelf and lit the kerosene lamp that hung from a bracket attached to the wall. Then he hunkered down in front of the pot-bellied stove, opened the small door and began pulling split logs and kindling from the wood box on the floor. He worked with quick efficiency, his jaw clenched tight against the seething emotions bubbling inside him.

The one-room cabin was a crude log structure, meant to house a cowboy through the summer months. An ancient hand pump mounted on the counter that served as a kitchen brought water into the cabin from a well, but that was the extent of the plumbing—or any other modern convenience. There was no electricity. The old pot-bellied stove did double duty as a heat source and a cook range. A white enamel chamber pot was tucked beneath the bunk built into the corner, but unless the weather was inclement most cowboys simply grabbed a roll of tissue and headed for the bushes when nature called. For those who were too fastidious—or too chicken—to bathe in the icy waters of a mountain stream, a galvanized tub hung on a nail by the stove.

When Zach had a good blaze going, he stood and dusted off his hands. "There, you should start feeling some heat soon."

"Th-thanks."

Maybe it was the brevity of her answer, or the pathetic quaver in her voice. Or maybe it was simply the sight of her sitting there huddled in that big coat, shivering, her creamy skin reddened by the cold and ice melting on those long ebony lashes. Whatever the reason, that one shaky word snapped the last thread of Zach's patience.

For the past several hours emotions had roiled inside him like a churning cauldron, but he had kept a tight lid on those feelings and turned all his energy and focus on finding Willa. Now that lid blew off like an exploding pressure cooker.

"Thanks? *Thanks!*" His fist came down hard on the table, making both it and Willa jump. "That's all you have to say?"

"I..."

"What the *hell* did you think you were doing, driving that herd up here?"

"D-don't you dare r-raise your v-voice to m-me," she flared back, but her chattering teeth robbed the protest of its heat and spoiled the effect.

"I'd like to raise more than my voice. What I ought to do is turn you over my knee and blister your butt."

"Y-you wouldn't d-dare!"

"No, I wouldn't. But only because you're female. Believe me, if you were a man I'd flatten you."

As it was, Zach itched to grab her by her shoulders and shake her until her teeth fell out. Knowing he had to put space between them, he swung away and stomped to the window, but he was too upset to remain still and began to stride back and forth across the small cabin. His boot heels struck the puncheon floor like hammer blows.

"Dammit, woman!" he raged, flinging his arms wide. "You countermanded my orders, put your life and the lives of those men in danger, worried Pete sick and nearly cost this ranch several hundred head of cattle. And for what? Because I had the gall to ask you to take one day off and go see a doctor? Damn. What a monster I am."

"Y-you didn't a-ask—"

"Quiet!" he roared. "I don't want to hear it!"

Willa was so startled, she shrank back in the chair and goggled at him.

Zach stalked from one side of the cabin to the other like a caged lion. Every cell in his body quivered with tension. He felt as though he was suddenly too big for his skin and might burst apart at any second.

"Up until now I have been patient with you, dammit. For four months you've criticized and argued and opposed me at every turn. You resent me and my brothers—especially me, it seems. You don't want us here. You don't think we have a right to this ranch. Okay, I got that. Hell, I even understand it. But let me remind you—*I* didn't write that damned will," he bellowed, thumbing his chest. "*I'm* not the one who gave you a raw deal. That was Seamus. Not me."

"If you hadn't—"

"I said *quiet!*" He jerked to a halt and jabbed his finger at the end of her nose. "Not another word until I've had my say."

Her mouth went slack and her eyes widened. Whether he'd startled her into silence or she was afraid to speak, he didn't know. At that moment he didn't care.

When he was certain she would remain silent he resumed his restless pacing. "Like it or not, this is the hand we've all been dealt. You either accept that or we all lose."

"I kn-know tha—"

This time he silenced her with a look. "I'm through being patient. From now on I'm not going to tolerate any more of your guff. Or any more stunts like the one you pulled today."

Willa opened her mouth to speak, thought better of it, and snapped it shut again.

Zach stopped in the middle of the floor and pressed the heels of his hands to his temples. "Dammit, woman, you drove those cattle up here just to defy me. Of all the reckless, stupid, irresponsible…" He shook his head, at a loss.

"I—I didn't expect it to snow."

The mumbled replied enraged him even more. "Give me a break! You've lived here all your life. You know spring in the mountains can be treacherous. Why the devil did you think I wanted to wait a few more weeks?

"No. Never mind, don't bother to answer that. You weren't *thinking* at all. You saw a chance to strike out at me and took it. Consequences be damned."

Guilt flickered across her face, and he knew he'd hit the mark. Cursing roundly, he started pacing again, but when he reached the opposite wall he swung back and pinned her with an accusing glare.

"Do you have any idea how close you came to losing your life out there?" he shouted, flinging an arm out toward the window. "If I hadn't found you when I did you wouldn't have lasted another ten minutes. And believe me, it was dumb luck that I found you at all. Hell, we both could have died out there. I'd been searching for you for hours."

Willa blanched at that, and pressed her trembling lips together. "I—I know," she murmured in a subdued voice. "I was s-so scared. Oh, Lord, I haven't even thanked you yet. I'm so sorry, Zach. I'm—"

"Forget it. I don't need your thanks." Zach stopped pacing and looked into those stricken violet eyes, his chest so tight he could barely breathe.

"Hell, I can't deal with this right now," he growled, and stomped for the door. "I've gotta go see to the horses." He paused to cram his hat down tighter on his head and arrange the scarf again, then he stepped out into the teeth of the storm.

After the brief respite it seemed even colder, and Zach caught his breath at the first slap of icy wind. Visibility was no more than a couple of feet. Keeping one hand on the outside of the cabin wall at all times, he untied the horses and led them around back and into the small lean-to. It wasn't the warm barn that Bertha usually enjoyed, but both horses would be sheltered from the wind and snow, and their shared body heat in the small space would keep them warm enough to survive.

Zach worked quickly, methodically, using the chores to keep his churning emotions at bay. By the light of a battery-powered lantern, he unsaddled the animals and rubbed each one down with a wad of hay, then covered them with horse blankets he found on a shelf. After breaking the ice on top of the rain barrel located just outside the door, he dipped up a bucket of water and gave each animal a drink. He then poured grain from the sack he'd brought with him into a galvanized trough.

Finally, though, he ran out of things to do, and his emotions caught up with him. Overwhelmed him.

When he thought about what could have happened—what had almost happened—a hard shudder shook his big frame.

The adrenaline that had kept him going for the past few hours drained away in a whoosh, leaving him suddenly shaky and weak in the knees.

With an agonized groan, he leaned against the gray gelding and rested his head against the animal's back.

While the two horses munched contentedly, Zach rolled his forehead against the coarse horse blanket, shaken to the depth of his being. It hadn't been anger that had made him tear into Willa, as she no doubt believed. It had been fear at how close he had come to losing her.

Zach groaned again, but he couldn't deny the truth any longer. He would have been concerned about anyone lost in a storm and done his best to find them. However it had been more than mere concern he'd experienced while searching for Willa. It had been gut-wrenching terror that he would not find her in time, and heaven help him, the thought of that had been unbearable.

The depth of his feeling stunned and appalled him. "Damn, Mahoney, have you lost your mind?" he raged at himself. "Willa Simmons is a pain-in-the-butt, smart-mouthed little spitfire. Any man who takes her on will have his hands full. She's not even your type, for Pete's sake."

The lecture didn't do one whit of good. Somehow she had gotten under his guard and stolen his heart, something he would have sworn no woman could ever do.

Zach shook his head. That he'd allowed himself to fall for Willa Simmons, a feisty little hellion who couldn't stand the sight of him, made him feel foolish.

Of all the women in the world, why this one? Though he'd always been a bit of a loner, he'd never had any trouble attracting women. The barrel racers who followed the rodeo circuit and the groupies who hung around the shows had gone to great lengths to gain his attention. For the most part he had ignored their overtures, although that had seemed to only make them more determined.

Not that he'd lived like a monk. While traveling the circuit he'd had a few long-term relationships, mainly out of need and loneliness, and because he preferred serial monogamy to one-night stands.

He'd liked all of the women well enough. A couple he'd been genuinely fond of, but his feelings had never gone deeper than that. In his thirty-six years he'd never let a woman get that close. Until now.

Not that he was in love. Okay, so maybe his feelings for Willa went deeper and were more intense than anything he'd ever experienced before. To even imagine his life without her in it brought pain, but that didn't mean he was in love with her.

Dammit, he didn't want to be in love with any woman. That was not an emotion he trusted. From what he'd observed, it blinded you to a person's true character, often hiding their less than admirable traits until it was too late.

That had certainly been the case with his adoptive mother. After being widowed, in a love-struck haze, she had married a charismatic charmer who'd claimed to be a man of God, but who was in reality a charlatan and a criminal. And a wife abuser.

Zach had learned from her mistake.

Although…now that he thought about it, no one could say that Willa had ever bothered to hide her flaws and put her best foot forward around him.

There was no pretense or guile in the woman. With Willa, you always knew where you stood. She didn't conceal her feelings or opinions behind a polite facade or pretend to be anything but what she was—feisty, willful and defiant, often rash. A real handful. She was also loyal, hardworking, honest, kind to old folks and children, although she was learning her way with the latter and still a bit awkward. She was also friendly and loving with those she cared about. Many times, when she hadn't known he was around, he'd seen her laughing and chatting with the men or giving Pete or Maria a hug and an affectionate kiss on the cheek.

Zach's mouth twisted. Hell, it was probably her unaffected, straightforward manner that had gotten past his guard. He knew all her faults, all her weaknesses and shortcomings, and despite them—maybe even because of them—he was crazy about her.

He'd felt the attraction from the first moment he'd seen her. Desire had slammed through him like a freight train going ninety when he spotted her standing on the stairs that day he and his brothers had come to the ranch to confront Seamus, but he'd chalked that up to nothing more than lust. A basic, animal attraction. Then he'd found out who she was, and realized that she hated him and his brothers. He'd thought her animosity would cancel out the attraction, but he was wrong.

Over the past months that pull had not faded, had in fact grown stronger, though he had refused to admit it until now.

Zach supposed that adage about opposites attracting was true. He tended to be reserved and played his cards close to his chest. Willa was an open book, candid and unrestrained, and out-going around those with whom she was comfortable. He tended to think things through and plan a course of action. Willa reacted impulsively, letting her emotions guide her. Not always wisely, perhaps, and sometimes with disastrous results, but always with genuine conviction.

One thing was certain, life with Willa might be a wild ride and give a man one headache after another, but it would sure as hell never be dull.

He made a disgusted sound. Yeah, right. Dream on, Mahoney. No way in hell that's ever going to happen. The woman would as soon give you a good, swift kick in the shins as look at you. Dammit to hell! Wouldn't you know he'd fall for the one woman who hated his guts?

She'd probably laugh her head off if she knew he was out here in the freezing cold, mooning over her like some infatuated teenager. Grinding his teeth, Zach straightened and squared his shoulders. The only thing he could do was to keep his distance and hope she never guessed that he cared for her.

Chapter Eight

Willa felt wretched.

She had behaved badly. Again. Zach had every right to be furious with her. To hate her, even, after what she'd done. He was right; she could have cost three men their lives. As it was, she'd come darn close to losing her own.

Tears of self-loathing welled in her eyes. She put her head down on the table and groaned. What was the matter with her? When would she ever learn to use her head and stop letting her emotions control her?

If she weren't so contrary, none of this would have happened, she thought glumly.

Willa sniffed, thoroughly disgusted with herself.

The truth was, from the beginning she had cast Zach in the role of villain and blamed him for everything. Partly because he was an available target and partly because that was easier than accepting Seamus's perfidy. Most of all, however, because he aroused feelings in her that she had never experienced before—hot, jittery, uncomfortable feelings that she didn't have a clue how to handle, except to strike out in anger.

She desperately needed to believe the worst of him, but she had to admit, doing so was getting harder all the time. Day by day, as she'd gotten to know him, it had became more and more obvious that Zach was not the grasping, greedy opportunist she had first assumed him to be, but a decent, intelligent, hardworking man who had a deep love for the land and ranching and the knowledge to manage both.

Yet, even knowing that, she still responded to him with prickly antagonism. It seemed to be an instinctive reflex over which she had no control.

Some of her behavior toward Zach could be traced to Lennie's door, as well. Darn him. If he hadn't planted the seed in her mind that Seamus had written his will as he had to manipulate her and Zach, maybe she wouldn't be so leery. It would be just like the domineering old devil to try to control them from the grave.

Well, it wasn't going to work. She would not—absolutely would not—allow him to do that. Which meant she didn't dare get too friendly with Zach. She couldn't risk falling for him, and Willa had a terrible suspicion if she ever let her guard down she might. Lord knew, he already stirred her emotions more than any other man ever had.

Nevertheless, her relentless antagonism toward him had to stop. The man had saved her life, for Pete's sake. And he'd risked his own to do it. They didn't have to be friends, but it wouldn't kill her to be polite. He deserved that much.

She sat up and wiped her teary eyes with her fingertips. When he came back she would apologize. She would also thank him for saving her life. And in the future, she would be polite to him, she swore. Even if it killed her.

She would start by making herself useful.

Willa jumped up and went to the counter and rummaged through the crude cabinets underneath and located a can of coffee and a blue-speckled enamel coffeepot, the kind they used on a campfire.

A short while later she was hunkered down in front of the potbellied stove, stuffing more wood into the firebox when the door banged open and Zach stepped inside carrying a load of firewood in his arms and saddlebags and a bedroll over his shoulder. A blast of frigid wind and snow blew in around him until he shouldered the door shut again.

Standing, Willa held out her hands to the heat rising from the stove's surface and peeked at him out of the corner of her eye. Without so much as looking at her, Zach stomped across the room and dumped the wood into the woodbox.

"I made some coffee. Would you like some?"

He glanced at her, his expression remote. "Later. Right now I need to bring in more firewood. We're going to need it tonight. While I do that, why don't you start dinner?"

"Dinner?"

He cocked one brow. "Don't tell me you can't cook."

"Oh, and I suppose you can?" she snapped before remembering her vow to be cordial.

"Nothing fancy, but I manage. I figure if you eat, you ought be able to feed yourself. You can't always expect others to put a meal on the table for you."

Put that way, Willa couldn't very well argue, but knowing he was right didn't take away the sting. Though she knew she worked as hard or harder than anyone else on the ranch, the matter-of-fact statement made her feel inadequate and lazy, as though she were some spoiled little rich girl who never lifted a finger.

Hurt and defensive, she ground her teeth and hitched one shoulder. "I guess not. But since Maria has always done all the cooking, I never had to learn. Anyway, I prefer ranch work."

"So do I." Willa was certain she saw disdain in his eyes, but he turned and headed for the door. "All right, I'll do the cooking," he said over his shoulder. "But you can at least make yourself useful and man this door for me."

Zach hauled in five more loads of firewood. When the woodbox overflowed he dumped the extra on the floor beside it.

"Do we need so much?"

"If you want the fire to last until morning, we do. I'm sure as hell not going out in that storm in the middle of the night to get more."

His tone instantly put Willa's back up. She opened her mouth to make a pithy comment, then closed it again and ground her teeth harder. "Yes, of course. I should have realized."

Zach raised an eyebrow. Clearly he had expected a more heated reply.

He stomped the snow off of his boots and knocked more off of his long duster before shucking out of the garment and hanging it, along with his scarf and hat, on wall pegs by the door, but he did not remove the heavy coat he wore underneath. The woodstove had raised the temperature in the cabin, but it still hovered around freezing.

In the kitchen area, Zach located another kerosene lamp, lit it and placed it in the middle of the rickety table.

He returned to the counter and primed the old pump with a jar of water kept under the sink for that purpose, then worked the handle up and down until water gushed out into a chipped enamel dishpan. After washing his hands, Zach pulled a kettle from beneath the counter, filled it with water and set it on one of the stove's two burners to heat while he went to work. The coffeepot simmered on the other.

"Can I help?"

Zach arched one blond eyebrow. His green eyes fixed her with a look that made her cheeks heat.

Determined to do something useful, she poured a cup of the strong "cowboy" coffee and set it on the counter beside him. Zach barely acknowledged the gesture with a curt "Thanks."

"You're welcome. I'll, uh…I'll set the table."

The meal of canned stew and biscuits that Zach prepared was surprisingly delicious. Either that, or Willa was so ravenous anything would have tasted like ambrosia. If you didn't count the bite of roast beef she'd had for dinner the previous night, she hadn't eaten since lunch the day before.

She had psyched herself up to apologize and wanted to get it over with. Throughout the meal she waited for an opening to broach the subject, but Zach's expression did not encourage conversation. Every time she tried to initiate a discussion he was cool and distant and responded with a curt reply meant to cut her off, so for the most part they ate in silence.

Finally she couldn't stand the hostile silence a minute longer.

"All right, that's it. I've had enough of your cold shoulder," she announced. "I'm sorry, okay? I'm really, truly sorry. You're right, I shouldn't have driven those cattle up here. It was a reckless, irresponsible, stupid thing to do.''

He stopped eating and fixed her with a hard look. "So why did you?''

Willa exhaled a gusty sigh and grimaced. "Just what you said. My temper got the best of me.''

He opened his mouth to speak, but she raised her hands and silenced him. "I know, I know. I had no reason to get so angry. You were just trying to look out for my welfare. But the thing is, I've had a lifetime of Seamus ordering me around and directing my life. When he died I swore I'd never let anyone do that again. I guess when I found out you'd already made an appointment for me with the doctor and arranged for Kate to drive me, you hit a nerve.''

"So you decided to strike back by defying me. But why the cattle? There were plenty of other things you could have done that would've angered me without risking lives and property. Hell, you came up here totally unprepared. You didn't bring any food with you or emergency gear or even a winter coat.''

"I know, I know. It was an impulsive decision. I was just so angry I wasn't thinking. I felt as though I had to do something or I was going to explode.'' She spread her hands. "Driving the cattle to summer range just happened to be the first thing that occurred to me.''

"Great. So every time you get ticked off at me over some imagined insult you're going to pull another stunt like this?''

"No! At least...I hope not. From now on I'm going to do my darnedest to think things through before I act. I promise.''

Doubt glittered in his green eyes. "I don't know.

That's one helluva temper you've got, lady. It's not going to be that easy to control.''

"But that's just it. I've never had what you'd call a volatile temper until—'' She stopped abruptly and caught her lower lip between her teeth. "Uh, that is…''

"Until my brothers and I moved in? Is that what you were about to say?'' When Willa reluctantly nodded, he just looked at her, his expression remote, unreadable. "In other words, I rub you the wrong way.'' He shook his head and snorted. "Well, that's not likely to change, is it? And I'm sure as hell not going anywhere. So there goes your good intentions.''

"Okay, fine, don't believe me. Don't accept my apology,'' she said in an offended voice.

"I didn't say that. I know you're sorry and that you didn't mean any real harm.''

"You do?''

"Sure. You don't have a malicious bone in your body. Trust me, if I didn't believe that, you and I would have had a showdown long before now. You're just frustrated because you feel you've been cheated. Hey, I agree. You have. But I can't do anything to change that. You need a target for all that anger, and since you hate my guts, I seem to be elected.''

"I don't *hate* you!'' she exclaimed, appalled that he would think such a thing.

"Really. You could've fooled me.''

Willa held his gaze for a long time, unsure what to say. She couldn't very well explain that he made her feel things she'd never experienced before, that he made her aware of her own body, her own femininity in ways that made her feel vulnerable and edgy. Or that she was afraid of where those feelings would lead.

She certainly couldn't tell him that she suspected Seamus had set them up, hoping to manipulate them into marriage. That would be too humiliating to bear, especially since she did not seem to have the same effect on Zach that he had on her.

No. It was better if she let him believe she disliked him.

"All right. So we won't ever be friends. But since it looks like we're going to be stuck here together for a while, do you think we could possibly call a truce, at least for the duration? I don't relish the thought of spending the next day or two locked in battle. It's too exhausting."

Zach regarded her over the top of his tin coffee mug. "Fine by me."

"Good."

They both returned their attention to the meal, and for several minutes a peaceful, if tentative, silence stretched out, the only sounds the scrap of spoons against tin. They were almost finished when, out of the blue, Zach said, "So, since we're being so cordial, mind if I ask you a friendly question?"

Willa shot him a wary look. "I suppose not."

"How *is* your wrist?"

"It's fi—"

His eyebrows shot skyward, and she stopped abruptly, chagrined when she realized the reply and her strident tone had been an automatic response. "Sorry. Habit. Actually, it hurts like the very devil."

"I thought it might. I noticed you've been favoring it. Let's have a look."

Before she realized his intent, Zach's took her hand and pushed her coat sleeve up as far as he could. "Mmm. No wonder it hurts. Your bandage has come loose. It needs to be rewrapped. Let's slip your arm out of this sleeve, okay?''

"I...okay.''

With Zach's help, she worked her arm free, but by then her wrist was throbbing. She gritted her teeth as he unwound the loose bandage. A livid purple discolored her skin halfway up to her elbow and over her hand, even in between her fingers.

"Can you flex your fingers?''

"I think so.''

"Good. Now slowly rotate your hand. How does that feel?''

"It hurts, but it's not too bad. Just a throbbing ache. It's only excruciating when it's under stress, like when I grip something or have to pull with that hand.''

"Mmm.'' He slid the kerosene lamp closer to her hand and leaned in for a better look.

Willa's breath caught. When her lungs began to function again her breathing was shallow and rapid. She stared down at the top of Zach's head, at that shock of wheat-colored hair, and her heart did a funny little flip-flop in her chest. Each individual strand glittered like burnished gold in the lamplight. This close, she could smell it—some sort of citrusy shampoo mixed with his tantalizing male scent.

"That's one heck of a bruise. It also looks a bit more swollen than last night, but that's probably because you used it too much riding up here.'' He gently pressed on the puffy flesh with his forefinger. "Does that hurt?''

Willa was so distracted the question didn't register at first. "Uh, n-no. It's just sore.'' In truth, all she could feel was the warm touch of that calloused finger against her skin.

"I think it's just sprained, but I'd feel better if you had a doctor look at it when we get off this mountain."

"I, uh, I will."

He glanced up at her. His face wore the same fathomless expression, but for once surprise and a touch of humor glittered in his eyes. "What, no argument?"

"It hurts."

"Ah." He carefully wound the Ace bandage and clipped it in place. "There. That will keep it immobile, which will help ease the pain."

He looked up again, and their gazes met. Held.

Their faces were so close she could feel his breath feathering over her skin like a caress. Neither moved. The air seemed to have grown suddenly thick. Willa's heart began to pound so hard she felt a vein in her neck pulsing, heard the heavy beat reverberating in her ears. Fluttering wings of panic beat in her stomach. Still, she could not move, could not look away from those hypnotizing green eyes.

A howling gust of wind rattled the door, and Zach's head whipped around toward the sound, breaking the spell.

"I brought a first-aid kit with me," he announced abruptly, and shot to his feet. "I'll see if I can find some painkillers for you."

He strode away and rummaged through the saddlebags he'd dumped on the floor beside the door. Willa closed her eyes and slumped in the chair, and the breath she hadn't realized she'd been holding came whooshing out.

"Here you go. Hold out your hand." Willa complied, and he shook two tablets out into her palm. "That should dull the pain somewhat."

"Thanks."

"No problem." He picked up their bowls and started

to move away, but she grasped his coat sleeve and stopped him.

"Zach, wait." She gazed up at him, feeling horribly awkward but determined to speak her piece. "I never thanked you for saving my life. I just want you to know that I appreciate what you did."

"You don't have to thank me. I would have done the same for anyone."

She didn't doubt that, but it hadn't escaped her that she would have died if he hadn't come after her...and then the Rocking R would have belonged entirely to him and his brothers. "That may be, but it was me you risked your life to save, and I am grateful. I just wanted you to know that."

He stared at her for a moment, his expression, as usual, unreadable. Finally he dipped his chin in a quick nod and carried the bowls to the counter.

Willa cleared the table of the remaining items, and while Zach washed up, she dried. They worked in silence for a while, but that soon began to grate on her nerves, and she searched for a safe topic of conversation.

"So...how long were you a rodeo rider?"

"Ten years."

"Really? Then you didn't start until you were in your mid-twenties. Isn't that a little old to take up such a dangerous occupation?"

He slanted her a look out of the corner of his eye and kept scouring the stew pot. "I was twenty-six. And, yeah, I guess you could say that."

She waited for him to elaborate. When he didn't she probed a little deeper. "So what did you do before that?"

"In college I majored in business and ranch management. After graduation I worked as assistant manager of the Triple C Ranch in Colorado."

Willa gaped at him. "You managed the Triple C?"

"Yeah. You've heard of it?"

"Of course I've heard of it. Everyone in ranching has heard of the Triple C. It's one of the few spreads in the country that rivals this one." Recalling the assumptions she'd made about his ranching experience, Willa felt absolutely foolish. "You might have told me."

"Would it have made any difference?"

She thought that over, and sighed. "Probably not."

"That's what I figured."

"With a job like that, why on earth did you leave it to take up rodeoing?"

Zach swished the tin bowl he'd just washed through the pan of rinse water and handed it to her. "Working on the Triple C was great, but I wanted a place of my own. After four years I realized that I needed to do something with the potential to earn large chunks of money fast. There are some rich purses in rodeos. Particularly the big ones like those in Houston or Dallas. If you consistently finish in the top five or so and avoid getting busted up, you can sock away a good chunk of change."

"And did you?"

"I did all right. I won my share of events, and I lived frugally. I figure, barring any major injuries, I was about two years away from having enough saved to buy a spread in Texas that I've had my eye on. Nothing on the scale of this place, mind you, but a sweet little setup all the same."

"Was your adoptive father a rancher? Is that how you got interested in the business?"

"No, he was a mining engineer. He was superintendent of one of the last gold mines in the Colorado Rockies. I think he was a little disappointed when I didn't follow in his footsteps, but mining just wasn't for me. As far back as I can remember all I've ever wanted to do was ranch. It's just something that's in my blood.''

Yes, it would be, Willa thought. She studied his profile, that strong face with its sharply chiseled features, and for the first time a feeling of acceptance settled over her.

The absolute rightness of Zach and his brothers inheriting the Rocking R suddenly struck her with such blinding clarity that she wondered how she could ever have denied it. This place had been carved out of the wilderness by generations of Raffertys before them. Had it not been for Seamus's controlling nature and rigidity, Zach, J.T. and Matt would have been born here, grown up here, and eventually have inherited the whole kit and caboodle. The Rock R was their heritage, not hers.

Oh, she had worked the land and given the ranch her all for twenty years, but it had never quite been hers. Not the way it was Zach's. Or Matt's or J.T.'s. If anyone was the interloper here, it was her, she realized with a pang.

''How about you?'' Zach asked, handing her a rinsed cup. ''I know you said you were born on a small ranch near here, but it's unusual for a woman to get so involved in the day-to-day operation of a place like you have. What sparked your interest in ranching?''

''Oh, that's easy. I was trying to impress Seamus.''

''Why, for Pete's sake? The man was a tyrant.''

''True, but he was also the only father figure I had, and I realized soon after my mother and I moved here that the only thing that mattered to Seamus was the Rocking R. So I set about learning everything I could about ranching.'' A wry half smile tipped up one corner of her mouth. ''At first I thought that would please him. Later, when I was a bit older, I figured if I made myself indispensable to him, he would have to love me.

"It didn't work, of course. At best, he tolerated me. I don't think Seamus was capable of loving anyone. It's just too bad I didn't realize that until I was grown."

"How old were you when you came here?"

"Six. My own father died when I was barely five years old. I don't have any memory of him at all—just a few old photos. My mother tried, but she couldn't work the ranch by herself, and a year after my dad's death the bank foreclosed. We were about to be turned out on the street when Seamus came to our rescue. I guess he figured since she'd already had one child, she would be a good breeder. He offered her marriage and lifetime security. All she had to do was give him a son.

"Mother didn't love him, nor did he love her, but our situation was desperate."

"I guess it's safe to assume your mother didn't produce the way Seamus planned."

"Oh, there was one pregnancy after another just like clockwork for five years, but the babies were all stillborn. And none of them was the son Seamus wanted. I understand that the same thing happened with his first wife, your grandmother, after Colleen was born."

"Sounds to me like the problem lay with Seamus."

"Yes, the doctor suspected he carried a defective gene, but Seamus refused to accept that. His determination to father a son cost two good women their lives. My mother died giving birth to her fifth stillborn daughter. Your own grandmother died with her sixth."

"You said he ran your life. How so?"

"He decided what I could do, where I could go and when. He even told me what I could and couldn't wear, with whom I could associate—which was no one outside this ranch."

"Why did you let him get by with it? You sure don't have any trouble defying me."

"I wasn't a meek little mouse, if that's what you mean, but I knew not to push him too far." Willa dried the Dutch oven and put it away. "At first I didn't rebel because I was trying so desperately to gain his approval. Later, after my mother died, I was afraid if I crossed him too much he wouldn't let me stay here. He hadn't adopted me, so he wasn't under any obligation. He could have sent me to an orphanage, and that thought terrified me. Also, by then, it seemed the only thing in my life that I could count on to always be there was this ranch."

Zach gave her a long searching look, but he didn't comment.

When they finished the dishes he added more wood to the fire. Then he dragged the rolled-up mattress off the bed and tossed it onto the floor in front of the stove. "We'll sleep here where we'll get maximum heat," he announced.

Willa's mouth fell open. "We? We! What do you mean, *we?* If you think I'm going to sleep with you, you can just forget it!"

Chapter Nine

"Relax. Your virtue is safe." Zach hunkered down on one knee and spread a silver space blanket out on the floor in front of the stove then untied the cords holding the thin bunk mattress and unrolled it on top. He didn't bother to look up.

"Darn right it is, because I'm not getting into bed with you."

"You don't have any choice. Neither of us has." He shook out the bedroll blanket and spread it on top of the mattress.

"That's what you think. Lay a hand on me, Mahoney, and you'll be walking funny for a week."

Zach stood up and dusted off his palms, his movements fluid and unhurried. Willa backed up a step.

"Oh, for the love of— Will you cut that out? I'm not going to force myself on you."

She didn't look convinced, and he rolled his eyes.

"Look, the temperature outside is about fifteen and dropping, and all we have is one wool blanket and the two space blankets I tossed into my saddlebags. This little stove can't heat the whole cabin. It was only intended for cooking, and maybe to knock off the chill on a summer night. Hell, you could freeze meat over there in the corners right now. The only way we're going to keep from turning into a couple of popsicles is to sleep right here," he insisted, pointing to the makeshift bed at his feet.

Willa crossed her arms and hugged them tightly to her middle. "We could sleep in shifts," she suggested hopefully.

"Trust me, before this night is over we're going to need to share our body heat."

Just the thought of that made Willa's stomach muscles quiver.

Zach went to the door and took his duster from the peg and slipped it on. "I'm going to step outside for a few minutes and give us both some privacy. I suggest you make use of the facilities while I'm gone," he said with a pointed glance at the chamber pot under the bunk frame. "And I'd hurry if I were you. I'm not standing around out there for very long."

He was out the door before she could reply. When it banged shut behind him Willa practically leaped across the room and dragged out the white enamel pot.

She had barely zipped up her jeans when he returned amid a blast of freezing air and snowflakes. He shed his duster and shook off the snow, but instead of hanging it back on the peg he carried it across to the mattress and dropped it onto the floor, then shucked out of his heavy inner coat and dropped it on top of the wool blanket. "Give me your coat."

"What for?"

"We'll be warmer, not to mention more comfortable, if we use our coats as cover. Now hand it over."

Willa complied reluctantly. Shivering, she rubbed her arms and watched him arrange her coat and his over the wool blanket then lay the open slicker over both. "Don't just stand there freezing. Take your boots off. By the time you're done the bed will be ready and you can jump in."

While she hooked the heels of first one boot then the other into the bootjack by the door, Zach shook out another silver space blanket and covered the slicker and coats.

By the time her boots were off Willa was so cold any qualms she had about sharing a bed with Zach had vanished. She scampered across the cold floor and dove into the bed.

Scooting over as close to the stove as she could get, she pulled the covers up to her ears. Mercifully, the coats still held their body heat, and as the blessed warmth soaked in she almost groaned.

Lying huddled in the cocoon of coats and blankets, Willa watched Zach squat down in the small space between the bed and the stove and build up the fire. He worked steadily, seemingly impervious to the cold. With each movement the muscles in his back flexed and rippled beneath his flannel shirt. From that angle his shoulders looked impossibly broad. Helpless to resist, her gaze traveled downward, tracing the beautiful taper of his back to his lean waist and narrow hips. He really was a fantastic male specimen, she thought, as a swarm of butterflies seemed to take over her stomach.

"There, that should hold us for a while." He rose, and Willa heard him cross the room and pull off his boots. A second later she heard his belt hit the floor with a clunk. She pressed her lips together as her heart rate kicked up another notch.

One by one, the kerosene lamps went out. Moments later a draft blew in and raced up her backside when the edge of the cover lifted and Zach slipped in beside her. Willa squeezed her eyes shut and lay as still as a stone.

When he was settled, Zach turned onto his side, toward her, and hooked his arm over her middle. At the first touch Willa nearly jumped right out of her skin.

"What do you think you're doing? Stop that!" she cried when she felt herself being hauled backward. She tried to scoot away but she was no match for his strength.

"Will you settle down?"

The deep rumble of his voice right above her left ear sent another shockwave rippling through her. With every word, his warm breath dewed the side of her face and stirred the loose strands of hair at her temple.

"This is a single bed. For both of us to fit on it, we're going to have to snuggle close. Anyway, we'll stay warmer this way." With his hand splayed over her belly, he tucked her into the curve of his body until they fit together like two spoons.

Willa's breath caught. The feel of that hard, utterly masculine body pressing against her back set every pulse point in her to throbbing.

She couldn't argue with his reasoning, though. Already his heat was seeping through the layers of their clothing. She felt it from the back of her neck all the way to the soles of her feet. Willa welcomed the warmth, but the intimacy of their position shocked her to her core. Never in her life had she been this close to a man.

Nor had she ever been so aware of her body, or its needs. She had to stifle a groan. It was foolish and crazy, stupid even, and if he knew, no doubt he would laugh, but heaven help her, it felt wonderful to be held in his arms.

She tried to fight it, but Zach's nearness filled her with a longing so intense it was almost pain. To her horror her nipples had hardened and were suddenly so tender they ached, and that private place between her legs throbbed and yearned.

Trying to ease the ache, she shifted, and immediately froze. She stared, wide-eyed, into the semidarkness, her heart pounding. Apparently, Zach was just as affected by her nearness as she was his. She felt the hard evidence of that pressing against her backside.

Awareness overwhelmed her. With acute sensitivity, she could feel every square inch of contact between their bodies, feel his chest rise and fall with each breath he took, hear its sibilant hiss in her ear. She could even feel the steady thump-thump of his heart tapping against her back.

His smell surrounded her, masculine and earthy, and so erotic it made her head spin.

Every nerve ending in Willa's body had come alive as though electrically charged. She closed her eyes and breathed deeply and tried to banish the scorching desire, but it was hopeless. She was so tense her entire body was stretched as taut as a piano wire.

"Dammit, woman, will you stop worrying," Zach growled in her ear. "I already told you, I'm not going to attack you."

"I...I know that."

"Oh, yeah? Then why are you trembling?"

"I..." Willa bit her lower lip and again willed herself to relax, but it was no use. The hot, shivering longing that suffused her would not be denied.

Though he didn't move, she sensed Zach's sudden tension.

"Willa?"

Her throat grew so tight it hurt. She could not have made a sound to save her life.

Rising up on one elbow, Zach eased back enough to pull her onto her back, but she stubbornly kept her face turned away. "Willa?" he repeated softly. He gripped her chin with his fingers and turned her face toward his. "Open your eyes, Willa, and look at me," he commanded in a voice like warm velvet.

Awash with embarrassment, she pressed her lips tightly together, but after a few moments she gave in to the inevitable. As though weighted with lead, her long lashes lifted and her feverish gaze met his. In the soft glow coming from the stove's firebox she saw his pupils widen, saw something flicker in those depths, something hot and a little wild. And unbearably exciting.

Not quite steady, his big hand cupped the side of her face. "Willa." This time he said her name in a husky whisper. His gaze roamed her face, delved deep into her eyes. His calloused thumb swept over her cheek, touched the corner of her mouth, and when her lips quivered she heard his sharp intake of breath.

Then his eyes grew heavy-lidded and his head angled to one side and began a slow decent.

Every cell in Willa's body trembled with excitement and anticipation. Her breathing grew rapid and shallow. Her heart pounded so hard the heavy tom-tom beat reverberated in her ears.

With his lips mere inches from hers, Zach stopped and waited, giving her one last chance to stop him.

In some tiny part of her brain that still functioned with a grain of sanity, Willa knew that stopping was the wise thing to do. The right thing to do. Zach had no idea that he might be playing right into Seamus's hands. At the very least she should warn him of what she suspected. He had a right to know that it was possible they had been set up. No doubt, he would be as appalled as she was.

She could not let them fall into the old man's trap. All it would take was a word from her, a shake of her head, and Zach would back off, of that she was positive.

He stared down at her, his eyes sizzling with desire, waiting. Willa opened her mouth to say the words that would end this now, before it was too late, but she couldn't do it. She simply could not. Lord help her, she wanted this. Needed this.

Instead she whispered his name, soft as a caress.

Something flickered in his eyes, something hot and hungry and so erotic it sent a shiver down her spine.

Then his lips were on hers.

There was nothing tentative or restrained about the kiss. It was firm and sure and spoke of easy confidence, his lips rocking greedily over hers as though he could not get enough of her. It was the kiss of a man who knew exactly what he wanted and intended to have it.

Though inexperienced, and on some level, aware that she was out of her league, Willa let her instincts guide her. Winding her arms around Zach's neck, she kissed him back with all the passion, all the pent-up longing that pounded through her, and when he silently urged her to open her mouth she complied without hesitation.

The first intimate touch of his tongue against hers sent a shock of intense desire jolting through Willa. She clutched him tighter and welcomed the sensual invasion, eagerly following his lead, twining her tongue with his in an ageless mating dance.

Then his hand closed over her breast, and when his

thumb rubbed back and forth over her nipple Willa's breath shuddered to a stop.

The pleasure was so exquisite she moaned deep in her throat.

Zach tensed at the sound and tore his mouth from hers. "Dammit to hell!" He jackknifed to a sitting position, braced his elbows on his updrawn knees and clutched his head between his hands.

Willa felt instantly bereft, and for a second she was so disoriented she couldn't think. She stared at his broad back and hunched posture and blinked several times. "Z-Zach?"

"I'm sorry. Damn, I'm so sorry."

"S-sorry? You're...sorry?" Around the edges of her consciousness, she felt the chill of humiliation creeping in.

"You have every right to be furious. Hell, I ought to be horse-whipped. I just finished assuring you that I wouldn't force myself on you. Then two minutes later, what do I do? I'm all over you, that's what. What kind of man does that make me? And to think, I pride myself on keeping my word."

He clutched his head tighter and cursed vividly.

Willa's eyes widened as understanding dawned. She reached out her hand to touch him, then thought better of it. "Zach, no, it wasn't like that. You mustn't blame yourself. I—I knew what I was doing."

He glanced at her over his shoulder and shook his head. "No. You had a bad scare tonight. And now here we are, trapped alone together in an isolated cabin in a howling storm. You're upset and not thinking clearly."

"That's not true. I—I wanted you to kiss me."

"Dammit, Willa, I wanted more than just a few kisses.

And believe me, if I hadn't stopped when I did, we would've done a whole lot more.''

''I know that,'' she insisted, trying to ignore the blush that heated her cheeks. ''And I wanted that, too. So you see, you have no reason to blame yourself.''

He shot her a sharp look, and for an instant she thought she saw desire rekindle in his eyes. Then he shook his head and it was gone. ''No. You're too vulnerable right now to make that kind of decision.''

His refusal to believe her was beginning to get under her skin. ''That's just not true. I'm not a child. I knew exactly what I was doing.''

''Oh, yeah, right. For Pete's sake, Willa, just this morning you would've like nothing better than to see me strung up by my thumbs. If you had been yourself you would've fought me like a wildcat, and you know it. So let's just drop it, okay. I promise it won't happen again.''

''Well,'' Willa huffed, and flounced over onto her side. ''So much for Seamus's big plan.''

''What?'' Zach twisted around and shot her a hard look. ''What plan? What are you talking about?''

''Nothing.''

''Nothing, hell.'' He grasped her shoulder pulled her onto her back again. ''What did you mean, 'So much for Seamus's plan'?''

Willa grimaced. Once again, she'd let her temper over-rule her good sense. Would she ever learn? ''It's just a silly theory that Lennie has about Seamus's will. There's absolutely no proof that he's right. I shouldn't have mentioned it.''

''Tell me, anyway.''

Willa gave him an annoyed look. ''Oh, all right. He thinks Seamus's will was nothing more than a scheme to trick you and me into...well...''

"Into...? C'mon, spit it out."

"Okay, if you must know, into marriage," she snapped.

"*What!*" His head jerked back as though he'd been slapped.

"Lennie believes that Seamus thought if he threw us together on a daily basis nature would take its course and you and I would eventually get married. If that happened, then the ranch would remain in the family, and I would be compensated for all my years of hard work and dedication." She shrugged. "Of course, he hadn't counted on your rigid sense of ethics," she added in a resentful voice.

"Why that sorry son of a—"

"There's no point in getting upset. We don't know if it's true. It could merely be Lennie's suspicious mind at work."

Zach shot her a look. "You knew the old man better than anyone else. What do you think?"

Willa was sorely tempted to lie so he would drop the matter, but she couldn't. She sighed. "Seamus was certainly capable of doing something like that."

"That's what I thought."

"But that doesn't mean he did. It's still just a theory."

"Yeah, one that makes perfect sense. It would explain why he had a change of heart about making me and my brothers his heirs." Zach mulled the idea over a few moments, his mouth grim. Then he exploded. "Damn that old coot! *Damn* him! I *won't* be manipulated."

"What does that mean?" she asked uneasily. "You wouldn't throw away the ranch because of a suspicion, surely."

"No. I'm angry, not stupid. I wouldn't do that even if I had proof that the old buzzard had tried to direct our lives to suit his own purposes. What I can do, though, is make damned sure his little scheme doesn't work.''

Willa took immediate offense. ''Trust me, you have nothing to worry about,'' she declared huffily. ''It does take two, you know.''

''Hell, I know that. Naturally I assumed that you wouldn't like being a pawn in Seamus's little game any better than I do. I am right, aren't I?'' he asked, watching her.

''Yes. Of course.''

''That's what I thought. Look, we might as well admit it. As unlikely as it seems, there is an attraction between us. After what just happened, I don't think either of us can deny that. But we sure don't have to act on it. Right?''

Willa nodded. ''Right.''

''Fine. Then we have no problem.'' Lying back down on the mattress, Zach turned onto his side and ordered bruskly, ''Now let's get some sleep. It's been a long day.'' As Willa turned over to face the stove again he draped his arm across her waist, but this time he didn't pull her close.

Lying motionless, she stared at the fire through the glass in the stove door. Zach couldn't have made his feelings clearer if he had spelled them out on a marquee: he wasn't interested.

Oh, he wasn't adverse to a roll in the hay when the opportunity presented itself. After all, he was a man. That didn't mean his emotions were involved. Men didn't necessarily equate sex and love. She might be a novice when it came to romance and male/female relations, but she'd spent her life almost exclusively among men. She'd overheard them talking enough to know that much.

Zach certainly wasn't interested in any sort of serious or permanent relationship. Not with her.

It shouldn't matter. In fact, she ought to be delighted, but the truth was, she wasn't. His rejection hurt.

Willa's eyes filled with tears. It was time to admit the truth, she thought dejectedly. At least to herself. Like it or not, welcomed or not, her feelings toward Zach had changed dramatically.

For two months, ever since that cold February night in the barn when he had kissed her, she had been restless and edgy, filled with a vague hunger that seemed to grow more insistent with every passing day. At first she had adamantly refused to admit that the encounter with Zach had been the cause, or that it had affected her at all. She simply had a bad case of spring fever, she'd told herself. It would pass.

However, instead of fading, the raw nerves and undefined yearnings had intensified. They tugged at her constantly, haunted her dreams, distracted her at the most inopportune times, made her feel vulnerable and desperate.

She'd tried to deny the feelings, tried to banish them by constantly whipping up her anger against Zach, but that ploy had failed miserably.

Now she realized that his kiss had stirred slumbering passions in her that, once awakened, would not be pushed aside.

Ever since that night, she'd wanted to feel his lips on hers again, wanted to experience that exquisite, heart-stopping pleasure. She'd buried those yearnings deep and had refused to acknowledge them. Until now...when it was too late.

A tear spilled from the corner of her eye and soaked

into the mattress. A sad, wry smile twitched the corner of her mouth. What a fool she'd been all these months.

Like an idiot, she'd told Zach about Lennie's stupid suspicions, and now any chance of him developing feelings for her was lost.

Long after Willa had drifted off to sleep Zach lay awake, staring into the semidarkness, his mind and heart in turmoil. The more he thought about what she'd told him the more convinced he was that it was true. That cantankerous old devil had set them up.

Oh, he'd been clever about it. He'd made J.T. and Matt beneficiaries, as well, so his scheme wouldn't be obvious.

Zach thought about the private detective's report he'd found in Seamus's file cabinet. It had contained a thorough dossier on each of them, including the most private details of his and his brothers' lives. The report had been dated three months after their first visit to the ranch. Had the discovery that one of his grandsons was single prompted the old man to hatch the scheme? Zach's mouth twisted. How convenient for him.

In her sleep, Willa made a small sound and shifted closer. The move put her enticing little bottom into firm contact with the fly on Zach's jeans. He nearly groaned when she wiggled into a more comfortable position, rubbing innocently against him.

In the faint light from the fire he studied the curve of her cheek, the delicacy of her eyelids and the way her lashes lay like lush ebony fans against her white skin. Gently, so as not to wake her, he tucked a loose tendril of hair behind her ear.

The hell of it was, he cared for Willa. She had become important to him in ways he could never have imagined. Each morning when he got up, the knowledge that she would be there made his day seem brighter. He looked forward to seeing her across the table from him at mealtime. Having her with him while they worked around the ranch, no matter how prickly she was, gave him an odd feeling of contentment. He like the way she looked, the sound of her voice, her laugh, the way she walked. He liked everything about her, even that fiery temper.

Just when he'd found a woman who meant the world to him, he finds out the old man had handpicked her for him. Just the thought of it made Zach see red. Damn you, Seamus, he raged silently.

The sly old coot had set a trap, and like an idiot he'd walked into it. But he wasn't about to take the bait.

Willa awoke alone the next morning. The fire had been stoked and was blazing brightly and a pot of coffee boiled on the stove. Zach's coat and slicker were gone, and she assumed he was seeing to the horses. Jumping out of bed, she made a dash for the chamber pot and sent up a prayer he would not return for a few minutes longer.

Twenty minutes later the door opened and he came in carrying another load of wood. He gave her a quick look and a muttered, "Morning," and went to the woodbox and dumped the split logs.

She polished off the leftover biscuit she was eating and washed it down with a swig of coffee before returning the terse greeting.

"That storm must have been just a freak weather system moving through," he announced as he straightened and dusted off his palms. "It stopped snowing around midnight, and now it's sunny and mild out there. The snow is melting fast. While you finish eating and tidy up, I'll go saddle the horses."

"We're leaving?" She had thought that they would

probably be stuck there for at least another day or two. Not that she was complaining. The prospect of another day and night alone with Zach was painful to contemplate.

"Yeah. It'll be rough going in spots, but it should get easier the lower we go. The heaviest snowfall was above seven thousand feet. Besides, there's probably a search party out looking for us already. So get a move on."

Normally Willa would have bristled at his tone, but she was distracted by a stab of guilt. Until that moment she hadn't given a thought to how distressed the folks back at the ranch must be. Kate, in particular, would be worried sick about Zach.

They rode single file with Zach leading the way. The temperature had climbed into the high sixties, and the snow was mushy and wet and melting into little rivulets everywhere. Though the horses plowed easily through the rotten snow, Zach kept a slow pace, keeping a sharp eye out, knowing the slightest misstep could be disastrous.

An hour out, and barely a quarter of the way down the mountain they came around a bend and met the search party coming up the trail from the opposite direction. The group consisted of three of their oldest hands, and Zach's brothers.

"Zach!" J.T. called the instant he spotted them, and spurred his horse forward. "Man, are we ever glad to see you, bro." His gaze darted behind Zach to Willa, and his grin widened. "And you found Willa. Thank God for that."

"Are you two okay? Either of you hurt?" Matt demanded as he and the others reached them. They crowded around, adding their own words of relief.

"We're fine. We found the line camp before dark and spent the night there."

Matt's face remained stern but the relief in his eyes was obvious. "Girl, you scared us all witless," he barked, only to relent a second later, his hard mouth stretching into one of his rare smiles. "But it sure is good to have you back safe and sound. Just don't pull another stunt like this again. Okay?"

"I won't. I promise." She was stunned and amazed by the brothers' concern. She had expected them to be worried about Zach, but not her.

When they arrived at the ranch she was even more surprised by the greeting she received from Kate and Maude Ann. Amid tears and murmurs of heartfelt relief, the two woman and Maria crowded around her the instant she dismounted and hugged her fiercely.

"Oh, Willa, we've been so worried. Thank heaven, you're all right," Maude Ann declared.

"I don't think any of us slept a wink last night," Kate added. "But I knew if anyone could find you in that storm it would be Zach."

The children attacked her en masse, wrapping their arms around her waist and legs and clinging so tight she couldn't move. When they finally released her, Pete stepped up.

He scowled and squirted a stream of tobacco juice into the dirt. "I oughta turn you over my knee, that's what I oughta do. Scarin' an old man thata way." Then he snatched her against his chest and hugged her tight, his gnarled hands clutching her as though he'd never let go.

"Willa. Oh, thank God."

She turned, and her eyes widened. "Edward. I didn't expect to see you here. Don't tell me they called you."

"No, no one called me. Although, I wish they had. I arrived this morning shortly after the search party left. When I learned what had happened my heart nearly stopped.'' He grasped her upper arms and inspected her. ''Are you okay?''

Willa knew she must look as though she'd been jerked through a knothole backward after the past forty-eight hours, especially to someone as fastidious as Edward, but she smiled and shook her head. ''Yes, I'm fine. But thanks for asking.''

''Good. I've been pacing the floor for the past four hours. We all have.'' He looked at Matt and J.T. ''Your wives filled me in on what else has been going on. Have you told them yet?''

Zach was instantly alert. ''Told us what?''

''No, not yet,'' J.T. replied, looking uncomfortable.

Matt scowled. ''We were going to give them a chance to relax and recover before we unloaded that on them. Thanks a lot.''

''Oh. Sorry…I didn't realize—''

''All right, somebody tell me what's happened. Now.''

''We got trouble, Zach.'' Matt said in a somber voice. ''While you were gone yesterday someone shot our best bull and gutted him like a fish.''

Chapter Ten

The senseless attacks continued with no letup. A week after the storm, someone dynamited the stock tank that Willa and the men had repaired earlier in the spring. Ten days after that, Zach, Matt, J.T. and the rest of the men returned one evening to find every tire on every vehicle in the ranch yard slashed. Three weeks later, someone spray-painted a satanic symbol on the side of the barn.

As spring gave way to summer the vandalism began occurring more frequently. More troublesome, the acts, and the notes that were often found nearby, had begun to take on sinister overtones.

Cattle were slaughtered and left in the pastures to rot. Others were mutilated pitifully and in so much pain they had to be put down.

One morning, about to leave on a shopping trip to Bozeman, Maude Ann and the kids discovered one of the barn cats had been killed and left out on the windshield of her van. On the front seat was a note warning that one of them could be next.

After that incident, Zach, with the wholehearted support of Matt and J.T., issued orders that the women and children were not to go anywhere alone, not even into Clear Water for groceries. Wherever Willa worked on the ranch she was to be in the company of at least two men at all times.

The instant the edicts were issued Zach glanced at Willa. "Any objections?"

That he had expected her to balk at the restriction was obvious, and she admitted to herself that as little as two months earlier she would have done so automatically, simply to oppose him. Abashed, she shook her head. "No. It makes sense. Whoever is doing this is obviously unbalanced. I'm not anxious to be his next victim."

That earned her a long, considering look from Zach and almost comical, stupefied stares from everyone else sitting around the table.

All of the attacks near the house had taken place while the men and Sadie, the dog, were working miles away. Pete spent his days in and around the barn, but the old man was hard of hearing and too frail to be of much protection for the women, so Zach assigned two men, armed with rifles, to remain at the ranch headquarters every day and to patrol the grounds.

After the first animal was discovered butchered they all feared for Sadie, who had recently whelped a litter of six, so Zach moved the dog and her pups into the house, much to the delight of the children.

After each incident the sheriff was called. He spent hours at the ranch, going over the sites and conferring with the men, particularly Matt, but they had no leads, other than the notes torn from a spiral notebook, which Matt had saved as evidence.

A feeling of uneasiness permeated the ranch and everyone on it. You could see it on the somber faces of the men, the way everyone constantly looked over their shoulder and scanned the area around them everywhere they went.

It was standard procedure for every man to carry a rifle in his scabbard while out on the range. In the high country you never knew when you'd run across a cougar or rattlesnake or some other unfriendly critter. Also, if an injury occurred you could fire the gun to signal for help. Now, however, the men had started strapping on handguns, too. The cowboys looked like an armed posse out of a Western movie, Willa thought wryly.

The precautions made no difference. The attacks continued with more frequency than ever. A watering hole was poisoned and the vet had to be called out when over thirty head of cattle sickened. An unusual number of horses turned up lame, the result of blows to the legs. A prime pasture was set on fire, and Zach and the men battled the blaze for over thirty hours. They were staggering with exhaustion by the time they finally put it out.

Zach was furious, and though he did not say so, he was worried, as well. So were his brothers. They discussed sending the women and children away until whoever was responsible was caught, but Maude Ann and Kate flatly refused to budge.

"Forget it. There is no way I am leaving you, J.T.," Kate declared. "Anyway, Willa can't leave. If she does you all lose the ranch."

"That's right. And if she stays, Kate and I stay, too. We won't leave her alone here with no women for moral support. Besides, the ranch is our home now, and that creep isn't going to run us off of it,'' Maude Ann added.

The men argued and pleaded. Matt and J.T. even tried issuing ultimatums, but Kate and Maude Ann stood firm, and in the end their husbands had to accept defeat.

Since the night of the storm, Willa's feelings had changed, not only toward Zach, but toward his family, as well. The concern his brothers and sisters-in-law had shown for her safety when she and Zach returned after the storm had disarmed her, and once she lowered her guard and her prickly hostility began to fade she started to see all of them differently.

Gradually, Willa discovered that she truly liked both women.

Maude Ann, a born earth mother, was warm and open and utterly natural. Kate, though a bit more reserved, was friendly and pleasant and just as congenial.

Willa was still cautious and reserved around the brothers, but after months of listening to their conversations she began to understand how the events of their lives had shaped them into the men they were.

There was Matt, the former police detective, with his penchant for rules and order and doing what was right. On the outside Matt appeared stern and unapproachable, but Willa had witnessed his gruff tenderness with the children numerous times, and she had come to realize that behind the stern facade was an old softie.

J.T. was a charmer. His quick grin and easy banter made him appear a lightweight, but that breezy manner hid a keen intellect and a kind heart. Willa suspected the devil-may-care attitude, like Matt's penchant for order and constancy, was J.T.'s way of dealing with the pain of loss.

Then there was Zach—the strong, silent type, a stoic

loner who carefully guarded his feelings. He was a difficult man to get to know, but Willa had learned enough about him to realize that Zach was a man of bedrock-solid ethics and morals, a man whom a woman could trust with her life—and her heart—if she could ever break through that protective wall he'd built around himself.

Of course, in her case, she admitted with a dejected sigh, even if she could manage to do that, he would probably still reject her, thanks to Seamus and his scheming.

Intellectually, Willa knew it was for the best. Neither she nor Zach would allow themselves to become Seamus's puppet. However, that message had not yet gotten through to her heart, or her body.

Whenever she and Zach were in the same room the air still hummed with a sizzling awareness that seemed to grow stronger with each passing day. Sparks of electricity arched between them if they accidentally touched, and when their gazes happened to meet, the dark emotions swirling in his eyes made her weak in the knees.

Beyond those brief, isolated moments, though, Zach was so preoccupied with the troubles that Willa doubted he gave her more than a passing thought when he wasn't around her.

Unfortunately, she couldn't *stop* thinking about him. He occupied her mind nearly every moment of the day and she dreamed of him almost nightly. In her mind she relived that kiss in front of the fire over and over. She thought often about how wonderful it had felt to sleep in his arms, to cuddle next to that big, warm body.

During mealtimes or whenever Willa worked in Zach's vicinity, her gaze was drawn to him like a moth to a flame. And each time her heart did a crazy little dance in her chest.

The reaction made her feel foolish and lovesick, but she couldn't stop herself. He was so utterly masculine, at times just watching him walk across the ranch yard with that rangy, loose-limbed stride caused her to catch her breath.

One evening after dinner, when she spotted him in the main corral working with Satan, she couldn't resist strolling over to watch. The Dolans and the Conways and all the children were already there, and some of the hands had gathered to watch, as well.

Zach did not attempt to saddle the stallion or ride him. He didn't even put a bridle on the animal. He merely stood in the middle of the circular corral while Satan trotted nervously around the perimeter, ears back and eyes wild with hate and distrust. Zach merely turned slowly in place, keeping the enraged stallion in sight at all times, talking to him in a soft, calming voice while he gently tossed a soft rope made of loosely braided cotton rags over the horse's back and pulled it back. He repeated the action again and again, letting the animal grow accustomed to the touch and the sound of his voice.

"What's he doin' that for?" Tyrone demanded from his perch on the fence rail.

"I'm not sure," J.T. replied absently. "Trying to calm him down, I guess."

"Is the horsie scared?" Debbie asked, her blue eyes wide.

"He doesn't want to be ridden, that's for sure," Matt replied.

Willa moved over to the group and climbed up on the fence with the kids. "Satan is scared, all right. He's scared he's going to be eaten."

All five children looked at her with horrified expressions, their eyes big as saucers.

"We don't eat horsies," Jennifer stated with childlike outrage. "We ride them."

"Yes, but Satan doesn't know that. He's mostly wild, and his instincts tell him to flee from all other animals, and that includes man. Or, if he's cornered, to fight with all his might because they may eat him. So what your uncle Zach is trying to do is teach him not to fear him or his touch."

Willa was amazed at Zach's patience. And his gentleness. He kept tossing the rope and murmuring to the stallion tirelessly. She could see that the horse was confused and trying to figure out just what this human was up to.

Finally, after perhaps twenty minutes, Satan grew tired and came to a stop, bobbing his head and snorting, but still keeping a wary eye on Zach. He continued to toss the rope, but now each time he moved a step or two closer. Watching him out of the corner of his eye, Satan continued to bob his head and blow softly through his nose.

Finally, when Zach was close enough, he slowly reached out and ran his hand down the horse's neck. A quiver ran over Satan's hide, but he didn't shy away.

Emboldened, Zach wrapped both arms around the animal's neck, stroking him constantly as he murmured encouragement in his ear. Willa was amazed that Satan tolerated the touch, but he just stood there, his ears moving back and forth.

"Why's he huggin' 'em?" Timothy asked.

"Shh. Just watch," Matt replied.

After perhaps ten minutes of stroking and soothing, Zach released the horse and turned his back and walked away five steps and stopped. Satan followed him and nudged his shoulder. Keeping his back to the horse, Zach changed direction and took a few more steps. Again Satan followed and nudged his shoulder.

Over and over, Zach repeated the maneuver, and every time Satan stuck with him. When he took a bridle off the fence post and slipped it on, the horse accepted it with merely a twitch of his ears. Constantly murmuring reassurance and stroking, Zach put the saddle pad and saddle on the horse. Satan shifted uneasily but he calmed under Zach's hand and allowed him to tighten the cinch.

He soothed the horse for a few minutes more, then grasped the saddle horn and put his foot in the stirrup. Everyone held their breaths.

Zach carefully lifted himself up and swung into the saddle. Satan sidestepped and bobbed his head, and his front hooves lifted a few inches off the ground, but he settled when Zach patted his neck and murmured to him.

For a moment they remained motionless while Zach stroked and murmured. Then he gave the horse a gentle nudge and the black stallion started walking. Another gentle nudge sent him trotting easily around the enclosure.

All around the others exclaimed in subdued tones of amazement. Willa watched horse and rider, her throat tight, her eyes misty. She had never seen anything so beautiful or so touching in her life.

In that moment of startling clarity, she realized that she wasn't merely attracted to Zach. She was in love with him.

He was everything she had ever dreamed of finding in a man, she realized—strong yet gentle, patient, intelligent, kind, hardworking, passionate and sexy. Everything about him appealed to her—his raw masculinity, his rugged good looks and lean, muscular build, that air of quiet authority that he wore with such ease.

Willa bit her lower lip and fought back tears. Dear Lord, she was in love with Zach—completely, irrevocably, head-over-heels in love with him. And it was hopeless.

Willa did her best to squash her feelings for Zach, or at least ignore them. To avoid him she reverted to her former behavior of retreating to her room immediately after dinner, and she volunteered for work assignments that took her out of his immediate vicinity. At mealtime, when avoiding him was impossible, she never spoke to him directly and tried never to make eye contact with him.

None of her efforts worked. Day by day she fell more in love. Too inexperienced with men and love to know what else to do, Willa nursed her feelings in silence. She thought about confiding in Maude Ann, but she was still too unsure of the tentative friendship between herself and the other women. Confiding in Kate was out of the question since she was Zach's adoptive sister. As for Maria, much as Willa loved her, she knew the old woman couldn't keep a secret for spit. So she said nothing and dealt with the emotional turmoil as best she could.

Except for winter, late summer was the slowest season on the ranch. The majority of the cattle were pastured in various high mountain valleys. The branding, castrating and inoculating had been completed. The hands took turns manning the line camps, working in one week shifts, and those who were not in the mountains spent the late spring plowing, planting, fertilizing and irrigating the pastures. In summer they completed any needed repairs, and made hay and stored it in the pole barns scattered around the winter range.

During spring and fall roundups, everyone worked from sunup to sundown. In mid-summer, however, many of the men found time on Saturday night to go in to town and raise a little hell at the local dance hall, Hody's.

After a day of dusty, hot work driving the haybaler, Willa had just showered, changed and joined the others in the kitchen when Zach walked in. Wearing clean jeans and a clean shirt, he had that shower-fresh scrubbed look and smelled of soap and shampoo.

Willa's heart gave its usual little flutter at the sight of him. Turning away, she went to the stove and poured herself a cup of coffee. She carried it to the back window and gazed out. Several of the men, scrubbed and spit-polished for their Saturday night outing, were climbing into pickups.

"My, don't you look nice, big brother," Kate commented. "Is that a new shirt?"

"Sorta. And thanks. Don't bother setting a place for me tonight. I'm going to go into town with the men, maybe shoot some pool and have a few beers."

J.T. grinned. "And maybe latch on to some pretty little thing to two-step with too, I'll bet. Huh, bro?"

Willa's head snapped around. He was going into town?

Unfazed by his brother's teasing, Zach shrugged. "There's always that possibility, I guess." His gaze met Willa's in a long, searing look. Then he blinked, and the contact was broken.

"I'd better get going. I'll see you all tomorrow."

As he went out the door Willa turned back to the window and watched him stride down the walk and climb into his truck. Her heart felt like a lead weight in her chest.

Willa worked like a demon through the remainder of the summer and through the fall roundup, wearing herself out each day so that she barely had the energy to eat before falling into bed and almost none to mope over Zach.

She volunteered for the dirtiest, most strenuous jobs— anything to keep her mind off of him. He had gone into town four more evenings since that first time, and each time he hadn't returned until after midnight. Willa knew because she'd still been awake and heard him come in. She wondered if he'd met someone—and who she was.

Eventually the roundup was over, the herd had been culled and all but the breeding stock and this year's crop of calves was on its way to market, leaving Willa to wonder how she would ever get through the winter, cooped up in the house with Zach.

She was nibbling at her dinner, mulling over that problem when Maude Ann interrupted her.

"So what are you going to wear, Willa?"

Willa didn't hear her at first. Then she noticed that everyone was staring at her expectantly, and she blinked. "What?"

"I said, what are you going to wear?"

"Wear?"

"To the After Roundup Dance at the Grange Hall? It's this Saturday night."

"Oh. I'm not going."

"What do you mean, you're not going. Of course you are. We're all going."

"No, you don't understand. I never go to these things. I haven't since I was fifteen." She didn't bother telling them that Seamus had disapproved and forbidden her to attend.

"Then it's high time you did," Kate insisted.

"No, I—"

"Willa," Zach said her name softly, and her gaze snapped to meet his. He was watching her, his green eyes steady and glittering with some deep emotion. "We're trying to build some goodwill and rapport with our neighbors and overcome Seamus's reputation around here. For that reason it's important that we all attend the Grange dance and socialize."

"But…but I don't have anything to wear." Though the classic female complaint, in Willa's case it was true. Other than the wool skirt and sweater she'd bought on impulse months ago, and the black dress she kept for funerals, the only thing in her closet were jeans and shirts.

"Is that all?" Maude Ann laughed. "Trust me, sweetie, that's a problem we can fix in no time with a quick shopping trip to Bozeman or Helena."

"No, really, I couldn't."

"C'mon, Willa, it'll be fun," Kate urged. "We'll go tomorrow, just the three of us."

"And an escort," all three men stated in unison.

"There. All done." Maude Ann stepped back and studied her handiwork with a satisfied smile.

Kate came rushing into Willa's bedroom from the hall. "Here, I finally found the necklace I was looking for. See, it'll will be perfect with your dr—" She stopped short, staring. "Oh, my. Willa, you look gorgeous."

"The's boo-ti-ful," Debbie declared dreamily. "Ithin't the, Jennifer?"

"Uh-huh. Just like a princess."

Leaning against either end of Willa's dressing table, elbows propped on the top and chins resting in their hands, the two little girls gazed at her in wide-eyed admiration. Lying stretched out on her belly across the bed, Yolanda did the same.

Willa stared at her reflection in the mirror. She barely recognized herself.

The "quick" shopping trip to Helena had turned into a whirlwind, all-day spree that had resulted in her being outfitted with a whole new wardrobe. Trying to resist Maude Ann and Kate in a shopping mode was pointless, Willa discovered. It was like trying to tame twin tornadoes with your bare hands.

They had simply overwhelmed her, dragging her from store to store, department to department, bullying her into trying on mountains of clothes. Willa had never seen anyone sort through racks with that kind of concentration and speed.

The two women worked as a team. While one helped her in and out of one outfit after another, the other kept bringing more and more things for her to try on, and each one was given a critical once-over by both women.

They hadn't stopped at clothes, either. They had dragged her around stores buying shoes, purses, jewelry, makeup, perfume, scarves, even a hat with a little veil hanging from the broad brim, though where in the world she would ever wear such a thing, Willa didn't know.

Then today she had been in the middle of giving Yolanda a riding lesson when Kate and Maude Ann had descended on her and dragged her inside, declaring it was time to get ready for the dance. Willa had protested that she didn't need four hours to shower and change her clothes, but she hadn't reckoned on Kate and Maude Ann.

The two women had hustled her straight into the shower, and when she'd stepped out she'd discovered that the serviceable, plain cotton undies she had laid out to wear had been replaced by a pair of bikini panties and a strapless bra made of scraps of black silk and lace. Kate and Maude Ann had then bullied her into donning a pair of outrageously sexy, strappy, red high-heeled sandals and her new silk robe.

Then the beauty regime had begun.

Willa had endured a facial, a manicure and a pedicure. She was lotioned and perfumed and her eyebrows plucked. Kate piled her hair on top of her head in an elegant arrangement with several tendrils hanging loose around her face and neck. When she was done, Maude Ann went to work with the array of new cosmetics that she had been cajoled into buying the day before.

The result was the stunning creature staring back at her from the mirror.

"Okay, time to get dressed. Stand up."

Still fascinated by her new look, Willa obeyed Maude Ann's command, docile as a lamb, and the next thing she knew the women stripped off her robe and slipped a little wisp of a red dress over her head and zipped it up.

Held up by two tiny straps, the dress hugged her upper body like a second skin before flaring out from her waist to fall in billowy folds around the middle of her calves.

Willa stared at her reflection, stunned. She had never dreamed she could look so elegant and attractive, or so...so...sexy.

Kate slipped the necklace around her neck and fastened the matching gold earrings in her lobes, then stepped back with a self-satisfied grin. "There. Perfect."

"Yes, and I have a gold-and-black evening shawl that will be the perfect wrap with that dress. Willa, honey, you're going to knock 'em dead tonight."

"Okay, we'd better get a move on. The men are downstairs, straining at the bit to leave. Maudie and I took care of our makeup and hair earlier, so just give us a minute to slip into our dresses and we'll all go down together.''

The reaction Willa received was worth every second of the torture Kate and Maude Ann had put her through.

The men were standing at the foot of the stairs when they descended. J.T. and Matt complimented their wives lavishly, but when they caught sight of her they both did double takes and their jaws dropped.

Willa barely noticed. She was aware of only Zach. He stared at her with an almost predatory intensity, his green eyes sizzling as they ran slowly over her, from the top of her fabulous up-do all the way down to her red-tipped toes peeking out of the strappy high-heeled sandals, then back again.

''Wow, Willa, I'm so used to seeing you in jeans I hardly recognized you,'' J.T. said. ''You look great.''

''Yeah,'' Matt agreed. ''You clean up real good, kiddo.''

Kate giggled and Maude Ann rolled her eyes. ''Matt, honestly.''

''What? What did I say?''

''Ignore these two bozos.'' Zach stepped forward and took her hand. ''You're beautiful,'' he said softly.

While her heart started beating in a snare-drum roll, Willa smiled shyly and murmured a quiet, ''Thank you.''

''Well, if we're all ready, shall we go? We can all ride together in the van.''

''Thanks, Maudie, but I'll take my truck, just in case any of us wants to leave early. Willa and I will follow you.''

Chapter Eleven

Zach didn't give her a chance to object. Taking the evening shawl from her, he draped it around her shoulders, placed his hand against the small of her back and ushered her out the door.

Which was just as well, Willa thought, sitting in the passenger seat of Zach's truck, watching him skirt around the front. She didn't know what she would have said, or even if she would have had the strength to object. The truth was, she wanted to be with him.

Zach climbed in behind and wheel and started the engine. While they waited for the others to get into the van he turned those steady green eyes on her. "You comfortable?"

Lord, no, she thought. How in heaven's name could she be comfortable, when she was tense as a drawn bow? "Yes. I'm fine, thanks," she lied.

The Grange Hall was only about five miles south of

the ranch entrance, halfway between the Rocking R and town, for which Willa was profoundly grateful. What in heaven's name had possessed Zach? He had been adamant about keeping his distance from her, and all summer, except for a few sultry looks, he had kept that vow. Now he had practically kidnapped her.

They made the short drive in silence. Zach was in one of his intense moods, and Willa was so confused and excited she was tongue-tied and in no shape to carry on a conversation. In any case, she had no idea what to say to him.

At the Grange Hall he parked beside the van and cut the engine. When he made no move to get out, Willa glanced his way and found that he was staring at her through the fading light. Instantly her nerves began to jump.

"You really are beautiful."

The husky murmur and the heat in his eyes rendered her mute. All she could do was stare back at him, mesmerized.

Next to them, the others climbed out of the van and slammed the doors, and the spell was broken. Without a word, Zach baled out of the truck and came around to her side.

Inside the hall the women were left standing alone while the men took their wraps to the coatroom. Maude Ann immediately took advantage of the opportunity and nudged Willa in the ribs.

"Zach is certainly being masterful tonight," she said with a teasing grin. "I think he's smitten."

"Oh, no, you've got it all wro—"

"Willa?"

She turned and saw a group of young men around her age approaching.

"It is you. See, guys, I told you it was Willa." He flashed her a grin. "Remember me. I'm John Finley. We went to school together."

"Actually, we all did," one of his buddies inserted. "I'm Bobby Lehmann, and this is Travis Howard and Neil James."

"Of course I remember you. Good grief, it's not as though I've been gone these past eight years. I see all of you in town from time to time."

"Yeah, but not looking the way you do now," Travis blurted.

Their dumbfounded expressions brought a wry smile to Willa's lips. When they had attended school together she had not been one of their crowd and none of them had given her so much as a second glance. Granted, that had probably been because she was Seamus's stepdaughter and he had kept her so confined. Still, their lack of interest had hurt.

Before she could introduce Kate and Maude Ann, John Finley, who had always been the most aggressive of the four, stepped closer and smiled. "How about it if you and I get reacquainted while we dance?"

Taking her acceptance for granted, he reached for her hand, but before he could make contact Zach's fingers clamped around his wrist. "Forget it, fella. The lady's with me."

John looked as though he was about to challenge the claim—until he met Zach's stare. "Hey, sorry, man. I didn't know. I just wanted to chat with an old friend, that's all."

"No harm done." Zach released him, and the four men turned away and disappeared into the crowd.

"You know, Zach, if you want to build a rapport with

our neighbors, that's not exactly the way to go about it,'' Maude Ann drawled.

"He'll get over it.''

"What's up? Did we miss something?'' J.T. asked as he and Matt joined them.

"Not really.'' Zach took Willa's elbow. "Let's dance.''

"I'm sorry, I can't.'' She gave him an apologetic look. "I don't know how to dance. I never had an opportunity to learn.''

"Then it's time you did. C'mon, I'll show you. It's easy.''

"No, Zach, really, I can't.'' Panic fluttered in her chest, but he ignored her protest and tugged her toward the dance floor.

"Zach—''

"Just relax and follow my lead,'' he said, turning her into his arms. "You'll do fine, I promise.''

Instead of assuming the normal stance, he wrapped both arms around her waist and pulled her close, and at the first contact with his body Willa was lost.

With a sigh, she closed her eyes and rested her cheek against his chest.

His hands roamed up and down her back, molding her to him from shoulder to thigh. Willa shivered and gave herself over to him as he began to sway in rhythm with the slow music.

He was right, she discovered. It was easy. Their bodies moved together as though they were one person. The country and western song had a heavy, sensual beat, and as the singer crooned out the crying lyrics of love lost, a tingle shuddered through Willa.

The feel of Zach's body pressed against hers, moving to the provocative rhythm, was so erotic she felt as though she were melting. His body was warm and wonderfully firm, and the clean scent of him surrounded her, making her senses swim.

Zach lowered his head and rested his chin against her temple, and Willa sighed again and snuggled her cheek against his chest. Dear Lord, this felt so good, so right.

The song ended and another began, this one faster. Instead of releasing her, as she expected, he swung her into the dance, twirling her around the floor in step with the energetic beat, leaving her no choice but to follow.

Willa had no idea how long they stayed on the floor or for how many dances. She didn't care. Dreamily, she was aware of the other couples gliding by, of the looks she and Zach were receiving, but they didn't matter. Often one of the couples would be Kate and J.T., and now and then, during the slow dances, Maude Ann and Matt, but even they registered on her consciousness only remotely. Willa's whole world had been reduced to just her and Zach. She floated through the evening on a cloud of happiness and pleasure, her body vibrating with a delicious excitement.

Suddenly the music stopped and the band leader whooped, "Okay, guys and gals take your places. It's time for a *line dance!*"

Easing Willa back a half step, Zach raised an eyebrow, but she laughed and shook her head. "I don't think I'm ready for that yet."

"Okay, I guess you've earned a break." He wrapped his arm around her waist and led her off the floor.

When they reached the sidelines Willa's nerves began to jump again. Now what? she wondered. How did one behave with a man after they had practically made love on a dance floor? Or perhaps she was making too much of it. Maybe Zach danced that way with all women. The thought didn't set well, but she had to face that possibility.

Suddenly she felt tongue-tied and awkward. She had no idea what to say or what to do with her hands, but Zach solved the problem for her.

"Would you like something to drink? I think they have punch and beer."

"Yes, please. Punch would be lovely."

He touched her cheek and looked into her eyes, and the proprietary gleam she saw there sent a thrill rocketing through her. "I'll be right back," he murmured. "Don't go away."

"I won't."

Floating on air, Willa watched him walk away. Winding his way through the crowd toward the drinks table on the other side of the hall, Zach stood head and shoulders above most of the other men, and to her eyes he was by far the handsomest.

"Haven't you made a big enough spectacle of yourself without drooling over that bastard?"

Willa jumped and swung around. "Lennie. I didn't see you there."

Flanked by two of his friends, Lennie Dawson leaned against the wall a few feet away, glaring at her.

He straightened and stalked over to her. Up close she saw the wild look in his eyes and uneasiness trickled down her spine. He was simmering with rage.

"Did you think I wouldn't be here? That I wouldn't see you hanging all over that Mahoney character? Flaunting yourself in front of him?"

"I wasn't—"

"Don't lie to me. I heard all about that night you spent with him up in the mountains," he snarled. "The way you kept turning me down, I figured you were just playing hard to get, so I backed off to give you a little time to come to your senses. And while my back is turned you start cheating on me with one of Seamus's bastards. Just like the old man wanted.''

Willa sucked in a sharp breath, but before she could deliver the blistering set-down that was on the tip of her tongue, Lennie raged on.

"Just look at you," he sneered. "You got yourself all floozied up for him, didn't you? You look like a painted slut.''

"Why you rude, egotistic, overbearing twit. I don't have to stand here and listen to your insults." She tried to walk away but he stepped in front of her.

"I'm not through talking to you.''

"Too bad, because I'm through listening. Get this through that thick head of yours, Lennie. What I do and with whom I do it is none of your business. I am *not* interested in you. Never have been, never will be. Not if you were the last man on earth.''

Rage contorted his face. "You bitch.''

Pain exploded in Willa's cheek as Lennie struck her across the face. Willa felt hands grabbing her to keep her from falling and heard the shocked gasps and murmurs from the people nearby, but before she could recover her balance Zach stepped between her and Lennie and smashed his fist into the other man's face.

"Hey!" Lennie's buddies yelped.

The blow sent Lennie flying backward. He landed hard on his backside at the feet of his friends, blood gushing from his nose.

Kate and Maude Ann pushed their way through the crowd and hovered protectively over Willa. "Are you all right?" both women asked.

Lennie struggled to his feet with the help of his cohorts. Wiping his bloodied nose on his shirtsleeve, he looked over the top of his arm at Zach with pure hatred. "C'mon, guys, let's get him," he snarled.

"Need any help?" Matt and J.T. stepped forward, flanking Zach on either side an instant before Lennie cut loose with a growl and he and his friends charged.

After that, everything happened so quickly it was almost a blur.

Zach blocked Lennie's blow with one arm and with his other fist delivered a punch to his stomach that doubled him over. J.T. elegantly ducked his man's first swing, sidestepped the second and felled him with a karate chop to the back of the neck as he stumbled past. At the same time Lennie's other friend came at Matt swinging an empty beer bottle, but a cane whack across his forearm sent the bottle tumbling to the floor and dropped the man to his knees, holding his arm and howling in pain.

Before any of the downed trio could move, Zach, J.T. and Matt jerked them up by the backs of their shirt collars, bundled them out through the open double doors of the hall and tossed them down the steps. Lennie and his pals landed in a tangled heap in the gravel-and-dirt parking lot.

Zach stared down at Lennie, his eyes glacial. At his sides his hands curled and uncurled, again and again. "I'm going to count to ten, Dawson." His voice grated from between clenched teeth. "If you're not out of here by the time I'm done I'm going to whip your sorry butt from here to Clear Water and back."

"That's...that's assault!" Lennie blustered. "I'll have you arrested!"

"One. Two."

"You all heard him," Lennie cried, addressing the

crowd that had gathered behind Zach and his brothers. "He threatened me."

"Three."

"Threat? What threat? I didn't hear anybody threaten Lennie, did you, Harvey?"

"Uh-uh, not me."

"Me, either," several others chimed in.

"Four. Five."

"You dirty little coward," another man jeered. "You're the one who started it all."

"Six."

"That's right. If anyone files assault charges it oughta be Willa."

"Seven."

"All right! All right! We're going."

"Eight. Nine."

The three men scrambled to their feet and nearly fell over one another hobbling across the parking lot for Lennie's pickup.

Within seconds the red truck careered out of the parking lot, sending up a shower of gravel, then burning rubber as it took off down the highway toward town.

Zach turned and began pushing his way through the crowd amid a flurry of compliments and back-thumping. Following him, Matt and J.T. received the same treatment.

"I'd like to shake you fellas' hands. He had it coming."

"Good job. Lennie Dawson ain't nothin' but a bully."

"That's right, he's been running roughshod over folks hereabouts for years."

"About time he got his comeuppance. Those friends of his, too."

Zach accepted the praise with gritted teeth and kept

moving. "Thanks, but if you'll excuse me, I need to see about Willa," he said over and over with an edge of impatience.

He found her sitting on the sidelines between Kate and Maude Ann, holding a wet cloth to her cheek and looking shaken. A cluster of curious women fluttered nearby.

Zach hunkered down in front of her and took her free hand. "How bad is it?"

"I'm okay. Really," she insisted automatically. Willa did not quite meet his eyes, and he realized that she was more humiliated than hurt.

"Her cheek is bruised, but I don't think the bone is broken," Maude Ann supplied.

Zach bit off a shocking curse, then shot to his feet, pulling Willa up with him. "I'm taking her home."

"Good idea," J.T. agreed.

"Yeah, we'll all go," Matt stated, but when he cupped Maude Ann's elbow to lead her out she held back.

"Whoa. There's no reason for us all to leave. I'm sure that Zach can look after Willa just fine."

"I agree with Maudie," Kate said.

Their husbands gaped at them. "You want to stay? After what just happened?" Matt demanded.

"Of course. Darling, it's all over now and the evening is young." Now that the excitement was over the band had started playing again and Maude Ann nodded toward the couples who were beginning to take to the floor. "Besides, Kate and I want to dance some more. Don't we, Kate?"

"Oh, yes. Definitely."

"Good, that's settled then. Have a good time." Hooking his arm around Willa's waist, Zach wasted no time leading her away.

Matt and J.T. gaped at their wives with identical bewildered expressions.

"I swear, Maudie, I've never known you to be insensitive. That poor girl has been traumatized and hurt. I would think that you of all people would want to comfort her."

"Yeah, you, too, Kate," J.T. added. "It's not like either one of you to think of yourself first."

The women exchanged a look and rolled their eyes.

"Poor darlings. They really are clueless, aren't they?"

"Totally," Kate agreed.

"What does that mean? Clueless about what?"

Maude Ann patted Matt's cheek. "Kate and I aren't being selfish, darling. Or insensitive. Actually, we're doing Willa and Zach a favor. For heaven's sake, hasn't either of you noticed what's going on between those two? There's enough heat between them to melt a glacier."

The two men looked thunderstruck.

"Are you telling us..."

"I don't believe it!"

The brothers looked at each other and shook their heads. *"Willa and Zach?"*

On the drive home Zach gritted his teeth and silently cursed Lennie Dawson. He still itched to throttle the little weasel. Unconsciously, his fingers squeezed the steering wheel as though it were Lennie's neck.

He had been returning with a cup of punch for Willa and a cold brew for himself when he saw the little creep pull back his hand and slap Willa. Zach knew the image was burned into his brain forever. He couldn't remember ever being so angry.

He only wished he had done more to the bastard than punch him, he thought, tightening his fingers around the steering wheel once again. Dammit, no one hit a woman in his presence. Especially not this woman.

He glanced at Willa, and his rage spiked anew. She sat huddled on the far side of the bench seat in a defensive posture with her arms folded over her middle, her face turned away, gazing out the passenger window at the dark night. The blow she took had knocked her elegant hairdo loose, and now it listed to one side and sagged over her right ear.

"You okay?"

She spared him only the briefest glance before turning back to the window. "Yes. I'm fine."

"Does your cheek hurt?"

"No. Not anymore."

Zach sighed and turned the truck in at the ranch entrance. Ever since leaving the Grange Hall he'd gotten the same type of uncommunicative response whenever he spoke to her. For the rest of the drive along the twisting, turning ranch road he remained silent, as well.

Zach parked the pickup out back and they entered the house through the kitchen. The instant they stepped inside, Willa murmured a quiet, "Good night," and headed for the front hall and the stairs, but he put a hand on her arm and stopped her.

"Willa, wait. Let me take a look at your cheek."

"That's not necessary. It's okay."

"Humor me."

Only the dim glow of the light above the stove that Maria had left burning for them illuminated the room. Zach flipped on the overhead light and cupped her face with both hands and tilted it up. Frowning, he inspected the red mark on her left cheek. "It's red but the skin isn't broken." He lightly touched the puffy area with his forefinger. "Does that hurt?"

Willa shook her head.

Merely looking at the angry red splotch brought Zach's anger rushing back. "Dammit, why did he hit you?"

"Lennie has a bad temper."

"Yeah, so you said before. But what set him off tonight?"

"Does it matter?"

"It sure as hell does to me. So tell me."

For a moment he thought she wasn't going to answer. Then she hitched one shoulder. "He was jealous. Of you."

"I see." Zach's thumbs stroked along her jaw, the tender underside. "And does he have reason to be?"

The deep timbre of his voice sent a shiver of longing through her. Willa stared at the plaid pattern of Zach shirt. His nearness was having its usual effect on her system, making her head swim and her pulses pound and filling her with trembling awareness. She wanted so much to lay her head on his chest and feel his arms enfold her again, but she didn't dare.

All evening she had been floating in a foolish, rosy-colored dream, but Lennie's sudden appearance had brought her back to earth with a thud, reminding her that a future with Zach was not in the cards.

"Willa?"

She tried to turn her head away, but he wouldn't let her.

"Look at me," he commanded in a husky whisper.

There was no place to go, no place to hide. She couldn't even summon up a spark of defensive anger. Defeated, she slowly raised her head and looked at him helplessly, knowing that all she was feeling was there in her eyes for him to see.

Something flickered in the green depths of his eyes,

something hot and intense. She felt his sudden stillness, the faint tremor in the hands cupping her face.

"Willa." This time he whispered her name like a caress. He examined her face, feature by feature, then his gaze dropped to her mouth, and his eyes grew heavy-lidded as his head tilted to one side and began a slow descent.

Watching him through the screen of her lashes, she waited, her heart pounding, wanting his kiss so much she could barely breathe, and at the same time aching with sadness at the futility of it all.

As his lips closed over hers, Willa moaned and stepped into the kiss, wrapping her arms tight around his lean middle.

Releasing her face, Zach slid his arms around her and pulled her tightly against him. All the quivering awareness, all the pent-up longing that had been building between them throughout the evening, throughout the long, busy spring and summer, exploded. He kissed her deeply, passionately, as though he would devour her.

Willa responded in kind, holding nothing back, greedily giving and taking all the pleasure she could in these few glorious moments, knowing that all too soon it would be taken from her.

Her hands clutched his back, roamed frantically over the broad expanse. Innocently, driven almost mad by the need to touch him, she snatched the tail of his shirt loose from his jeans and slipped her hands underneath. With a sigh of satisfaction she ran her palms over his bare flesh, glorying in its warmth, its firmness, her fingers alternately clutching and kneading.

A low groan vibrated from Zach's throat and he tore his mouth from hers. "I want you," he rasped. "Dear heaven, how I want you."

"I—I want you, too."

"Then come upstairs with me. Now. Let me make love to you."

The husky words vibrated with so much passion a shiver rippled through her. "I want to, Zach, but…how can we, when this is probably what Seamus planned?"

"The devil with Seamus. I've been giving this a lot of thought. Hell, I've hardly thought about anything else since that night in the line camp. I finally realized that if we deny this thing between us just because we suspect the old man plotted to get us together, then he's still controlling our actions, and we end up hurting only ourselves. It would be like cutting off your nose to spite your face.

"This has nothing to do with Seamus, or this ranch, or with the two of us being in close proximity day to day. It's not as though you're the only female in the area. I've met a few others since I've been here. I even took a couple of them out.

"I tried to tell myself that I just needed to be with a woman. Any woman. That if I started seeing someone else I would stop thinking about you constantly."

Hurt coursed through Willa. Merely suspecting that he was seeing someone else, she had suffered searing jealousy every night that he'd gone into town, but knowing for certain, hearing him admit it, was so much worse.

"I see," she said, her voice frosty with hurt. "In that case, maybe you should be asking one of those women to sleep with you." She tried to pull away but he grasped her shoulders and refused to let her go. Willa turned her head away, refusing to look at him.

"Willa, listen to me. It didn't work. Nothing happened. I didn't want either of those women. They both let me know that they wanted to go to bed with me, but I wasn't interested. And do you know why?''

She gazed at him warily out of the corner of her eye, her expression still mulish and distrustful. ''Why?''

''Because they weren't you.'' Crooking his finger under her chin, he turned her face toward his again. He looked into her eyes, and his voice deepened. ''It's you I want. Only you.''

Hope fluttered in her chest. She searched his face, his eyes, and all she saw there was unflinching honesty.

''To hell with Seamus and his plotting. This is just me wanting you and you wanting me,'' he continued in the same low tone.

Happiness began to percolate, effervescing from somewhere deep inside Willa like tiny champagne bubbles. Slowly her mouth curved into a smile and she slid her hands up over his chest and clasped them behind his neck. ''Take me upstairs, Zach.''

Before all the words were out of her mouth he swooped her up into his arms. Willa gazed at his determined profile, her heart thudding, excitement and dread nearly suffocating her. She had to tell him. He had a right to know. She had to.

Zach shouldered open the swinging door and strode into the hall, and when he'd gained the foyer he took the steps two at a time.

He did not slow his pace until they were inside his room. Coming to a halt beside the bed, he looked deep into her eyes. ''Are you sure this is what you want? If not, say so now. I'm not sure I'll be able to stop if we go on.''

Tell him. You have to tell him, now before it's too late.
''Zach, I...there's something you should know. I...''

''Yes?''

"I..." She gazed at his rough-hewn face, flushed with passion, the desire blazing in his eyes—for her—and instead of the words she intended to say she answered his question, truthfully from her heart. "I want you to make love to me. I've never been more sure of anything in my life."

He pressed a quick, hard kiss on her mouth, and placed her on her feet. Willa was so nervous her knees were weak, and when he slid his hands over her shoulders and up the sides of her neck she shivered. "You looked beautiful tonight," he whispered. "But I've been wanting to do this all evening."

She felt his fingers in her hair, and a second later the pins scattered across the floor and what was left of her elegant hairdo came tumbling down. He picked up handfuls of the slippery strands, lifted them, let them slide through his spread fingers and cascade around her shoulders and back like an ebony silk curtain, all the while watching as though mesmerized. "Lovely," he murmured.

Then his gaze drifted to her face, and he bent his head and kissed her again, as though unable to resist. Willa sighed and leaned in closer, then smiled against his lips as she felt his hands winnow through her hair again. Not until the kiss ended and she felt a tickle of cooler air against her lower back did she realize that he'd unzipped her dress. Instinctively, she crossed her arm over her chest to hold up the sagging bodice.

Zach smiled. "Shy? Don't be. Not with me. I want to see you. I've dreamed about this for months."

"You...you have?"

"Mmm. Watching you in those tight jeans every day has been driving me slowly out of my mind."

His words thrilled her. All this time, she thought with

amazement, while she had been almost sick with love for him, Zach had been fantasizing about her.

Gathering her courage, she swallowed hard and slid first one strap, then the other off her shoulder, all the while holding his gaze. As the dress slithered to the floor she saw the fire leap into his eyes. Trembling with nerves, she stood in front of him wearing only the sexy little black lace panties and bra and red, strappy high heels.

"Ah, sweetheart." Zach reached out and ran his forefinger along the top edge of the bra, leaving a line of fire on the pearly mounds of flesh that swelled above it. "You take my breath away."

His trailing finger reached the clasp at the center front of the bra and flipped it open, and the strapless scrap of lace fell to the floor. Willa shivered and resisted the urge to cover herself.

Then Zach's hands were there, cupping her breasts, lifting, stroking. He bent his head and kissed the soft flesh, ran his tongue around one rosy aureole, then pulled it into his mouth. Willa's head lolled back and she squeezed her eyes shut, moaning at the delicious sensation that tugged all the way to her feminine core. Had she not been clutching his shoulders for support she would have surely collapsed in a heap.

With a sudden urgency, Zach released her, and as the cool air struck her wet nipple she moaned and reached for him, but he ignored her plea and swept her up into his arms and moved closer to the bed. With one knee sunk into the mattress, he paused and looked into her eyes. His face was dark and rigid with passion, his eyes glittering like diamonds. "I meant to go slow, but I can't. Not this time. I've wanted you too long."

"Oh, Zach."

He laid her down on the mattress, and in one smooth

motion stripped away the lacy panties and sandals. Then he went to work on his own clothes. Willa watched him, fascinated, her heart pounding wildly in her chest.

He yanked off his boots and socks and straightened. Gripping the lapels of his Western shirt, he gave them a yank, and the gripper snaps came loose with a rapid rat-tat-tat-tat-tat, like a tiny machine gun firing. He snatched off the shirt and tossed it over his shoulder. Next he hooked his thumbs under the waistband of his jeans and underwear and shoved them to his ankles and kicked them off. All the while, he watched Willa watching him.

The mattress dipped, and he came down beside her. He took her mouth in a ravenous kiss and ran his hand over her body, cupping her breast, sweeping his thumb across the nipple until it stood up like a pebble, then abandoning the soft mound to skim over the long curve of midriff and waist and hip.

He trailed kisses over her cheek, her jaw, down her neck. "You taste heavenly," he murmured, nuzzling the silky valley between her breasts. He explored her navel, her hipbone, the silky juncture where her thigh met her body. Then his fingers found that nest of tight, black curls.

"Zach. Oh, Zach."

Willa shifted restlessly, almost delirious. She was swamped with so many new and wondrous sensations she couldn't think. She could only respond, and at his silent urging, she parted her thighs for him. Then his fingers stroked that warm, wet part of her that yearned for him, and she moaned and arched against his hand.

A low, desperate growl rumbled from Zach, and he quickly moved into position between her thighs. Willa was on fire, her body hot and feverish, but gossamer wings of panic fluttered around the edges of her mind when she felt his sex nudge her. She struggled to think, to remember.

"Zach...I..."

Then it was too late.

He thrust into her, and she felt a searing pain. It lasted only a moment, but she could not hold back the cry that tore from her throat.

"What the—"

Braced on his arms above her, Zach stilled and stared down at her in horror. "Willa? What—?"

He started to withdraw, but she clutched his shoulders and pleaded, "No! Don't stop. Please, don't stop."

"Dammit, Willa—"

"Please." She gazed up at him, her eyes entreating, and arched her hips, taking him deeper. "Please."

Zach gritted his teeth, but when she lifted again he was lost. With a groan he started to move, slowly, watching her face for signs of distress, but all he saw there was relief and building pleasure. He watched her eyes glaze with it, her lips part. She began to move with him, arching her hips to meet every thrust.

"Put your legs around me," he rasped.

She obeyed, and her eyes widened as he thrust deeper, faster. Her breathing became labored and rapid, and she began to turn her head from side to side on the pillow and to make small, frantic sounds.

Zach stared down at her in awe, amazed and unbearably excited by her innocent ardor. He could see the passion building in her, hear it in her desperate little moans.

"Oh. Oh. Oh, Zach. *Zach!*"

"Go with it, baby. Let go," he growled.

Willa cried out, and he felt her sweet, pulsing contractions tighten around him, and his control began to slip. Arching his back, he threw his head back and pressed deep, and a low, guttural sound of ecstacy rumbled from his throat as his own climax overtook him.

Zach collapsed on top of her and struggled to catch his breath. Willa sighed and wrapped her arms around him and ran her palms up over his back.

That feather-light touch instantly jarred him back to his senses, and he withdrew from her and rolled out of bed.

"Zach?"

Jaw set, he stalked across the room and snatched up his jeans and stepped into them. He heard a rustling sound, and from the corner of his eye he saw Willa sit up in the bed and pull the sheet up to her armpits.

"Zach?"

The anger and guilt bubbling inside him boiled to the surface and he swung on her. "A *virgin!* Why the hell didn't you tell me?" he shouted.

"I...I..."

"Dammit, you're twenty-six! How can you still be a virgin?"

"I—I told you I haven't dated much. Seamus...Seamus didn't approve. After I turned twenty-one and could defy him I had a few dates, but I never went out with any of them more than once. I think he scared them off somehow. So..." She broke off and pressed her lips together and watched him nervously.

"And you let him get by with that?"

"I—I'm sorry you're disappointed."

"Don't be ridiculous. I'm not disappointed. I'm angry. Dammit, you should have told me. I never would have touched you if I'd known you were a virgin."

"I see." Willa ducked her head and stared at her fingers, which were nervously plucking at the sheet.

"Damn." Zach paced to the window, then swung back

and plowed both hands into his hair, holding his head as though to keep it from exploding. "Well, the damage is done now. There's only one thing to do. We'll get married as soon as possible. Tomorrow, if I can arrange it."

Willa's head jerked up. "What?"

"I'll call Edward in the morning. Maybe he can pull some strings for us."

"Forget it." Tossing back the sheet, Willa jumped out of bed and snatched up her dress from the floor.

"Okay, if you don't want Edward to help, we'll go through normal channels."

Willa stepped into the dress and yanked up the zipper. "No, I mean forget the whole thing. I'm not marrying you. Period. This is the twenty-first century, for heaven's sake! I will not marry a man simply because he feels obligated to make an 'honest woman' out of me." She grabbed up her bra and panties and stomped for the door. "So you can take your proposal and stuff it, Mahoney!"

"Willa, come back here. That's not what I meant."

Ignoring him, she kept going. Zach cursed and stomped after her down the hallway. "Will you stop and listen to me. Dammit, I didn't even use any protection. You could be pregnant."

She stormed into her bedroom, and turned back, blocking the door. "If I am, then I'll deal with it. Alone."

Zach opened his mouth to argue, but she slammed the door in his face and turned the lock. He spewed a string of curses and banged on the door with the side of his fist. "Dammit, woman, open this door!"

"Stop that! You'll wake up the children. Just go away. I have nothing more to say to you."

He stopped pounding and looked down the hall toward the children's bedrooms and cursed again, this time under his breath. "All right, all right. I'm going," he said, pitching his voice just loud enough for her to hear him through the door. "But this isn't the end of it. We're going to talk about this in the morning."

He stalked back into his room and slammed the door. Too agitated to sit, his hands clenched at his sides. "Stubborn woman," he snarled at the ceiling. What the devil was the matter with her? After what they had just shared, he knew she cared for him. So why was she being so obstinate?

He reached the window and turned to pace back to the other side of the room, but after only two steps he spotted one of her shoes. Zach bent, picked up the red sandal and sat on the edge of his bed. He stared at the tiny shoe, turning it around and around in his hand. How did women walk in these things? It had a three-inch heel and was nothing more than a couple of straps and a thin sole.

The corners of his mouth twitched. It sure was sexy, though. The silvery innersole bore the impression of her toes, and he smiled wider this time, remembering the sassy red nail polish on them. When she had come sashaying down those stairs in that swirly red dress and these little-bit-of-nothing shoes it had been all he could do not to ravish her on the spot.

He'd never felt this way about a woman before. He was crazy about her, and she was tying him in knots.

Zach sighed and rubbed his thumb back and forth over one of the red straps. "Dammit, Willa, why won't you marry me?"

Chapter Twelve

Leaning back with his chair tilted on its rear legs, Zach sipped his coffee and watched the hall door over the rim of the mug.

Tying on her apron, Maria came into the kitchen through the side door that led to her quarters. When she spotted Zach, she jumped and let out a squeak and slapped her hand over her heart.

"Señor Zach! You startled me. You are early this morning."

"Yeah." He nodded toward the stove. "I already made the coffee." Immediately, his gaze returned to the swinging door. He had a hunch Willa would try to sneak out early. He'd come downstairs almost an hour ago to make sure that didn't happen.

Maria followed the direction of his gaze, and wisely went about her business, saying nothing.

Just as Zach suspected, a moment later Willa pushed

through the door. Two steps into the room she stopped short. He cocked one eyebrow. "Going somewhere?"

"What are you doing here?"

"Waiting for you." He gave her a searching look and his tone gentled. "Are you okay?"

"My cheek is fine."

"That's not what I meant. After last night, I thought you might be a little...uncomfortable."

Willa gave him a go-to-hell look and headed for the back door.

The front legs of Zach's chair hit the floor as he sprang to his feet and blocked her path. "You aren't going anywhere until we have that talk we should have had last night."

"Forget it, Mahoney. I'm leaving." She sidestepped first one way, then the other, but each time he mimicked the action. "Will you stop that!"

Maria stopped working and watched them with avid curiosity, her gaze bouncing from one to the other.

"We have to talk, Willa."

"We most certainly do not! I have nothing to say to you. Now get out of my way."

"Or you'll what? Face it, sweetheart, I'm bigger and stronger than you are, and just as stubborn.

"You wouldn't dare use brute force on me."

"Wanna bet?"

"Why you sorry, low-down, good-for-nothing—"

"Hey! Hey! What's all the racket about?" Matt demanded, limping into the kitchen. J.T., Kate and Maude Ann followed behind him. "We could hear you two yelling at each other all the way upstairs. You wake those kids before it's time for them to get up and I'll personally knock your heads together." He limped over to the stove to get some coffee. "So what's the problem here?"

"Your brother won't take no for an answer. *That's* the problem."

"What?" Both Matt and J.T. stiffened and drilled Zach with identical icy stares. The women looked stunned. "What did you do to her?"

A guilty flush crept up Zach's neck and face. "This is between Willa and me, so just stay out of it."

"I have nothing more to say to you. Get out of my way."

"Oh, no, you don't," he warned, matching her side-step again. "You're not going anywhere until we settle this."

"It is settled!" she yelled.

"Dammit, will you calm down and listen to reason?"

"Reason? *Reason!* Don't you dare talk to me about reason, you...you...throwback! Now get out of my way!"

She feinted to one side, then darted around him on the other. Zach made a grab for her arm, missed, and snagged the back of her shirt instead, jerking her to a halt. Willa shrieked and twisted around, swinging.

"Hey, that's enough! Break it up, you two." Matt stepped between the pair.

J.T. grabbed Zach's arm. "Let her go, Zach."

"Dammit—"

Matt jutted his head forward until he and Zach were nose to nose, eyeball to eyeball. "You heard him," he growled. "The lady wants to leave. Let her go. And remember, there are two of us."

Jaw clenched, Zach stared back, weighing his chances. "Damn," he finally snapped, and released the shirt. Willa shot out the door like a bullet.

"*Muchacha!* Your breakfast!"

Ignoring Maria, she kept going and ran to her pickup.

An instant later the engine roared to life, and the tires kicked up gravel when she stomped on the gas and sped out of the yard.

"Great. Just great." Zach turned cold, furious eyes on his brothers. "Don't either of you ever do anything like that again."

"Hey, bro, you can't expect Matt and me to stand by and do nothing while you manhandle a woman."

"I wasn't going to hurt her, for Pete's sake. I just wanted to talk to her."

"That's not how it looked from where we stood," Matt replied. "What the devil happened between you two last night, anyway?"

"Obviously not what we thought was going to happen," J.T. drawled.

Kate put her hand on her brother's arm. "Zach, what's wrong? You and Willa were getting along so well at the dance before that thug Lennie hit her. Why is she so upset with you now?"

"Damned if I know." Zach raked his hand through his hair and began to pace. "All I did was ask her to marry me, and she hit the roof."

"You asked her to *marry* you?" Kate stared at him with her mouth hanging open.

"Jeez, bro, isn't that kind of sudden?"

"I know. I know. I didn't intend to ask her this soon, but then after we got home last night we—" He broke off and scowled at them. "Look, just forget it, okay. This is a personal matter between Willa and me. I'll work it out."

"Oh, no, you don't. You can't just leave us hanging," Maude Ann insisted. "Besides, how can we help you if you don't tell us what the problem is? So spit it out. What happened when you and Willa got home?"

Zach glared at them, but all five just waited with expectant expressions. Finally he sighed and raked both hands through his hair again. "After we got home, I took a look at her cheek and tried to comfort her and...well...one thing led to another and—"

"Aha! So what we thought was going to happen *did* happen. Jeez, bro, you must not have done it right if she's that mad."

"Knock if off, J.T., and let him finish," Matt barked.

Zach shot J.T. a quelling look, and started pacing again. "Anyway, the thing is...it was Willa's first time. But she didn't tell me, and by the time I realized it, was too late."

Matt gave a long, low whistle.

"Oh, man, that's a heavy responsibility," J.T. murmured, sobering.

"Yeah, well, I chewed her out for not telling me. I told her if she had I wouldn't have touched her, but the damage was done, so we would get married. That's when she hit the roof and started acting completely irrational."

Maude Ann rolled her eyes. "Big surprise. No wonder she's got her nose out of joint."

"Oh, Zach, how could you?" his sister groaned.

"What? I was trying to do the right thing."

"Jeez, bro, I sure hope you didn't say *that* to Willa."

"Man, you really bungled things." Matt shook his head and gave him a pitying look. "Hell, Zach, even I know you don't ask a woman to marry you without first telling her that you love her."

"He's right," Kate said. "No woman wants a man to marry her because he feels it's his duty. She needs to know that she's loved and wanted so much that her man can't bear the thought of a life without her."

"I can't! Dammit, I've never felt this way about any

woman before. Surely she knows that I wouldn't have ask her to marry me if I didn't love her.''

''Oh? And just how would she know that?''

Zach glared at Maude Ann, unable to come up with a reasonable answer. After a moment he heaved a sigh, grimacing. ''Ah, hell. I guess I really shot myself in the foot, didn't I? I swear to you, I was already thinking marriage, but I was going to court Willa for a couple of months first, then propose. What happened between us last night just made it seem more urgent, that's all.''

''Then I suggest you tell her that,'' Kate advised. ''But I warn you, don't be surprised if she doesn't believe you.''

''Damn. So, it's hopeless?''

''Not necessarily,'' Kate replied. ''All I'm saying is, be prepared. It's going to take a lot of effort to convince her. You may be in for a long, hard struggle.''

''I'll damn well lay siege to her if I have to,'' he declared.

Zach began to pace again, muttering under his breath about Willa's stubbornness and his own stupidity. Halfway across the room he stopped and glared at his brothers. ''Wipe those grins off your faces. You two are really enjoying this, aren't you?''

J.T.'s grin widened. ''Hey, after the grief you gave me when I wanted to marry Kate, can you blame me? Anyway, I gotta tell you, man, seeing my calm, always-incontrol brother so frazzled is a pure delight.''

Except for a light in the kitchen, the house was in darkness when Willa drove into the ranch yard that night.

She parked beside the barn and went inside and flipped on the dim overhead light. Immediately Bertha whinnied and her head appeared over the front of her stall. ''Hi, girl,'' Willa murmured, stroking the mare's forehead. ''Did you miss me today?''

''It's about time you showed up.''

Willa jumped and spun around, her hand over her racing heart. ''Zach! What are you doing here?''

''Waiting for you. I knew you'd look in on your horse before you sneaked up to your room.''

''So you lay in wait in the dark to ambush me,'' she snapped.

Zach shrugged. ''Whatever it takes. So, where were you all day?''

''I went to a movie in Helena. Not that it's any of your business.'' She'd also spent hours moping in a park and more just aimlessly driving around, but she wasn't going to admit that to him. She didn't dare let him know how much he'd hurt her.

She stomped around him to the feed bin, half expecting him to reach out and grab her, but he kept his distance and merely watched her.

''By the way, I've already fed your mare.''

''Oh.'' She dropped the scoop back into the bin and closed the lid. ''In that case there's no reason for me to stay.'' She swung around and headed for the door with a determined stride.

''Willa, I love you.''

The quiet declaration stopped her in her tracks and sent a shaft of pain through her heart. She turned slowly and looked at him, her eyes accusing. ''Don't you dare say that to me. Not now.''

''I know, I know. I should have told you last night. My only excuse is, I was rattled. But it's true all the same.''

''I don't believe you.'' Her voice was low and quivering with hurt and anger. It was all she could do to not burst into tears.

"Nevertheless, I do love you. I swear it."

"Stop it! Stop saying that!"

She headed for the door again, but before she'd taken two steps Zach was blocking her path. She hadn't known a man his size could move that fast.

"Willa, listen to me—"

"No! You'll say anything to get your way, all because of some outdated code of honor. Well, I'm sorry if you have a guilty conscience about what happened, but I refuse to have a martyr for a husband. Now get out of my way."

"Okay, I will, if you'll answer just one question?"

She eyed him warily. "Oh, all right. Go ahead."

Zach looked deep into her eyes. "Do you love me?"

Willa sucked in a sharp breath. "That's not fair. You can't—"

"Do you?"

She tried to turn her head away, but he grasped her chin and refused to let her. "Look at me, Willa," he commanded in a voice like velvet. "Look at me."

When at last she raised sullen eyes to meet his gaze he went on in the same softly insistent tone. "If you can look me straight in the eye and honestly say, 'I don't love you, Zach' then I'll never bother you again. Can you say that, Willa?"

Her chin began to quiver and her eyes grew moist. "I...I..."

"Say it, Willa."

Her eyes accused him. "Why are you doing this to me?"

"Say it," he whispered.

She tried, but she couldn't force the words out. Finally she closed her eyes and shook her head. "I...I can't."

"Thank God for that," Zach exclaimed, and snatched her into his arms. He cradled her close and rubbed his cheek against the top of her head. "If you'd said that to me it would have killed me."

He loosened his hold just enough to lean back and look at her. Willa's heart jumped when she saw the gleam in his eyes.

"Zach, no—"

"I have to. I've nearly gone insane these past twenty-four hours. If I don't kiss you soon I'm going to blow apart."

"You don't understand. This changes noth—"

Zach's mouth settled over hers, swallowing up the words. She tried to resist, pushing at his shoulders, but it was a weak effort at best and pointless. This was Zach, and she loved him so much it hurt.

The lushness of the kiss, its power, its seductiveness were impossible to resist. At the first touch of his lips against hers, the tingling heat coursed through her veins and set her pulse to beating like a tom-tom.

After a night of crying, followed by a day of licking her wounds, her emotions were running just below the surface, making it impossible to hold back her response.

With a groan, Willa succumbed and wrapped her arms around his neck, kissing him back greedily, hungrily, her passions soaring. Vaguely, she felt herself being lifted, carried, then they were lying together in one of the empty stalls on a pile of fresh hay. It crackled beneath them as they kissed endlessly and clung to each other, its pungent grassy scent rising all around them, filling the air with its sharp sweetness.

There was no time for foreplay, and no need. Driven

by the anxiety and raw emotions of the past twenty-four hours, their desire reached fever pitch within seconds. They worked frantically to get free of their clothes. Soon buttons and zippers and clasps were dealt with, but needs were desperate, demanding, and neither could wait long enough to strip completely. Shirts were yanked open, jeans and underwear shoved down and kicked off partway. Then, in a move as natural as breathing, Willa opened to him, and Zach sank into her silky warmth.

For several moments the only sounds in the dimly lit barn were the stomp of hooves and an occasional soft whicker from the horses stalls, the crackle of hay, and lovers' soft sighs and gasps and whispered words of passion.

The end, when it came, was explosive, eliciting a long, moaning cry from both of them. Then only the hiss of their labored breathing broke the ponderous silence.

After a moment Willa became aware of a piece of straw poking into her back and shifted. Zach raised up on his forearms and smiled down at her, one blond eyebrow cocked. "Am I too heavy?"

Their intimate position, combined with the wild disarray of their clothes and the dawning awareness that they had just made love in the barn, a literal "roll in the hay," brought a blush to her face. Barely able to meet his gaze, she shook her head.

Zach's chiseled lips turned up at the corners. All the hard edges in his face seemed softer. He had that relaxed, slumberous look of a satisfied male. Lowering his head, he placed his forehead against hers and looked into her eyes. "Tell me again that you love me."

"Zach, don't." She pushed at his shoulders. "Let me up."

He rolled off of her, and she sat up and fastened her

bra and started buttoning her shirt. Zach sat up, as well. She knew he was watching her, but she kept her gaze focused on her task.

"Willa? What's wrong?"

She glanced at his puzzled expression and sighed. "Zach, nothing has changed."

"What do you mean? You do believe that I love you, don't you?"

"What I believe is, you're a moral and honorable man who always tries to do what's right. Right now you think that means marrying me." Her jeans and panties were bunched below her right knee. She stood and stuffed her left foot into the empty pant leg and pulled them up.

"How can you say that. After what just happened?"

Willa looked up from buttoning the waistband on her jeans, her face sad. "Oh, Zach, all that proves is you desire me. That's not a difficult response to get from a man. And it's certainly not enough to convince me that we could build a life together."

Over the next few days Zach was even more quiet and distant than usual, but Willa knew he hadn't given up. He watched her with brooding intensity whenever they were in the same room or working within sight of each other.

Everyone else had picked up on his black mood and they all watched what they said and tiptoed around him as though they were walking on eggs, making the atmosphere in the house extremely uncomfortable.

The only solution Willa could think of was to avoid Zach as much as possible, and each morning she grabbed a biscuit and headed for the barn before the others gathered for breakfast.

Four days after making love with Zach the second

time, she entered the barn at daybreak and was surprised when she didn't see Pete. "Pete? Are you here?" she called as she headed for Bertha's stall.

She was halfway there when someone grabbed her from behind, clamping one hand around her waist and the other around her mouth, cutting off her instinctive scream.

Her first thought was it was Zach, but then she realized that the man was smaller.

"I've been waiting for you, bitch," Lennie growled in her ear. "You've been leaving early these past few days, so I figured this would be the best time to catch you alone."

Willa struggled to twist free, but Lennie laughed and tightened his hold painfully. "Go ahead, fight me. It won't do you any good. You're coming with me."

Revulsion shivered through her. He'd been watching her.

"The trouble was that stupid old man was always here before you left the house and you never ride out without three or four cowboys with you. But I took care of the old geezer."

Pete! Dear Lord, what had he done to Pete?

"Now we're going up into the mountains, just you and me. And when I'm done with you, Mahoney or no other man will ever touch you again. C'mon. Let's go. My truck is hidden over behind the pine grove."

At first, all she'd felt was revulsion and disgust, but now real fear coursed through her and she began to twist and buck and kick.

"Stop that! It won't do you any good. Dammit! I've got a gun. If you don't stop I'll shoot you right here— *Ow!*"

He hopped on one foot and grabbed his leg where

Willa's boot heel had made hard contact with his shin. The instant his hand left her mouth she threw back her head and screamed.

Zach was halfway to the barn when the bloodcurdling sound stopped him in his tracks, raising the hairs on the back of his neck. Willa! His hesitation lasted only a fraction of a second, then he pounded for the barn.

The screams were cut off as suddenly as they erupted, just as Zach charged inside. The sight that greeted him brought him skidding to a stop. Lennie Dawson had Willa in a choke hold, with a gun to her temple.

"Stop right there, Mahoney, or she's dead!"

"Let her go, Dawson."

"Not on your life. She's coming with me."

Zach shook his head, his eyes fixed on Lennie. "I don't think so."

"I'll shoot you if you don't get out of the way," he screamed. "Damn you! If I can't have Willa, no man will. Especially not you."

The wild look in Lennie's eyes unnerved Zach, though he was careful to not let his uneasiness show. Eaten up with jealousy, the younger man hovered on the brink of insanity.

"Zach, please go. Please," Willa pleaded. "He means it."

"No. I'm not going to let him take you. He'll have to kill me first."

"That's a better idea, anyway," Lennie raged. "This ranch should have been mine. Willa should have been mine, and you stole both of them. You deserve to die, damn you!"

"Put the gun away, Dawson," Matt ordered. He and

J.T. entered the barn and took up a position on each side of Zach.

"Get out of here!" Lennie shrieked. "My quarrel is with him, not you two."

"Anyone who tangles with our brother has to deal with Matt and me, too," J.T. informed him.

"And with us, as well," Maude Ann stated calmly. She and Kate stepped inside the barn and stood shoulder to shoulder with their husbands and Zach, flanking the men on each side.

Appalled, the three men paled. "Maudie, you and Kate get out of here. Now," Matt bellowed.

"Jeez, Kate, have you lost your mind?"

"Sis, J.T.'s right. Get out of here. If you want to help, go call the sheriff," Zach said.

"He's on his way. I called as soon as we heard Willa scream and Matt and J.T. took off for the barn. And Maudie and I aren't leaving, so forget it."

"That's right." Maude Ann looked Lennie right in the eye and tilted her chin at a challenging angle. "Mr. Dawson, you really should have given this more thought before you decided to harm any of us, because we're a family, and that includes Willa. And families protect their own."

In the distance the wail of a siren could be heard, growing steadily louder. Zach took a step forward, and the others moved with him. "Drop the gun, Lennie. It's over."

"No! No, stay back! Or I'll shoot you all!"

Zach shook his head and edged forward another step. So did everyone else. "You may get one of us, maybe even two, but you can't stop us all."

"At least I'll get you."

"Please, Zach, go back. Go back," Willa sobbed.

"Shut up!" Lennie tightened his hold on Willa's neck, nearly choking her. "I'm gonna enjoy this." Lennie turned the gun directly at Zach and took aim at his heart.

Clawing at the arm encircling her neck, Willa struggled to get air and at the same time raised her knee and kicked back as hard she could. She landed a vicious blow squarely on Lennie's kneecap. He howled and the gun's booming report echoed through the barn. Zach let out an "Oof," spun around and went down.

"Zaaach!" Willa fought like a wildcat, clawing and scratching and kicking to get free, but Lennie stubbornly hung on. Cursing her and hobbling, he raised the gun again, but before he could fire, Matt and J.T. jumped him and wrestled him to the ground, taking Willa down with them.

Calling Zach's name over and over, she wriggled and squirmed and frantically worked herself free of the pile of men and scrambled on her hands and knees to his side. "Zach. Oh, Zach," she sobbed. With Kate and Maude Ann's help, they rolled him over onto his back, and Willa cried out when she saw the bloodstain spreading on his shirt.

"Easy," Maude Ann cautioned in her calm, physician's voice.

"What in the cat hair is goin' on?" Groaning, Pete staggered out from behind a stack of hay bales, holding his head.

"Pete! Thank God. Are you all right?"

"Far as I can tell, Willie."

"What happened?"

"Well now…one minute I was dippin' up grain outta the feed bin, an' the next thing I know, I'm waking up behind the hay bales to a godawful noise what sounded like an explosion. If that ain't bad enough, now some fool's comin' with a siren wailing like a banshee. Dang, I got me a knot on my noggin you could wear a hat on. I think somebody conked me.''

"That was Lennie. And he shot Zach."

Pete frowned, focusing on Zach's prone body. "How bad is he?"

"It probably looks a lot worse than it is," Maude Ann answered. "Kate, would you go get my medical bag? It's in the armoire in our room. And call an ambulance while you're there."

The sheriff's car screeched to a halt outside the barn as Kate ran out the door. She paused just long enough to say something to him and gesture toward the barn, then ran for the house, where Maria was standing on the back porch, wringing her hands.

"What's going on here?" Sheriff Denby demanded, taking in Zach's prone and bloodied form and Lennie struggling to break free from Matt and J.T.

When they explained what happened, the sheriff smiled contemptuously at Lennie. "Always knew you'd get in real trouble someday, Dawson."

"You can kiss my—"

The sheriff slapped Lennie upside the head. "Watch your mouth in front of the ladies, boy." He pulled the younger man's arms behind his back and snapped a pair of handcuffs on him. "Lennie Dawson, you're under arrest for attempted murder, attempted kidnapping, felony menacing—"

"And assault," Pete added. "He whopped me over the head."

"And felony assault. You have a right to remain silent. If you relinquish that right…"

When the sheriff finished reciting Lennie's Miranda rights he shoved him down onto the floor and asked Matt and J.T. to keep an eye on the prisoner while he checked out his truck.

Kate raced in with the medical bag. "The kids heard all the ruckus and they're pretty upset. I told Maria to keep them at the house, and that you would be there soon."

"Thanks." With Willa kneeling beside Zach, clutching his hand, Maude Ann went to work. She unbuttoned his shirt and peeled it back, but when she began swabbing the entry wound with a sterile pad his eyes fluttered open. "Willa?"

"I'm here, darling." She squeezed his hand and smiled tearfully. "I'm right here."

"Are you...all right?"

"Yes, I'm fine. Don't try to talk. The ambulance will be here soon to take you to the hospital."

"I...love you."

Willa's lips quivered and a tear spilled over onto their joined hands. "I know. I love you, too."

Maude Ann cleaned out the wound, applied antiseptic and packed it with sterile gauze. Zach groaned when she and Kate rolled him onto his side. "The good news is we won't have to dig out the bullet. It went straight through. And it doesn't appear to have hit any artery or major muscle."

The sheriff came back into the barn carrying several plastic evidence bags. "Looks like Lennie here is your vandal. I found this in his truck—yellow spray paint, butchering knives, dynamite, and a hide with your brand on it."

"I don't get it, Dawson. Why try to run us off? What did you have to gain?"

Lennie gave Matt a surly look. "You mean beside the satisfaction of hurting your brother? That's easy. Money.

Edward Manning paid me five thousand up front, and I was to get another ten when the bunch of you turned tail and ran.''

"I *knew* something was fishy about that guy," Matt declared. "I *knew* it. I had my suspicions about him from the moment we met him."

"Well, I for one think he's lying," Sheriff Denby said. "I mean, c'mon. Edward Manning is a well-known and respected man in this state. Seamus trusted him implicitly. Hell, he was the only one the old man did trust. Manning is also a wealthy man. He inherited a fortune plus a successful law firm from his old man.

"Not only that, for years he's been positioning himself to make a run for the governor's office. Some say he's going to throw his hat into the ring the next election. Why would he risk all that when he's got nothing to gain by running you off the ranch? No, I think our boy Lennie here is just blowing smoke."

"I'm telling you, I was acting under orders from Edward Manning. He said get rid of at least one of Seamus's heirs, and to use any means necessary to do it."

"Now why would Mr. Manning do that?" the sheriff demanded.

"I don't know. You think he'd tell me? I just do his dirty work."

"Then it's your word against his."

"I'm telling you, I'm not taken the fall for this alone. I was acting under orders from Edward Manning!''

"Yeah, yeah." The sheriff hauled Lennie to his feet and gave him a shove. "C'mon, get moving. I got a nice cell in town with your name on it."

"Sheriff, hold on," Matt said. "Look, I'm not trying to horn in on your territory or step on anyone's toes, but would you mind if I do some checking on Manning on my own? Just to satisfy my own curiosity?''

"I'm telling you, it's a waste of time. But, hey, if you want to give it a shot, be my guest."

Two days later Willa sat beside Zach's hospital bed watching him doze, when the Dolans and the Conways walked into the room.

"How's he doing?" J.T. whispered.

Zach's eyes fluttered open. "I'm okay."

"Are you sure?" Kate studied him worriedly. "You still look pale to me."

"Don't fuss, sis. I'm fine. Or at least I will be when they let me out of here."

"He's cranky because they've been keeping him sedated," Willa supplied, chuckling.

"I wanted to talk to you," he growled. "But they've kept me so groggy I haven't been able to string two coherent sentences together."

"Well, cheer up," Maude Ann said. "I spoke to Dr. Bailey, and he told me if there is no sign of infection in your wound, you can go home tomorrow."

"In the meantime, here's something that should cheer you up." Matt tossed a file folder onto Zach's bedside tray.

"What's this?"

"The scoop on Manning. At face value, he appears to be exactly what everyone assumes—a wealthy, successful attorney with a bright future ahead of him. I did some digging, though, and found out the man is broke."

"How can that be? What about his father's fortune and the law firm? And the retainer he gets from the Rocking R is nothing to sneeze at."

"It seems our friend Manning has expensive tastes. He

likes to run with the big boys. The movers and shakers. Thanks to a series of bad investments and his extravagant spending, Edward has lost the fortune his old man left him. To maintain his lifestyle and keep up appearances, he's borrowed heavily.

"With his political ambitions within reach and his back to the wall financially, he's desperate for money.

"If we were to forfeit the ranch it would be sold in a sealed-bid auction, and Edward would be solely in charge of the whole thing. It would be a simple matter for him to rig the bidding in favor of his buyer. I suspect he stood to receive a hefty kickback from the sale of ranch, but even without that, his fee as executor of the trust could run into the millions annually."

"That son of a—" Zach bit off the rest of the expletive and demanded, "So do we have enough to have him arrested?"

"Yeah, but on minor charges. All he's done so far is solicit someone to harass us, and Lennie's testimony is uncorroborated. It would be his word against Edwards—a bullying vandal and would-be murderer looking to make a deal versus a well-respected pillar of the community. Who do you think a jury will believe? Even if we did manage to get a conviction, all Edward would get is a fine and a slap on the wrist.

"As to the conspiracy to commit fraud, all we've got is motive and opportunity. Without hard evidence, we wouldn't stand a chance in court. A good defense attorney will rip our case to shreds."

"So there's nothing we can do," Zach demanded angrily.

"I didn't say that. We can't send him to prison, but we can have the satisfaction of making him squirm and derail his political ambitions. In fact, J.T. and I have already taken care of that little matter.''

"Yeah, you should of been there, bro," J.T. chimed in, grinning. "We paid Mr. Manning a visit this morning and laid it all out for him. We dismissed him as our attorney, of course, but we also warned him that if he even thinks of running for public office we'll file charges against him and make the public aware of his underhanded dealing. You should have seen his face," J.T. crowed. "I think that hurt him worse than a prison term would."

"Yeah, you're probably right." Zach looked at each of his brothers, gratitude and a new respect, even a hint of affection in his eyes. "Good job. And I want to thank you both for your help. You, too, Maudie and Kate. If you hadn't been there—"

"Hey, bro, you don't owe us any thanks."

"J.T.'s right." Matt gave Zach's uninjured shoulder a squeeze. "That's what brothers do. They stick together."

After Zach's family left he took Willa's hand and looked deep into her eyes, his face serious and just a touch anxious. "I think I'm awake enough now to talk."

She smiled and smoothed back a lock of hair from his forehead. "Okay."

"I seem to have a vague memory of telling you again while Maudie was patching me up, that I love you."

"Mmm, you did."

"And of you saying that you knew. Or was I hallucinating that last part?"

"No, you weren't hallucinating."

"Then you do believe that I love you?"

Willa's eyes grew moist as she gazed down at him. "Oh, my darling, of course I believe you. How could I not, when you risked your life to save me."

"Okay, now that we've got that settled, maybe I can do this right this time." He brought her hand to his mouth and pressed a warm kiss against her palm, looking into her eyes all the while. Then he pressed her hand against his heart. "I love you, Willa, and I will until the day I die."

"Oh, Zach." Her voice quavered with so much emotion she could barely speak.

"Will you marry me, sweetheart?"

Tears slipped over each of her lower eyelids and trickled down her cheeks. "Yes. Oh, yes, my love. I'll marry you."

Zach cupped his hand around her nape and brought her face down for a lingering kiss that made her heart thunder. When their lips parted, he looked into her eyes. "Soon?"

Willa laughed. "Anytime you say."

Three weeks later, on a bright October afternoon, Willa stood at her bedroom window and stared out, marveling at the people wandering through the ranch yard. In all her years at the Rocking R, there had never been this many guests on the ranch at one time, not even for her mother's funeral.

And more were arriving all the time, people with whom they did business and neighbors from miles around, new friends all, thanks to the determined efforts of Zach and his brothers to mend the fences that Seamus had destroyed years ago. There were so many guests the cowboys had taken down a section of fence and turned the home pasture into a temporary parking lot.

Willa's gaze wandered over to the meadow by the pine grove, where a flower-bedecked arch had been set up in front of two groups of folding chairs on either side of a long red carpet, and her throat grew tight with unbearably sweet emotions.

Someone tapped on her door, and a second later Kate and Maude Ann rushed in. "It's time. Tyrone and Timothy are seating the last of the guests now."

Willa smiled and picked up her bouquet and followed Maude Ann downstairs, while Kate held up her train. Pete was waiting for her in the foyer, looking scrubbed and uncomfortable in his tux, but when he saw her his faded old eyes grew misty. "Willie, girl, if you ain't the prettiest thing God ever made, I don't know what is."

She kissed his cheek, making him blush, and whispered, "I love you, too," and looped her arm through his.

Moments later Willa stood serenely beside Pete and watched her attendants, all dressed in long emerald-velvet gowns, walk down the red carpet aisle. First came little Debbie, solemnly strewing rose petals, then her bridesmaids, Jennifer and Yolanda, followed by her two matrons of honor, Kate and Maude Ann.

The stirring opening notes of "The Wedding March" sounded and, proud as punch, Pete led her down the aisle.

Every head turned in her direction, and gasps and sighs sounded all around, but Willa barely heard. Through the layers of tulle and lace, all she saw was Zach. He stood in front of the arch with Matt and J.T. and the minister, looking so handsome in his tux he took her breath away, his intense green eyes fixed on her as though willing her to come to him.

Through the misty veil, Willa glanced around—at the five children she had once resented, at Maude Ann and Kate and Matt and J.T., whom she had considered grasping usurpers, all watching her with pride and affection, waiting to welcome her with open arms into their family, and her heart overflowed.

How much had changed in the past ten months, she thought dreamily. Not just in her life, but for all of them. Zach and Matt and J.T. had forged a strong brotherly bond, the children finally had the safe and loving home they deserved, her own years of isolation and loneliness had ended and she and Kate and Maude Ann had become the dearest of friends.

And most miraculous and wonderful of all, she and Zach had found each other.

Willa and Pete came to the end of the aisle, and when Zach reached for her hand she smiled serenely at him through the veil. They had all started out at odds with one another, but now they had become exactly what Maude Ann had said they were, she thought happily. They were a family, bound together by ties of love.

* * * * *

*Don't miss Ginna Gray's
next book!*

THE WITNESS

*will be available in
September 2001 from
Mira Books!*

*Turn the page for
an exciting preview...*

One

The shots came from just beyond the door—two sharp pops in rapid succession.

Lauren Brownley's head jerked up. She stared at her reflection in the mirror above the sink. Her eyes were so wide they seemed to fill her white face. The only gunfire she had ever heard before had been on television or in the movies, but she recognized the sound instantly, and it sent a chill down her spine.

Her first instinct was to run. She shut off the faucet and darted a frantic look around the ladies' rest room for an escape route, but other than the high window that opened onto the alley, there was none.

Out in the lounge someone cried out in agony. Lauren's scalp crawled. She stared at the door, gripping the edge of the counter behind her with wet hands. It was after-hours. Except for her boss, Carlo Giovessi, who had retreated to his office when they had parted company ten minutes ago, the Club Classico was supposed to be empty.

Dear God, had he encountered a burglar? If so, which one of them had been shot?

After casting another desperate look around, Lauren swallowed hard and crept across the tile floor to the entrance. She reached out to push open the door but at the last instant jerked back her hand. Her heart beat double-time when she realized the mistake she had almost made. If there was a burglar out there with a gun, the last thing she wanted was to reveal her presence.

The moaning on the other side of the door hit another crescendo that made Lauren jump and flick off the light. In the darkness, she pressed her lips together and eased the door open a crack.

Lauren caught her breath. Three men stood on the dance floor near the piano. Two of them she had seen around the nightclub, but she had no idea who they were. The third man—the one with the gun in his hand—was Carlo.

At his feet a man writhed on the floor clutching his bloodied legs with both hands. Lauren nearly gagged when she realized that he had been shot in both kneecaps.

Groaning and gasping, the man rolled onto his side, facing her. Surprise shot through Lauren. It was Frank Pappano!

Two months ago, when she had first started playing the piano in the lounge, Carlo had introduced Frank as a business associate. Since then she had seen him around the club frequently, but she didn't know him. Nor did she want to.

Frank was considerably younger than Carlo, somewhere in his mid-thirties, and handsome enough, if you liked the swarthy type. On several occasions he had tried to flirt with her, but she had pretended to not notice. There was something cold and soulless about Frank that made her skin crawl.

Even so, he didn't deserve to be shot. She couldn't believe Carlo had done such a thing.

Lauren leaned her forehead against the doorframe and closed her eyes. Dear God, what a fool she'd been. She had read the allegations in the newspaper and heard the talk, and since coming to work at the Club Classico she'd noticed the rough characters going in and out of Carlos's office, but she had blocked it all out. Like an ostrich with its head in the sand, she thought with disgust.

Granted, deep down she had felt uneasy, but she'd refused to examine the matter. After all Carlo had done for her, merely having suspicions had made her feel disloyal.

And now just look at what your blindness has done for you.

Oh, God, she couldn't believe this!

"You shot me! Jesus Christ, Carlo! Why! Ah-hhh, my knees! My knees!"

Carlo Giovessi's shock of white hair and distinguished face gave him the look of a stern patriarch even when he was enjoying himself, which made his slow smile even more chilling. "Don't play games with me, Frank. You know why. You stole from me. I can't allow that."

Without taking his gaze from Frank, Carlo snapped his fingers, and one of the other men handed him a square, plastic-wrapped bundle. He opened the package, picked up some of the contents and trickled white powder down on Frank. "This last load of coke you picked up for me is mostly sugar." He hefted the package experimentally and pursed his lips. "Too bad you got greedy. It might've worked if you hadn't skimmed off so much. That was stupid, Frank."

His demeanor changed in a blink, and he delivered a vicious kick to Frank's leg. Frank's scream made the hairs on Lauren's neck stand on end.

"You slimeball," Carlo snarled. "Did you really think you could steal almost half my coke and get away with it?"

"No, Carlo. I didn't skim. Swear to God, man! It...it must've been those damned suppliers! They're the ones ch-cheating you. Not me. You know I wouldn't do that! Ah-hhh, Lord, my knees!"

"I'm running out of patience, Frank. And you're running out of time."

Even in the dim light, Lauren saw Frank's face pale.

"I'm doing you a favor. You know I don't soil my hands with this sort of thing anymore. But this...this is personal. Because it's you, I decided to handle this myself. I owe you that much."

Frank's groans turned to blubbery weeping. "Jeez, Carlo, I'm sorry. I'm sorry, man. Please. Please, don't kill me."

"You've worked for me a lotta years, Frank. I took you off the streets when you were just a kid. I trained you. Christ, I treated you like a son, you scumbag."

"Please, Carlo, don't kill me. Don't kill me. Please! *Please, man!* I'm beggin' you! It'll never happen again! Swear to God! I'll do anything! *Anything!* Just don't kill me!" He rolled on the floor, clutching his knees, his contorted face streaming sweat. "Oh, God, oh, God, oh, God."

"Save your breath, Frank. You were a dead man the first time you stole from me. Now it's just a question of when and how you die, and that's up to you. You tell me where you stashed my goods and I'll kill you quick. Stall, and you'll soon be begging me to kill you."

"Lord, Man, if you'll just listen—"

"Those are your only choices, Franco," Carlo said with deadly calm. "And I warn you, lie to me, and I'll kill your family, too. I don't want to do that. You know how fond I am of Maria and little Frank and Mario. It always distresses me to kill women and children, but you know I don't make idle threats. So, unless you want that pretty little wife and those boys of yours to suffer, too, then you'd better not lie." Carlo leaned forward and smiled. "You got three seconds."

Lauren watched the scene unfold with disbelief and horror, her fist pressed against her chest. She saw Frank shudder and squeeze his eyes shut. He muttered something under his breath and crossed himself, then took a deep breath. "It's...it's in a warehouse on...on Patton and East Third."

The words had barely left his lips when another loud pop exploded and an obscene hole appeared in the center of Frank's forehead.

Though Lauren had known the shot was coming, she jumped. Her hand flew to her mouth but she was not quick enough to stifle the gasp that burst from her. Frank jerked, then slumped on the floor. Frozen in place, Lauren stared at the dead man, and felt bile rise in her throat. That hideous black hole in his forehead seemed to blossom as blood began to ooze from it.

"What was that?" Carlo's gaze shot around the lounge and came to rest on the rest rooms, zeroing in first on the mens' then the ladies'.

Lauren flinched and stepped farther back into the darkness as terror overtook shock. Dear God, she had just witnessed a cold-blooded murder! She had to get out of there! Now, before they discovered her....

Look in the back pages of
all June Silhouette series books to find an
exciting new contest with fabulous prizes!
Available exclusively through Silhouette.

Don't miss it!

Where love comes alive™

*P.S. Watch for details on how you can meet
your favorite Silhouette author.*

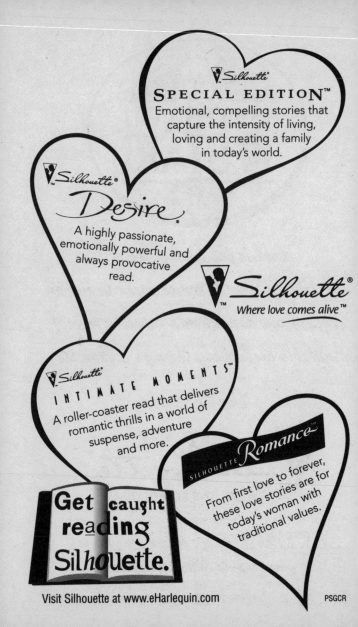

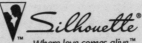